PRIVILEGE

Special Tactical Units Division, Book Two

By Sandra Marton

COPYRIGHT

Copyright © 2016 by Sandra Marton

All rights reserved.

CHAPTER ONE

7:30 pm, a spring evening, The Landing Zone
Bar & Grill, Santa Barbara, California

IT WAS SATURDAY night, and the LZ was jumping.

Every vinyl-covered booth was taken. So were the high-backed stools that lined the long, old-fashioned zinc bar. AC/DC was blasting from what looked like a 1940s jukebox but was really a digital miracle that could belt out early Elvis, up-to-the-minute Foo Fighters and everything in between at the touch of a button. The two pool tables way in the back of the long, narrow room were seeing action. The beer and ale were cold, the burgers were hot…

So were the women.

Some were wives and girlfriends, here with their men, because this was, after all, a Saturday night.

Some were what could most charitably be called groupies.

The thing was, the Landing Zone wasn't just a bar, it was *the* bar for the guys based at Camp Condor, on the beach just a handful of miles away. Condor was the home base for the military's Special Tactical Units Division. STUDs for short, and, yeah, the guys in the units took a lot of grief over that name.

Chayton Olivieri, who had commandeered a booth ten minutes ago, raised his bottle of Stone IPA to his lips and took a long, thirsty swallow.

Truth was, they were proud of it.

Becoming a STUD was hard. Hell, *hard* didn't come close to describing it. Most of the men in the units had been recruited as SEALs, as had Chay. And if SEAL training was the toughest in the world, STUD training took that level of difficulty and upped it a notch.

On average, of the twenty guys who entered a STUD class, five or six would be lucky to make it through.

The LZ was almost always packed with guys in training, guys who'd just graduated, guys newly returned from the kinds of missions you didn't talk about, not only because you were sworn to secrecy but because the last thing you wanted to do now that you were home was relive what had gone down in some shithole of a place with a name most civilians couldn't pronounce.

The bottom line was that if you filled a bar with hard-bodied military operatives who looked like Special Forces recruitment ads, who had a dangerous edge to them even when they were partying, you had a place that drew women like flies to sugar.

And most of the women were tens.

Nines, anyway.

Like the brunette with the endless legs sitting at the bar right across from Chay.

He'd been watching her for a couple of minutes.

She knew he was watching her. He could read the signs. Like the way she crossed those great legs and swung one back and forth the couple of times she'd glanced at him over her shoulder.

Nice.

She was easy on the eyes, especially to a man who'd spent the past six weeks looking at mountains, valleys, men out to kill him, and women wrapped head to toe in voluminous black.

Pretty face, if a little too heavily made up for his tastes, but his tastes weren't written in stone. Long straight hair that hung to her ass. She was wearing something red and almost sheer on top—he'd already seen the thrust of her nipples against it—and what he figured was supposed to be a skirt below the sheer red thing.

Actually, below her belly button.

The skirt ended at the tops of her thighs. After that came those long legs. And finally a pair of spike heels.

Chay drank some more ale.

All in all, she looked fine.

She'd look even better once he got her out of that top

and that skirt, but he'd tell her to keep the stilettos. And the thong. Experience told him she was sure to be wearing one. It would be lace. Or silk. Black. Or red.

He grinned to himself.

When it came to thongs, he wasn't a choosy kind of guy.

He wasn't choosy about women, either.

Well, not true.

He was into eye candy. Nothing wrong with that. And he liked women who were fun to be with. Uncomplicated. Undemanding. He wasn't the kind who signed on for more than a couple of nights, maybe a couple of weeks, max.

There wasn't room in his life for a woman who wanted more, not just because of the demands of his career but because he wasn't into anything more involved than that.

And he sure as hell wasn't into women who were always testing a man. No matter how good a woman looked, if she was confrontational, argumentative, if she was a constant challenge or, to put it bluntly, a constant pain in the ass, why would he want to be with her?

Chay took a long pull at his bottle of ale.

A smart dude avoided babes like that.

Easy enough, because no matter how hot they looked, the warning signs were easy to read and once Chay read them, he stayed away.

Hell, he stayed away in general.

Here tonight. Gone tomorrow. That was his motto. The same motto lots of guys in the units lived by. The motto his best friend, his blood brother, Tanner Akecheta, had lived by...

Until six months ago.

Tanner had not only fallen for a women, gone into a relationship, he'd gotten married. Amazing. Even more amazing, Tanner was happy.

If he was happy, then Chay was, too.

As far as he could tell, Tanner's wife, Alessandra, seemed like the right woman for him—once you got past the fact that it was hard to see how there could ever be a right woman for a man. Tanner kept urging him to take some time off, head up to their ranch in the Dakotas, spend some time riding, fishing, hunting, just hanging out.

Tanner had met his wife on a mission. He'd rescued her from kidnappers in a Central American hellhole called San Escobal. Chay had been the COM Op in charge, communicating with Tanner via satphone, coordinating their rescue. He'd worked from an office at Camp Condor, meaning he'd ended up spending time with Alessandra's family.

With her sister, Bianca.

Chay took a long, cooling swig of ale.

One thing was certain.

Tanner's wife and her sister couldn't possibly share much more than their last name. Last names, to be accurate. They were both Bellini-Wildes and man, when it came to not getting that two-name thing right with the sister, you were in deep shit.

Fact was, you were in deep shit with her most of the time.

The good news? She was hot. To look at, anyway, because the bad news was that she had all the warmth of an ice cube, plus she was a pain in the ass. A world-class pain in the ass.

The brunette took a quick glance over her shoulder, held a couple of seconds' worth of eye contact, flashed a smile, then went back to talking and laughing with her girlfriends.

Chay drank some more ale.

Another few minutes, he'd make a move.

Jesus, the sister. What a piece of work.

Bianca Wilde. Bianca Bellini Wilde, if you didn't want her to rip you a new one, but forget that.

It made more sense to think of her as Bianca the Tigress.

Talk about confrontational women...

She'd turned up at Camp Condor, marched right into his space and tried to take over. At first he'd thought it was because her old man was a four-star and she figured that gave her special rights, but in no time at all he'd realized her attitude had nothing to do with that.

It had to do with her.

The Tigress was, to put it charitably, a ball-buster.

He'd put her in her place quickly enough.

She'd driven him up the wall, demanding information she had no business demanding, telling him how he should be handling things, interfering every minute and every way she could, making his life hell until, finally, he'd taken her on, gone head-to-head with her, told her she was a total, complete, absolute pain in the ass and if she didn't want him to pick her up and literally throw her out of his office, she'd better back off.

The look on her face when'd told her that had been just wonderful.

The thought of tossing her out had been equally wonderful.

Or maybe it had been the thought of picking her up. Hoisting her off her feet, lifting her in his arms, finding out if there wasn't a way to convert all that icy need to control the world into heat and flame.

Of course, he hadn't touched her. Why would he?

Chay looked around, saw his waitress and signaled for another ale.

Which was why it was impossible to explain what had happened at the wedding. The bride's sister. The groom's best friend. Of necessity, they'd ended up sitting next to each other. Being called to the dance floor. Posing for pictures and smiling through their teeth.

They'd managed to be polite for the sake of the bridal couple.

Then everybody had gone outside to see the newlyweds off.

Somehow, he'd ended up alone on the porch with the Tigress. And man, she'd done her best to put him in his place while he'd done his best not to react…

And then, somehow or other, she'd ended up in his arms.

All these months later, he could still remember that

kiss.

The feel of her body against his.

The softness of her mouth.

The almost overwhelming desire to take her. There. Right there. No preliminaries. No explanations. He'd wanted to pull up her skirt, unzip his trousers and bury himself inside her.

The kiss had ended, fast.

So had those ridiculous imaginings.

The cause? He still couldn't figure it out. Too much champagne, maybe. There sure as hell was no other way to explain it. She'd made some lady-of-the-manor crack about him never touching her again. He'd followed up with some smartass remark. Then she'd gone back inside the house and he'd driven to Dallas, and he hadn't thought about Bianca Bellini Wilde again…

Come on, dude.

Yeah. He had. He'd thought about that kiss, too, for no reason he could come up with. Replayed it, especially the part where she'd kissed him back. Or maybe she hadn't. Maybe he'd imagined it. Maybe…

"Here you go, handsome."

He looked up, smiled and said "Thanks" as the waitress plopped a bottle of ale on the scarred wooden table.

Jesus.

Chay lifted the bottle, brought it to his lips and took a drink.

Why was Bianca Bellini Wilde in his head? Truth was, she'd been there a few times—okay, several times over the last few months. And that was crazy. Crazy. Especially tonight, his first night back in the world…

"Such a waste."

The voice was female, a sexy purr.

The brunette was standing next to the booth, or maybe it made more sense to say she was damn near draped over it, the sheer red top gaping enough so he knew with certainty that she was braless beneath it.

"This big booth," she said. "So much space for one man." She smiled and ran the tip of her tongue lightly over her bottom lip. "Don't you believe in sharing?"

He knew the correct answer. He'd say, *I believe in sharing everything, baby. Where would you like to start?*

And she'd laugh and say she was here for the weekend, she had a room nearby, one of the motels on the ocean, probably, and her girlfriends would know enough to stay away.

Or maybe not. Maybe they'd come along, too. Maybe that was her idea of sharing and that was fine.

The brunette leaned towards him.

He could smell her perfume.

Sweet. Cloying. So sweet and cloying it made bile rise in the back of his throat—and suddenly, he was back in a meadow in the high mountains he'd left not forty-eight hours ago.

The meadow had been a place of death. Bodies. The burnt remains of vehicles lying, underbellies up, like big dead bugs.

And yet, for all the destruction, flowers had somehow

pushed their way above the soil. Their smell was sweet. Sickly sweet, almost like the smell of blood.

Chay and the seven other men in his until had been making their way cautiously through the flowers when he'd heard something behind him.

Or sensed it.

The guys in his unit joked about that ability of his. The sensing-some-other-presence thing.

"It's what comes of being an Indian," he'd say, and they'd all laugh, but yeah, he was an Indian. Part, anyway. Lakota Sioux. And even as a kid he'd had that sensing-thing. It had saved his ass a couple of times back home in South Dakota, the feeling that a mountain lion was approaching him from behind or that a bear was noiselessly following his trail.

That day in the meadow, the feeling had come to him again.

Something was coming up behind him.

He'd spun around quickly.

No cat. No grizzly.

A kid.

A boy.

Young.

Ten. Twelve at the most. And when he saw Chay looking at him, the kid began to run. Straight for him and the others, and he had a bulge under his shirt that could have been anything from a stack of *naan* or a jug of *doogh* or, Christ, a bomb, a bomb, and he was almost on them so that Chay knew he had all of one second to decide which of those fucking things it was and…

"Hey."

And it turned out he'd made the right decision, which was maybe his problem tonight because he could still hear the roar of explosives after he'd shouted a warning and the kid had kept coming, so he'd pulled the trigger and, fuck, all these days later, he could hear the *BANG*, see the flames, smell the stink of burning flesh—

"Hey, dude."

Chay shot out his arm, grabbed hold of something warm and slender…

"Hey. What are you trying to do? Break my arm?"

He blinked. His hand was wrapped around the brunette's wrist.

"Crap," she said. "All I did was snap my fingers."

The world came into focus.

He let go of her. She pulled back, rubbing her skin, staring at him as if he'd turned into an alien life form.

Chay drew a deep breath. "Sorry."

"You'd better be sorry."

Her gaze was assessing. A second passed. Then she tossed her head. "Well, okay. I mean, you want to buy me a drink…" She smiled, leaned in. Her perfume engulfed him. "We can start over. How's that?"

"That's…" He took another long breath. "The thing is… Sorry. Not tonight."

The brunette looked at him as if he'd spoken in Sanskrit.

Shit.

"What I mean is, thanks for the offer..."

Double shit. Now she was looking at him as if he'd lost his mind.

"Look," he said, "I'm just not into this tonight..."

Jesus H. Christ.

"Some other time," he said, and she straightened up, slapped her hands on her hips and gave him a look that he figured was pretty much the same as the one Medusa had wanted to give Perseus.

"Not even in your dreams," she said, and then, probably for good measure, she leaned in again. "I was just trying to do my patriotic duty. Otherwise, why would I even talk to an idiot whose cock is probably the size of a fruit fly?"

She turned on her heel and flounced away.

Chay tried to laugh. At himself, for being the idiot she'd called him even though she was wrong about the size of his cock.

He'd never had any complaints whatsoever about that.

Yeah, but he couldn't laugh. Couldn't even smile.

Chay closed his eyes.

Maybe it was time to get out of here.

Maguire and Sanchez had said they'd meet him, but they'd understand. What he needed was some air. A long walk on the beach. Maybe he'd shuck his clothes and head into the surf. The Pacific was cold at night. The surf was rough. For all he knew, maybe that was what he needed. Cold air. Rough water. Something, anything to empty his head of that fucking meadow.

"Dude, if you're an ad for meditation, you are doin'

one shitty job."

Chay's eyes flew open. He shot to his feet, hands fisted, adrenaline pounding, all six feet two inches of him ready, hell, eager for a fight…

"Hey. Olivieri. Take it easy, man. It's me."

Chay shook his head—and brought into focus the face of his oldest friend, his best buddy, his blood brother, Tanner Akecheta.

"Akecheta?"

Tanner, who he hadn't seen since that wedding months ago, grinned.

"Not unless you know some other dude who'd be dumb enough to say hello to somebody with an expression like yours on his face."

For a couple of seconds, Chay kept on staring. Then he grinned.

"Fuck," he said, and the men grabbed each other in the kind of embrace that would have pleased a pair of male grizzlies. "Dude," he said, when they finally stepped apart, "what are you doin' here? Why aren't you back home in South Dakota, chasing cows or horses or whatever it is you do on that ranch of yours?"

"You know damn well what I do, Olivieri, because you did enough of it when we were growing up. Here's a better question. What are you doing here?"

Chay took an exaggerated look around him.

"Let me think a minute," he said. "Uh, having a beer? I don't know, man. I mean, why else would I be in the LZ?"

Tanner laughed. "You were supposed to be away. Deployed until late next week. Meaning, we weren't going to get to see each other."

"Yeah. Well, we got picked up early."

"Mission went faster than expected?" Tanner's smile tilted. "Or mission aborted?"

"It went," Chay said, with a flatness to his voice that said he didn't want to discuss what had gone down. "Here's *my* better question. What are you doing in California?"

" Dude, didn't you get any of my emails?"

"Bad wireless where I was," Chay said with a wry smile. "What emails?"

"The ones I sent, telling you I was going to be here for a few days."

"Never got one."

The men sat down across from each other. "Do I want to know where you spent the past few weeks?" Tanner asked.

Chay shrugged. "The same garden spot where we put in three wonderful months when you were still with the unit."

Tanner's hand automatically went to his thigh and the wound that had almost killed him.

"Lucky you. I bet it was even more fun this time around."

The image of the kid flashed through Chay's mind. He reached for the bottle of ale, wrapped both hands around it, felt the coolness of the glass burn into his soul.

"It was okay."

Tanner eyed his friend. He knew that those words were

a long way from the truth.

"You want to talk about it?" he asked softly.

Chay shook his head. "No."

"Yeah. That's cool." Tanner cleared his throat. "So what's the deal? Am I supposed to sit here and watch you massage that bottle to death?"

Chay laughed. A real laugh, and that struck him as a very good thing. He lifted his hand, waggled it. The waitress appeared almost immediately, which was another great thing about the LZ. The waitstaff knew how to keep the clientele happy.

"What can I get you?"

"An ale for my friend. And maybe some peanuts. That okay with you, Akecheta?"

"Sure."

The waitress headed for the bar. Chay leaned across the table.

"So what are you doing here? I hope you're gonna say you decided to come on board as an instructor."

"No. Well, yes and no. I've agreed to do a couple of days to help destroy the egos of the new class."

Both men laughed.

"Yeah," said Chay. "I remember how that goes. But seriously, only a couple of days?"

" I have to get back to the Flying Eagle."

"Your ranch."

"Right."

"You're happy there?"

"I thought I'd miss everything. The missions. The unit. The whole thing." They sat back as the waitress put the ale and a bowl of nuts on the table. "And, hell, I'm not gonna lie," Tanner said, after she'd left. "I do miss it, sometimes. The unit especially."

Chay nodded. "Figures you would."

"But then I look around me. The land, the hills…"

Chay's eyebrows rose. "If you launch into a tune from *The Sound of Music*, you'll be in real trouble."

Tanner laughed.

"Okay. Maybe I'm going overboard, but—"

"No," Chay said quietly. "I'm just giving you a hard time. It's beautiful country. I've never denied that."

"Yeah." Tanner cleared his throat. "And we're fixing things up. The house. The outbuildings. Come for a visit. Wait'll you see what we've done with the place."

"We." Chay smiled. "Married life turns out to be good, huh?"

"It's not married life. It's Alessandra."

"Anybody ever tell you you get a goofy look on your face when you say her name?"

"No." Tanner grinned. "And if anybody ever did, I'd probably slug him." His smile tilted. "The thing is, I had no idea. I mean, you know, the one-man, one-woman thing…"

"I'm glad it's working for you," Chay said, taking a swig of ale.

"But not for you."

"Me? Hell, no. You know me, dude. I like my life exactly

as it is."

"Especially since you're so smooth with the ladies."

Chay shot Tanner a look. Tanner was trying not to laugh.

"Dammit," Chay said. "You saw what happened a couple of minutes ago."

"Some of it. What was that all about? You swearing off women?"

With anyone else, Chay would probably have tossed off a glib answer, but this was Tanner. They'd shared too much in their lives for glib answers.

""I'm just... I don't know. I'm just feeling out of it tonight."

"Dude, you change your mind, you want to talk..."

"No. I'm cool." Chay forced a smile. "This is great. Seeing you, I mean. But where's Alessandra? Don't tell me you left her on the ranch."

"No way. She's here. She just made a pit stop in the ladies' room. You know how women are. They can't pass up the chance to check out each and every—"

"Each and every what?" Alessandra Bellini Wilde Akecheta said as she appeared beside the booth. Both men shot to their feet, and she smiled at Chay. "Hello, handsome."

"Hey," Tanner said lightly, "watch that stuff."

"Alessandra," Chay said, returning the smile. "It's great to see you again."

Alessandra rose on her toes and planted a kiss on his jaw.

"It's great to see you, too." She leaned back and her husband wrapped his arm around her waist as he drew her close against him. "I keep asking Tanner when you're going to come and visit us."

'I will. Soon. I promise."

"I'd love that. I can't count how many times we go somewhere and Tanner talks about being there with you when you two were boys."

"I hope he hasn't told you anything that would ruin my pristine reputation."

"Of course not," Alessandra said, and they all laughed.

Tanner eased his wife into the booth. Chay took the seat across from them.

"So," he said, "how was your trip down?"

"It was great," Alessandra said. "We took a quick detour to El Sueño. You know. The Wilde ranch in Texas." She leaned her head against her husband's shoulder. "Turns out we might be doing some business with Jake."

"Your stepbrother."

"Half-brother. Yeah. He's thinking about getting into breeding Appaloosas. The way we do."

We, Chay thought. Amazing. So was the way Tanner was looking at his wife. They really were happy. Maybe Tanner had found the one woman in a million a guy could live with—assuming a guy wanted to live with a woman at all. Not that that would change his viewpoint, but if that was what Tanner wanted, good for him.

"So," he said, "are you guys hungry?"

Alessandra nodded.

"We're starved. According to my husband, the burgers here are the best in Northern California."

"The passage of time will screw up a man's memory," Chay said, laughing. "No, seriously, they're good. Or, if you want something else, we can go to that Thai place just up the road. Or that little Italian place up the coast a few miles."

"Honey?" Tanner said, looking at his wife. "Your choice."

"I'm fine with whatever you guys want, but why don't we wait and ask... Oh. Here she is now. Bianca? We're talking about where to have dinner...Whoops. Sorry. You remember Chay, don't you?"

Bianca Bellini Wilde, aka Bianca the Tigress, looked down at the man she absolutely, positively loathed, the man any woman with half a brain instantly recognized as a card-carrying male chauvinist, the man she had been assured she would not have to set eyes on because he was out of the country—deployed, in the language of her new brother-in-law—and asked herself what, exactly, she had done to deserve the punishment of having him turn up here.

And how had this trip—this much anticipated vacation—gone so wrong? First the calls to her cellphone in Texas. Ugly calls. Frightening, too, though she'd never admitted just how frightening to Alessandra or Tanner.

Now this. Lieutenant Chayton Olivieri, in the flesh. The man who had embarrassed her. Humiliated her.

Bianca set her jaw.

She'd been helpless in the face of those phone calls.

This was different.

The lieutenant wasn't into scaring women. He was into dominating them. Too strong a word, maybe, but what else would you call a man who lived and breathed machismo, who couldn't get through his head the simple fact that not all women were interested in the Neanderthal approach?

Her one satisfaction was that he was staring at her with the same look of shock she suspected was on her own face.

Good, Bianca thought with grim satisfaction.

She hadn't seen him for months, but she hadn't forgotten that he'd made her miserable every minute of every hour they'd been forced to spend in each other's company.

Now it was her turn to return the favor.

CHAPTER TWO

"OF COURSE. CLAY. Clay Oliver."

Smiling, even though she felt as if her lips were glued together, Bianca stuck out her hand as Olivieri rose to his feet. All six feet something of him. She'd forgotten how tall he was. Well, not forgotten, maybe just underestimated. Not that it mattered. What mattered was the flash of irritation in those dark green eyes.

Lovely to see.

Especially because she certainly hadn't forgotten his name.

She'd simply mangled it deliberately.

"It's Chay. Chayton Olivieri, Ms. Wilde. *Lieutenant* Chayton Olivieri."

His hand closed around hers. His grip was firm, so firm that she knew the only way she'd get her hand back would be by making a fool of herself in a tug of war she'd never win.

She'd just have to wait until he decided to let go.

Okay. One point to the big guy. He was, yes, big and muscled and tough, but perhaps he wasn't entirely stupid.

"Oh," she said sweetly, "sorry. I'm bad at remembering names."

She saw her sister blink. Well, why wouldn't she? Bianca wasn't bad at remembering anything, and Alessandra knew it. Names. Dates. The titles of books she'd read a decade ago. In fact, she had close to a photographic memory. It was one of the reasons she'd graduated from New York University with a perfect four-point-oh GPA, why she was heading for her doctorate at a speed her adviser called amazing.

"Unless the names are important, of course," she added, with a quick and, she hoped, blinding smile.

Olivieri's green eyes narrowed to slits that all but glowed with intensity. Her sister made the kind of sound a carp might make if it found itself gasping for air on dry land.

Her brother-in-law threw out a lifeline.

"Bianca," he said brightly. "Excellent timing. We're just deciding where to have dinner. Thai? Or Italian? You have a preference?"

Chay Olivieri's eyes were still locked on hers. She wanted to say that what she wanted for dinner was nothing, but why let him think he'd won the round? She shrugged her shoulders.

"Whatever you decide is fine."

Tanner and Alessandra exchanged looks. "Uh," Tanner said, "how about the two of you sitting down?"

He made it sound like they were on a date. She started to say she was fine standing up, but the lieutenant chose that moment to let go of her hand, step aside politely—as if he weren't a hulking brute—and motion her into the booth.

A booth where she'd be trapped between him and the wall.

"That's all right," she said quickly. "I mean, if we're leaving to go somewhere else…"

"We're going to have a beer first," Olivieri said. His eyes met hers again. The burning intensity had given way to cool mockery. "If that meets with your approval, of course, Ms. Wilde. Or should that be Bellini-Wilde?" His smile was tight. "I wouldn't want to get that wrong."

"Chay," Tanner said, "listen, bro—"

"Can I get you ladies something?"

Alessandra looked up at the waitress. "Ale for me, please," she said. "The same as they're having."

The waitress nodded and looked at Bianca. "What about you, miss? What would you like?"

Hemlock, Bianca thought. An enormous glass of it for the man whose body was pinning her to the wall. Or would have pinned her to the wall if she hadn't taken off her shoulder bag and set it between them.

"Miss?"

"Uh, I'd like some water, please."

"Sure. Ice?"

"Just a little ice. And lemon. Oh, and make that sparkling water."

The waitress cocked her head. "Club soda?"

"Sparkling. San Pellegrino, but if you don't have that brand—"

"We might have seltzer."

"No," Bianca said politely. "That's not the same as—"

"She'll have club soda," Chay said curtly, "with ice and lemon."

Bianca glared at him. "That isn't what I want."

"It's what you're getting."

"Hey," Tanner said softly, "dude…"

"Bianca," Alessandra said quickly, her voice cutting across her husband's, "how about something else? Ale, maybe? Or a soft drink?"

Bianca hesitated. Was she going to ruin her sister's evening? More to the point, was she going to let the barbarian seated next to her ruin it? No. She would not. She would, as the Americans said, go with the flow.

"I'll have some wine."

Everybody seemed to relax. The waitress nodded, pencil poised.

"Sure. What kind?"

Bianca folded her hands on the tabletop. "What kind do you have?"

"House red. House white. I think Charlie might have some rosé."

"No. I meant, what types of wine do you have? Say, in the reds. Merlot? Malbec? Maybe a pinot noir? Or perhaps a cabernet. What cabernets do you—"

Chay's voice cut across hers. "The house red is fine."

The waitress nodded. "Great choice. One house red, coming up."

Silence descended over the table, or something that was as close to it as you could get with the Stones blaring from the jukebox.

"*I can't get no satisfaction,*" Mick sang.

Neither can I, Bianca thought grimly.

She'd caught the look Alessandra had sent her about the water-and-wine thing. *Must you be so finicky?* the look said. The accusation was an old one. And definitely unfounded. There was nothing wrong with keeping things organized. With knowing what you wanted.

Let things slip and life turned into chaos.

Amazing that Alessandra had not absorbed that simple lesson from their childhood.

As for the lieutenant... He deserved whatever she dished out.

"Well," Tanner said briskly, "here we are. All of us in one place for the first time since Alessandra and I tied the knot."

"Oh. That's right," Bianca said. "That's where we last saw each other. The ensign and I."

"It's lieutenant," Chay said coldly.

"Of course. *Lieutenant.* I forgot. I met you at my sister's wedding."

"You met me at Camp Condor."

Bianca batted her lashes. "Really? Were you the one who went out and got us sandwiches?"

Alessandra made a hissing sound.

Chay's jaw tightened. "I was the one whose job you kept trying to do."

"Oh. Right. You were the radio operator."

"I was the COM Op," Chay said through his teeth.

"And then," Alessandra said brightly, "you saw each other again at the wedding. In fact, you guys must have spent a lot of time together that weekend."

"One red," the waitress said as she put a glass in front of Bianca.

Bianca raised the glass to her nose, sniffed it, then put it down.

"Did we? Spend time together?" she shrugged. "I can't recall. There were so many people there, so many men from your unit, Tanner. I know it's awful to admit, but it was hard to keep track of who was who."

"How about a reminder?" Chay growled before he could stop himself.

Tanner and Alessandra looked at him as if he'd gone nuts. Bianca turned pink. Chay said something short and succinct under his breath, shot to his feet and mumbled about needing to go to the men's room.

He stalked away.

The one-toilet men's bathroom was empty.

Chay locked the door, went to the sink, turned on the cold water and ducked his head under the faucet.

The woman was trying to get under his skin. Under his skin? Shit. She was trying to attach electrodes to his balls.

He straightened up, turned off the water, snagged a handful of paper towels and dried his hair, face and hands.

That performance just now.

San Pellegrino. And a wine list. The LZ was exactly what it was. No pretensions here. That was one of the reasons the place meant so much to the men in the units. What was she trying to prove?

That the queen controlled her world.

And all that crap about not remembering him.

She remembered him, all right, first from Camp Condor, where she'd made it clear she figured she could have handled the communications part of the operation much better than he could.

And she certainly remembered him from the wedding, thanks to that damn kiss.

Chay glared at his reflection in the mirror.

He wasn't proud of it. He'd never kissed a woman who hadn't looked as if she'd wanted kissing before, but, dammit, by the time it happened, he'd been going crazy. Not with lust. With more unwanted, uncomfortable togetherness than one human being could handle.

All those hours of tolerating each other. Sitting side by side at a rehearsal dinner that seemed endless. Hitting the dance floor—not slow dancing, for which he'd been almost pathetically grateful—but moving to the music together because it was expected. Smiling phony smiles for a trillion pictures, laughing phony laughs at a trillion jokes.

Bad.

All of it.

He'd been counting down the minutes until he never had to see Bianca the Perfect again. She was a control freak. And like most control freaks, she was positive she knew everything.

He'd watched the florist try to escape her; the bandleader get a panicked look each time she approached. He'd seen the caterer flinch when she eyed the wedding cake and again when she went from table to table, surreptitiously straightening forks and knives that didn't need straightening.

Okay. He had to admit she'd seemed polite enough in dealing with all those people, but didn't it occur to her they knew how to do their jobs? Her every action said she was the person who should be in charge of the world, that nobody else was up to it.

She'd dealt with him like that too.

No. Not like that.

Worse. She'd abandoned any pretense at politeness with him.

Disdainful glances. Icy words. An attitude that said he was in her way. Man, she was all attitude. And by the time the party was winding down, he'd been longing to see the last of Bianca Bellini Wilde.

That was what he'd been thinking when he and all the other guests went outside to see off the bride and groom.

"Goodbye," the guests shouted. "Be happy. Be well." And some of the guys from the unit had shouted more basic things, things that made everybody laugh.

Everybody but the Tigress, who'd been as aloof and

apart as if she were alone on the crowded porch.

The guests, the Wildes, the Bellinis had all gone back inside.

Bianca hadn't.

For reasons Chay still couldn't explain, neither had he.

They'd exchanged a few words. Chilly, not nasty.

And then…and then, he'd kissed her.

Okay. Not the smartest, smoothest move he'd ever made. He certainly hadn't had a real desire to kiss her. What man would want to kiss such a self-centered, know-it-all ice queen?

To this day, he couldn't come up with an answer for why he'd done it.

Impulse was the best he could manage, just a reaction to her looking at him as if he were a lesser form of life. He wasn't into the *me Tarzan, you Jane* thing, but if that was how she thought of him, so be it.

Or maybe she'd flattened his male ego one time too many. Whatever the reason, he'd reached for her, hauled her none too gently into his arms and kissed her.

Stupid? Of course, but no-think moments were usually stupid.

He hadn't even considered how she'd respond. If he had, he'd have figured she'd slug him.

But she hadn't.

Yeah, she'd struggled to get free. Struggled for maybe a tenth of a second. Then, she'd made a little sound that had gone straight through him.

And she'd melted in his arms.

Her body had softened against his.

Her lips had clung to his.

She'd lifted herself to him, clasped one hand around the nape of his neck and parted her lips to the demand of his, and then it was over, it was done...

Except...the taste and feel of her had been in his head all these months and wasn't that a bitch that he should remember a woman, a kiss, a moment that should never have happened, and now here she was, all that same disdain, that same fire, that same lush mouth and soft body and, Jesus, he could show her that what she felt for him wasn't disdain at all...

A fist pounded against the door.

It had been pounding for a while, Chay realized.

He ran the cold water again, cupped some in his hands and rubbed it over his face. Then he yanked another length of paper towel from the dispenser, dried his hands and face, and unlocked the door.

"Dude," said a guy he recognized as a STUD trainee, "I've been knockin' at that fucking door for an hour."

"A couple of minutes, maybe," Chay said. "And remember who you are, lowlife."

It was standard hazing talk from an established STUD to a trainee. Still, judging by the way the guy's eyebrows reached for his hairline, Chay figured his tone, his expression must have kicked things up a notch. He considered apologizing, couldn't come up with a valid reason for one and, instead, punched the guy lightly in the biceps as he moved past him.

"Good bladder training," he said.

The guy choked out a laugh. Chay shot him a smile, then threaded his way to the booth through the crowded bar.

He needed another cold ale.

Maybe he even needed some time off.

Captain Blake, the CO at Condor, had offered him a break.

"One, two weeks," he'd said. "Get away from here, do something different. Might be good for you."

Maybe it wasn't a bad idea. Maybe it was something to consider. Maybe—

Hell. The booth was ahead of him. And Tanner was seated in it, alone.

"What'd I do?" Chay said, sliding into the opposite seat. "Scare off the ladies?"

"Another pit stop." Tanner hunched forward over the table. "I think Alessandra figured the only way to stop the war was to come up with an excuse and get her sister off the battlefield."

"Yeah." Chay reached for his bottle of ale, shoved it aside instead and said, "Shit!"

"You always were good with words, Olivieri. I couldn't have said it better myself."

"I'm sorry, dude. I didn't mean to make Alessandra uncomfortable."

Tanner sat back. "What in hell was all that? You and my sister-in-law went at each other like a pair of street fighters."

Chay considered downplaying the accusation, but how

could he? They *had* gone at each other, and he'd have to figure Tanner as a dumbass if he hadn't recognized it.

He sighed, sat back, and shrugged his broad shoulders.

"Well, the thing is, we, you know, we don't get along."

Tanner barked out a laugh. "Amazing. I've never known you to deal in understatement before."

The look on Chay's face made it clear he wasn't amused.

"When I was COM Op for you during that San Escobal thing, she was damn near impossible."

"Yeah. I remember you saying she was in your space all the time."

"She was, to put it bluntly, a total pain in the ass."

"Doing what? Leaning on you because her old man's a general? I wouldn't have figured Bianca for that."

"She never mentioned him. It was her. I finally figured out that's just the way she is."

"Like, what?"

Chay folded his arms over his chest. "She's sure she knows everything, that she's smarter than everybody else."

"Yeah," Tanner said thoughtfully. "See, here's the thing. She really *is* smart. Alessandra says she graduated top of her undergrad class, and she's close to getting her doctorate."

"Do I give a damn about her doctorate?" Chay said, glowering. "She knows as much about what we do as a mouse knows about whales, but does that stop her from trying to interfere? Hell, no. Does it stop her from trying to do a job she knows nothing about? No way. She's got a one-track mind and the track it plays says *I know how this should be done and if you don't like it, that's too damn…* What?"

"Oh, nothing much." Tanner took a swig of ale. "I mean, I can't imagine why someone like you would have a problem with any of that. You're such an easy-to-deal-with guy, always ready to take advice, always so modest and humble and unassuming."

Chay glared across the table. "I am never difficult to…" His mouth twitched. "Jesus. Okay. I get it. I sound like a jerk, but, dammit, women aren't supposed to be like that."

"No." Tanner said. "Of course not. Women are supposed to be docile and sweet."

"Hell, Akecheta. Don't put words in my mouth. That's not what I meant." Chay shook his head. "We're like oil and water, you know? She rubs me the wrong way and I do the same to her."

"Yeah." Tanner cleared his throat. "But, you know, speaking of rubbing… She's a good-looking woman, dude. Did you maybe come on to her and get the door slammed in your face?"

Chay thought about that kiss. Thought, again, about how the Tigress had reacted. He even thought about clueing Tanner in, telling him that yes, he'd made a move and she'd dissolved right into it…

No. He wouldn't tell that to anybody. Not to protect himself. To protect her. She was a first-class bitch, but he was an officer and a gentleman, even though he'd managed to forget both those things on the porch at El Sueño.

"So? Did I touch on something, bro?"

Chay managed to smile. "You know better. How could such a thing ever happen? What woman in her right mind would turn down a Chayton Olivieri move?"

Tanner went on looking at him for a couple of seconds. Then he smiled, too, and lifted his bottle of ale in salute.

"See what I mean? So modest. It's one of your finest qualities."

"You left out *brilliant*," Chay said.

Both men laughed. They clinked their bottles of ale together, but before they could drink, a female voice interrupted them.

"Male bonding. Such a charming thing to see."

The sisters stood next to the table. Alessandra was the one who'd spoken in a high, deliberately cheerful voice. Bianca stood next to her, arms folded, expression stony and unforgiving.

So what else is new, Chay thought, but he kept smiling.

"It's bromance," he said. "You're just jealous."

"Of course they are," Tanner rose to his feet. "Ladies. How about getting out of here and having dinner somewhere else? That Thai place. Olivieri? You agree?"

Chay hesitated. *Forget it,* he wanted to say. *You guys take off. I'm gonna stay right here.*

But this wasn't about him. Or about the Tigress. It was about old pals getting together for a few hours. Just a few hours. He could deal with that.

He nodded, reached for his wallet and tossed some bills on the table. Tanner reached for his wallet, too, but Chay waved him off.

"Drinks are on me. So, how about getting some food. Sound good to you guys? Tanner?"

Both men looked at the women. Alessandra looked at Bianca.

"What about it?" she said softly. "You up for some dinner?"

They all waited. At last, the Tigress inclined her head. Only that. Not a word. Not a smile. Not anything that would keep Chay's gut from knotting. Just that one haughty gesture. The queen acceding to the request of the peasants.

"Fine."

The word was clipped and the tone she used made it a lie, but Tanner went with it.

"Great. Excellent. We'll take my truck."

"No." Chay spoke quickly. Everyone, including Bianca, looked at him. "No," he said again with what he hoped was a smile. "If we go to the restaurant separately, you guys can go straight to your hotel afterwards. Besides, I, ah, I'm meeting Sanchez on the beach for a run in the morning. At zero dark hundred. I'll probably want to call it a night before you do."

He could tell that Tanner wasn't buying the excuse, but Tanner was his blood brother. Blood brothers stood up for each other.

"Sure," Tanner said. "That makes sense."

It did, but what happened next sure as hell didn't.

Tanner put his arm around his wife's shoulders. "Ready to go, sweetheart?"

"Ready," Alessandra said. "Bianca?"

The Tigress took a breath so deep it was audible.

"You two go ahead. I'll ride with the lieutenant."

Three heads swung toward her. Three pairs of eyes focused on her face.

"Really. I need the change." Her smile was big and bright and, Chay knew, as phony as his had been a few seconds ago. "I've been riding in that truck for so long, I'm starting to think I need to buy cowboy boots."

"Yeah," Tanner said, "but—"

"Tanner?" Alessandra grabbed her husband's arm. "Honey, I'm starving. You promised me a meal, remember?"

Her smile was as artificial as Bianca's.

Tanner shot Chay a *What in hell's going on?* look. Chay shot the same look right back at him.

"Lieutenant?" Bianca said. "Is that okay with you?"

What could he do except nod his head in agreement?

"Well," Tanner said, "if everybody's cool with the arrangements—"

"For heaven's sake," Alessandra hissed. She flashed another smile, slid her hand into her husband's and all but dragged him toward the door.

Chay waited until they were out of sight. Then he turned towards Bianca.

"Kind of sudden," he said, because why pull any punches now that they were alone? "Your change of heart."

"I haven't had a change of heart. Not about you, Lieutenant."

"Then why ride with me instead of Tanner and your sister?"

"We were making them uncomfortable."

Chay folded his arms over his chest. "Isn't that a specialty of yours? Making people uncomfortable?"

Color stained her cheeks. "That's quite a statement from a man who went out of his way to make me uncomfortable just a few minutes ago."

"What are you talking about? I never…" The comment he'd made about knowing a way to remind her of the last time they'd met danced in his head. "Oh. That."

"Yes. That."

"Yeah, well, you can only push me so far."

"*I* pushed *you*?"

"*Oh, I remember you now,*" Chay said in a high, mincing voice. "*You were the gofer who brought us sandwiches.*"

The color in her face deepened. "I never called you a gofer."

"And the waitress… I'm only surprised you didn't get up and show her how to serve our drinks."

"Unbelievable! This is what I get for trying to pour salt on troubled waters."

"It's oil. Oil on troubled waters. The salt thing is about what you never want to pour on open wounds."

Bianca threw out her hands. "*Chi se ne frega!* Who cares? I am trying to make a point here."

"Which is?"

She drew another deep breath. The action drew her

breasts up tight against the shirt she was wearing.

He hadn't really noticed what she was wearing before.

He did now.

The shirt was an indeterminate shade of brown, somewhere between what he figured women called beige and tan. The short sleeves did justice to her arms, which were trim.

Everything about her was trim.

Nice breasts. Slender waist. Gently rounded hips.

He couldn't see her legs, because she had on pants the same color as the top. There was no way to judge whether her legs were as trim as the rest of her, but though the gown she'd worn at the wedding had been floor length, she'd lifted the skirt when she'd stalked back into the house and the glimpse he'd had of her ankles had been okay.

Better than okay.

It had made him want to see more.

He remembered the color of that gown, too. Purple. No. Pink. Not pink either. He had no idea what the color was, but it had been great for her, the perfect foil for her golden hair...

Jesus.

Who gave a damn about her looks? Okay. She was easy on the eyes despite the way she dressed. Even the shoes. If the brunette who'd been hitting on him had on spike heels, what would you call these? Not flats. They were kind of wedged. From head to toe, she was dressed the way she probably dressed for the office. Nothing that would draw a man's eye. Even her hair. She wore it drawn back into a low ponytail, something a woman with silky-looking, soft-looking long waves of golden hair should never do.

None of those things changed the fact that the lady was what you'd get if you crossed Marie Antoinette with a wolverine.

The thought made him laugh.

Her chin lifted.

"What," she said coldly, "do you find so amusing, Lieutenant?"

"Nothing. Everything." He sighed. "Actually, I was thinking that you're right."

She blinked. "I am?"

"Yes."

"Right about what?"

"About us making Tanner and his wife uncomfortable."

He could almost see a little of her defiance slipping away.

"Tanner's my best friend. I might not see him again for months. And Alessandra is your sister."

She gave a stiff little nod.

"Exactly. And we live thousands of miles apart, me in New York, she in North Dakota."

"South Dakota."

"Whatever," she said with a touch of her usual impatience. "The point is, it's far away. It is why I agreed to fly to Texas and meet them there so we could spend time with our family, and then to drive back to South Dakota with them and see their ranch."

"Sounds like a great trip."

"It was okay."

"What? Not fun to see the family again?"

"No. I mean, yes. Of course that was fun. But I had a couple of phone calls…" She clamped her lips together.

"A couple of phone calls…?" he prompted.

"Business calls," she said briskly.

There was more to it than that, Chay thought. It was that old *sensing* thing again, or maybe it was the surprise in her eyes, as if she'd said more than she'd expected to say.

He wanted to ask her about that, but a silky gold curl somehow escaped the ponytail and curved against her cheek.

It was a major distraction.

His fingers twitched with the desire to tuck it back.

Foolish.

Not just foolish. Ridiculous.

"… a truce."

"Sorry?"

"I said, what I suggest is a truce."

"A truce," he said. "You want a truce."

"I said I'm suggesting one."

He almost laughed, but her expression was dead serious. Okay. He could play serious too.

"The difference being?"

"The difference being, I'm suggesting we behave ourselves tonight."

Damn. Not laughing was tough.

"You mean," he said carefully, "the war will pick up where we left off if our paths ever cross again?"

She ran the tip of her tongue over her lips. This time, more than his fingers twitched.

"I mean," she said, "the odds are that won't ever happen. You know. That our paths will cross. So why even consider it? There's no reason to look beyond tonight."

Chay considered the request. For once, this woman who was always certain her ideas were sensible had actually come up with one that really *was* sensible. Tonight was a one-off. There was no way they'd ever see each other again, which meant they could afford to treat each other politely for the next few hours.

Unless he kissed her, in which case civility would fly out the window, but he'd get a taste of her again...

Man. Was he out of his fucking mind?

Chay cleared his throat and stuck out his hand. She gave it the kind of look he'd seen guys give giant camel spiders in Afghanistan.

The twitch behind his fly died a quick death.

"It's just a hand," he said brusquely, and held it up, palm out. "No secret weapons. You're safe."

Bianca looked at the lieutenant.

Yes. She certainly was.

She knew it because she was not the kind of female he undoubtedly specialized in. The kind who would melt at his feet. She saw him for precisely what he was. A man who objectified women. Who collected them the way some men collected cars.

A man who brought out the absolute worst in her.

Her thoughts flew back to the fuss she'd made over ordering a simple glass of wine. And yes, being honest, she had to admit it had been a fuss.

True, she believed in organization. And in exercising control over her environment. But she'd gone overboard with the wine thing.

Why?

Was it because the lieutenant made her feel flustered?

She could see how he'd have that effect on some women. Women who might find him attractive…and, yes. She knew some might. Lots of women were drawn to bad boys. You didn't need to be a candidate for a doctorate in psych to know that.

That face. The high cheekbones. Eyes so green they flashed like emeralds. That long, leanly muscled body. That low, slightly rough voice.

And that swagger.

He moved with a lazy grace. A lion on the hunt. Self-assured. In command.

And, *Dio*, the way he took what he wanted. That kiss he'd forced on her. What kind of man would do something so primitive?

A man like Chay Olivieri, a voice within her whispered.

Her gaze swept over him.

He had on a worn leather bomber jacket over a tight black T-shirt. Faded jeans that clung to his narrow hips and long legs. Scuffed boots. He looked tough and dangerous, and since she was *not* a woman attracted to bad boys, why did that make her heart skip a beat?

Not that what he wore dictated who he was.

The day he'd kissed her, he'd been wearing dress whites. He'd looked like the naval officer he was, but he'd behaved like a barbarian.

No warning. No lead-up. No polite moves at all.

He'd simply hauled her into his arms and kissed her. As if kissing her had been his right.

She'd been stunned. So stunned that it had taken her a few seconds to react. That was surely the only reason she hadn't punched him in the belly or kneed him in the groin or shoved him away.

It couldn't have been the feel of his strong arms around her, or the hardness of his body, or the silken feel of his mouth.

The hot, exciting, amazing feel of his mouth...

"Well?"

The sudden sound of his voice made her jump. She blinked and looked at him.

"Is it a truce?" he said brusquely. "Or are we just waiting for the start of round two?"

Bianca hesitated. She'd heard people speak of warning bells ringing in their heads and if asked, she'd have said the notion was laughable.

But warning bells were ringing in her head right now.

Not bells exactly. This was more like a tiny voice whispering *Bianca, Bianca, don't be foolish. Walk away. Turn around, phone for a taxi. Walk away.*

And that would be even more foolish.

This man was her sister's husband's best friend. And, in ways that had been impressive—even if she'd never admit it to him—he had helped save her sister's life.

Besides, what was one evening? What could possibly happen in a few short hours?

"Truce," she said.

She put her hand in his…

And felt the heat of his touch, the heat of him, sear its way straight down to her toes.

CHAPTER THREE

THE PARKING LOT, a sea of pickup trucks and low, lean sports cars, was dimly lighted. Bianca jerked away when Chay reached for her elbow.

"The light's bad," he said, "and the lot's uneven. They've been talking about resurfacing it for years, but they still haven't done it."

"I'm fine."

He lifted his hands in surrender. "Suit yourself."

He had a long stride. Matching it wasn't easy. Did he know she was taking two steps to his one? Was it deliberate? And he was right about the lot. It was a muddle of dips and broken concrete, but she could manage. She could—

"Oof!"

Her heel caught in something. He grabbed her arm before she went down.

"Dammit," he growled, "what's the big deal about

accepting my help?"

What, indeed? He was right. His hand on her elbow was meaningless. It was a simple act of courtesy and there was no sense in making more of it than it deserved.

Besides, surely they'd be at his vehicle soon. Would it be a truck with oversized tires or a car that looked fast even standing still? Either would suit him. She'd taken a fascinating course. Psychology of Marketing 101. A man like this would—

He stopped walking. She all but fell into him.

"Here we are," he said.

Here they were, where? Bianca almost said, because they were standing before a motorcycle.

A huge, black, shiny motorcycle.

"A motorcycle?" she said, her voice rising in disbelief.

So much for that marketing course. Of course, Chay Olivieri would ride a motorcycle. How come she hadn't thought of that?

"A '91 Harley Davidson FXDB Sturgis."

He offered the name in much the same way she'd have offered the title of her dissertation, with a detached coolness that you could tell masked a sense of pride.

Only one difference.

Interpersonal Bonding Among Millennials in the Age of the Internet couldn't kill you. A Harley Whatever-It-Was could.

Bianca folded her arms. "Forget it."

"Excuse me?"

"I am not riding that—that thing."

"Technically," he said, as he unhooked a pair of helmets

from a bar and offered one to her, "you won't be riding it. You'll be a passenger."

Just what she needed. Advice on vocabulary from a man who owned a not-very-subtle stand-in for male genitalia.

Although why a guy who looked like he did would need any kind of stand-in…

A series of hard-hitting guitar chords rose into the night.

Chay dug in the pocket of his jeans and took out an iPhone. "Yeah?" He listened, nodded, said, "See you in ten," and tucked the phone away. "That was Tanner. The Thai place is jammed. We're meeting them at a little Italian place farther up the highway."

"Not on that thing."

"That *thing*," he said tightly, "is one of the finest bikes ever made."

"How nice for you."

Chay folded his arms. "What's the problem?"

She had never been on a motorcycle. That was the problem. Especially one that looked like a beast from hell. More to the point, she'd never understood why anyone would want to ride one. Motorcycles looked as if they took charge of their riders. With cars, even trucks, it was the other way around.

"There's no problem," she said, hoping she sounded nonchalant. "I just prefer a car. Or a truck."

"Because?"

Dio. The man was persistent.

"Because they're more comfortable."

He raised one dark eyebrow. "So you've been on a bike before?"

Hell. Say "yes" and he'd only ask more questions. Say "no" and he'd get that smug, superior look on his face and tell her she'd missed the opportunity of a lifetime.

"That isn't the issue," she said. "I simply prefer a car."

He made a show of looking around.

"Well, that's going to difficult, seeing as the bike is what we've got."

"What *you've* got." Bianca opened the small black bag that hung from her shoulder and plucked a smartphone from its depths. "I've got a phone, meaning that in no time whatsoever I'll also have a taxi."

He nodded. "Who's your carrier?"

"What?"

"I said, who's your carrier? Your cellphone provider."

"I don't see where that's any of…"

She frowned. Jiggled the phone.

"Something wrong?"

He spoke politely. Far too politely, especially now that there was a smirk on his face.

"My phone isn't working."

"No. I didn't think it would. Cell coverage sucks here— if you don't have the right carrier."

Bianca held her phone skyward. Waved it. Glared at it. She swung towards him, eyes narrowed with suspicion.

"Did you do something to my phone?"

He laughed. She blushed. She was not in the habit

of asking stupid questions. Had an hour with Chay Olivieri reduced her to this?

"I wish I could take credit. I mean, I'd love to be a magician who can kill a smartphone with a look, but nope, I can't. Everybody around here knows the deal. The coverage sucks for the next couple of miles."

Bianca breathed in. Breathed out. He could almost see her telling herself he was either lying or joking. She turned the phone off. Turned it on. Did the little dance people do when their phones crap out.

"The twenty-first century Mashed Potato."

She stared at him. "What?"

"That dance. The one people do when they're trying to find a network. Fun to watch, but it won't work. Not here."

Bianca felt her lips twitch. She wanted to laugh, but behaving politely for an evening when other people were around was one thing. Laughing with the enemy was quite another.

Instead, she muttered something in Italian and dropped the phone into her purse.

"So," Chay said politely, "you change your mind about how we're gonna get to that restaurant?"

"You could," she said coldly, "use your phone to call a cab for me."

He shrugged, leaned back against the motorcycle and folded his arms over his chest.

"Yup. I could."

Dio, she despised this man! Despised him! He was so

disgustingly smug, so arrogant, so convinced that he was God...

"Must I beg?" she snapped.

He gave her a long, assessing look. The remnants of that irritating smirk vanished.

"There's a thought. I mean, having you beg might be interesting."

His voice was soft. Rough. The sound of it took her back to that weekend, to the wedding, to the way he'd kissed her and she'd told him never to try that again and he'd said he wouldn't, not until she asked...

Without warning, he stood away from the Harley, dug out his phone and tossed it to her.

"There's an Uber icon in the top row," he said briskly. "They'll send somebody for you."

She nodded. For some inexplicable reason, her throat had gone dry.

"Just tell the dispatcher you're at the Landing Zone. The drivers all know where it is."

She nodded again, found the icon, touched it, put the phone to her ear. "Yes," she said, to the person who answered. "I need a car, please. I'm at a bar. The Landing Zone. Fine. Uh-huh. Oh. Just a minute." She looked at Chay. "Where am I going?"

"What do you mean, where are you going?"

"The restaurant. What's the name of it?"

The restaurant. He'd been there half a dozen times since it had opened. *That little Italian place* was what everybody called it.

Surely it had a name.

Unfortunately, he had no idea what it was.

He told that to the Tigress. She looked at him as if he'd just announced he was from Mars.

"What do you mean, you don't know the name? You must know it. You've been there before, haven't you?"

He shrugged. "Yeah. But I never think of it as anything but the Italian place."

She stared at him. Then she put the phone to her ear and said, very politely, "Sorry to have bothered you." The polite tone vanished as she shoved the phone in his direction. "Call Tanner. Ask him."

Right. Ask Tanner the name of the restaurant. *Why do you need it?* Tanner would say, and then he'd have to explain that Bianca was the one who needed it so she could tell an Uber driver where to take her.

Well, hell.

All of that would become clear when they arrived separately, he on his Harley, she in a car. Unless he waited for her outside the place because he'd certainly get there first. So, yeah, he could wait until she arrived, and then they'd go inside together—unless, by some chance, Tanner and his wife had decided to wait outside, too…

"This," he said grimly, "is getting complicated."

"In what way?"

"The idea was not to make Tanner and your sister uncomfortable, right? Well, arriving at the restaurant separately might not fill the bill."

Bianca didn't answer. Then she sighed, looked skyward, as if she might find an answer to their dilemma scrawled on the night's black canvas.

Finally, she nodded.

He was right.

She could almost hear the questions, especially from her sister—a sister who, given the same set of circumstances, would undoubtedly view riding the Harley as a thrill.

Except, as Lieutenant Arrogant had pointed out, she wouldn't really be riding it. He would ride; she'd just hang on for dear life.

Hang on to him—she'd seen the way couples rode these things.

And maybe, just maybe, that was the real issue.

That she didn't like the idea of putting herself into someone else's care.

Into a man's care. Into this man's care.

Oh, hell.

Maybe the real issue was envisioning herself sitting tucked behind him, wrapping her arms around his hard body, pressing herself against his back...

The hot images in her mind fled, replaced by uncomfortable images of herself trying to deny the truth of those images to her sister. Alessandra had always possessed an uncanny knack of seeing through her.

Bianca took a deep breath.

"Okay."

"Okay, what?"

"I'll get on that thing."

"It's called—"

"I don't care what it's called." She waved her hand at the Harley. It looked as if it had gotten even bigger. "It will be more exponient to do this together."

"It's *expedient*. And—"

"I knew that," she said sharply. "I misspoke. That was all."

That wasn't all. Chay didn't know her very well. Hell, he didn't know her at all. But he'd already figured out that when she was upset or nervous, her all but perfect English developed flaws.

"But there will be rules."

Jesus H. Christ. "What rules?"

"You will not go too fast."

"Not a hair over ninety," he said, straight-faced. "What else?"

"You will go slowly on curves."

"Curves are my specialty. What else?"

"I do not want you to think I am wary of riding this—this—"

"Harley," he said politely. "A Harley Davidson 1991 FXDB Sturgis."

"Whatever. I am not wary of it, but—"

"Of course you're wary of it," he said impatiently. "You're scared you'll fall off. Or that we'll crash. When you're afraid of something, admit it. Face it. Deal with it."

She looked at him in surprise. Psychology, from

Lieutenant God?

"Just relax." His tone softened. "I've been riding most of my life." His teeth flashed in a quick smile. "Hell, I've been riding damn near all of my life. And I haven't had an accident yet."

Well, it wasn't really a lie. He hadn't had an accident worth mentioning and the one that, okay, maybe was worth mentioning hadn't been his fault.

"So we're okay with this?" he said.

She nodded. "Okay."

He held out a helmet. "Safety rule number one. Always wear a helmet."

She took the helmet from him it and pulled it on. The band that held all those long, soft golden strands at the nape of her neck came loose just as he reached for the chinstrap.

A silken curl brushed across his knuckles.

Something sizzled deep inside him. He jerked his hand away.

"Could you go a little faster?" he said sharply.

"*Cristo*! Are you always so impatient?"

"I'm not impatient. I just want to catch up with Tanner and your sister before breakfast."

"Very amusing."

"I'm glad you think so." Chay unzipped his leather jacket and shrugged it off. "Now get the jacket on."

Bianca stared at him. 'Why would I want to wear that?"

"It's leather."

"Yes," she said with a bright, infuriating smile. "I can

see that. Bikers always wear leather, and I thank you for the offer, but I have no need to try to look macho, or whatever the female equivalent is called."

He knew he'd just been insulted. Baited, maybe, but why rise to that bait? An insult only mattered if you were going to have to keep dealing with the person who'd insulted you. Well, he wouldn't. After tonight, he'd never have to see Bianca Bellini Wilde again.

Maybe there was a God after all.

"Bike safety rule number two. Leather isn't about looks. It's about protection. Leather can keep your skin from scraping off if we take a tumble. Skin is soft. Asphalt isn't."

Excellent. That stopped her. It also turned her a little pale. Time to retreat a little or he'd never get them the fuck out of here.

"Not that we'll take a tumble," he added quickly. "It's just a precaution."

"But what about you?"

"I have no intention of crashing my bike."

"Nobody intends an accident to happen."

"Jesus, woman, must you argue over everything? Put your arms into the sleeves. That's it."

He clasped her shoulders, turned her towards him. The jacket seemed to have swallowed her whole. She looked small and frightened. He thought of the women whose eyes always lit at the sight of his big Harley, and how eager they were to ride it with him.

"The Bountiful Babe Machine," Declan Sanchez had

dubbed it one unforgettable weekend, and the guys had all guffawed.

It didn't take a genius to figure out that the Tigress would not find the designation amusing.

"Listen," he said, his tone softening, "I know you're afraid of getting on the bike, but—"

Her chin lifted. "I am afraid of nothing, Lieutenant."

"Yeah, well, just in case you are—"

"Perhaps you didn't hear what I said."

"How could I not hear you?" he said, his voice rising. "You're shouting."

"I am speaking emphatically. I am not shouting."

"Look, you admitted it just a few minutes ago. You said you were fearful, and I said the best way to deal with fear was to face it, and—"

"*I* didn't say that. *You* did. It's what you always do, Lieutenant. You make assumptions and—"

Dammit, he thought, there was only one way to shut her up.

Cover her mouth with his.

Kiss her.

And kiss her. Kiss her until it happened just the way it had happened all those months ago at the wedding. Kiss her until she moaned and leaned into him, until she parted her lips, opened for him, to him…

Chay swung away and grabbed his helmet. He jammed it on his head. Closed the chinstrap. Then he threw his leg over the bike.

"Zip up the jacket," he growled. "Check the helmet strap. Now climb… Wait." He reached out. She jumped back. He grabbed her pocketbook, tugged it off her shoulder, then slipped the strap over her head so the purse fell across her body. "Okay. Take a look at the bottom of the bike. See those steel pegs? Stand on one with your left foot. Good. Now put your leg over the bike. That's the way. Okay. Excellent."

He could feel her shifting her weight, trying to get used to the feel of the seat.

"Got your feet set?"

"Yes. But what do I hold onto?"

There was a faint tremor in her voice. He wanted to reach back, touch her hand, tell her she'd be fine, but he knew better.

She'd jerk away, put up those I-don't-need-anybody walls.

Stroking a tigress could be bad for a man's health.

Besides, she really would be fine.

He was one damn good rider, and he had no intention of breaking any speed limits tonight.

True, he'd never installed a passenger seatback on the Harley. She'd have to lean forward and hold onto him. There were grab bars, but she didn't know that. And he, bastard that he was, couldn't come up with a reason to point them out.

"Lieutenant? Did you hear what I said? What do I hold on to?"

He turned the key. The big engine roared to life; the power of it throbbed beneath him.

"Me," he said, raising his voice over the sound of the bike.

She said something. *No.* Or maybe something harsher. He shifted into gear and let the bike roll forward.

And felt the first tentative touch of her hands at his waist.

He gave the bike a little gas.

She reacted instantly, leaning into him, pressing herself to him, her breasts against his back, her open thighs around his hips, her arms wound tightly around him. As he started out of the lot, he thought that if she held him any tighter, he might find breathing difficult.

But the unvarnished truth was that he'd been finding it difficult to breathe since the first time he'd set eyes on Bianca Bellini Wilde.

Chay frowned, shifted gears, and sent the big motorcycle into the night.

CHAPTER FOUR

"YOU?" ALESSANDRA SAID. "On a Harley?"

The sisters were standing before a mirror that stretched above a line of sinks in the ladies' room of Chay's "little Italian place." Its actual name, *Piccola Italia*, Little Italy, was so close to what he'd called it that Bianca would have laughed if she hadn't arrived at the restaurant too breathless to do anything except wonder how she'd survived the ride.

Breathless because the ride had been scary.

Surely not breathless for any other reason…

"Hey."

She blinked and met Alessandra's eyes in the mirror.

"I said, I'm still amazed. That you rode Chay's Harley. Tanner just assumed he had his truck. I mean, if we'd known he had the bike, we'd have insisted you go with us."

"Yes," Bianca said, as if the entire episode didn't amaze her, too, "but he didn't have a truck, so what is there to be amazed about? The motorcycle was the only vehicle available."

Alessandra poked her in the side with her elbow.

"You know what I mean. You're just not, you know, you're not the motorcycle type."

"And what type am I, pray tell?"

Alessandra rolled her eyes. She knew that tone of voice. It belonged to the highly intelligent, highly educated, highly irritating Bianca Bellini Wilde, soon-to-be Bianca Bellini Wilde, PhD.

"Give me a break. You'd sooner ride an elephant than a motorcycle."

Bianca leaned forward and frowned at her reflection. The helmet had wrecked her hair. She's lost the band that held her ponytail. Now what?

"And," Alessandra added, "this isn't just any motorcycle. It's a Harley."

"What's the difference?"

"Harleys are…well, they have a reputation. For being big. Good-looking. And bad." Alessandra shot Bianca a sideways glance. "Kind of like your lieutenant."

"For heaven's sake," Bianca said quickly, "he is not *my* lieutenant! Why would you call him that?"

"I don't know." Alessandra smiled. "Maybe because it looks more involved than that."

"What looks more involved than that?"

"Your relationship."

"*Mannaggia!* There is no relationship. Why would you even suggest such a thing?"

Alessandra dug into her purse, found a tube of gloss, leaned closer to the mirror and applied it to her lips.

"Well, he has this way of looking at you."

"As if he would like to wring my neck," Bianca said. "Yes. I've noticed."

"And there's the way you look at him…"

"As if I would like to return the favor. Really, Alessandra, you have such a vivid imagination."

"And the way you go at each other…"

"Like wolves fighting over a carcass. Oh yes," Bianca said grimly, "that is surely the sign of a relationship."

"It can be. Tanner and I squabbled endlessly when we met."

Bianca opened her purse and dug through it. "I know I have a comb here somewhere…"

"I mean, we sniped. And argued. And fought. And look at us now."

"Research shows that squabbling, as you call it, may be an indication of sexual attraction, but—"

"Aha!"

"But," Bianca said firmly, "it is equally an indicator of dislike."

"What about those looks?"

"For heaven's sake! What looks? Your imagination is not just vivid, it is overactive. The lieutenant does not like me. I do not like him. End of story." Bianca frowned. "Do you have a comb? I cannot find mine."

Alessandra looked at Bianca in the mirror. "You cannot

find yours?"

"No. Otherwise, why would I ask for—What?"

"What you just said. You cannot find your comb. You never speak that way unless something's thrown you off balance."

"I do not know what you are talking about."

Alessandra rolled her eyes. "There. You just did it again. 'I cannot find my comb. I do not know what you are talking about.' That formality. That perfect diction."

"Something is wrong with speaking correctly?"

"It's what you do when you're nervous."

"You do the same thing."

"Yes. But you're the one doing it right now."

"No, I am not. I am not doing…" Bianca narrowed her eyes at her sister's smug expression. "What's your point?" she said, though it took all her determination to say *what's* instead of *what is*.

"My point," Alessandra said, "is that Chayton Olivieri is hot. And he has the hots for you."

"Ridiculous."

"That he's hot?"

"That he has anything but disdain for me. And trust me, the feeling is mutual."

"But you admit that he's hot."

Bianca ran her hands through her helmet-flattened hair. It tumbled over her shoulders and she flashed to a moment in the bar when she'd realized a strand of hair had come loose. She'd brushed it back, looked up—and found the lieutenant's eyes on her hand. On that strand of hair. Whatever he'd been thinking had been there, blazing in his eyes, and for a heartbeat, just for a heartbeat, she'd wondered what would happen if she whispered his name and went into his arms...

"Bianca?"

"What?"

Alessandra handed her sister a comb. "Can you at least admit that he's hot?"

"I admit that there are some women who might find him attractive." Bianca said, digging the comb into her hair and dragging the teeth through the tangles. "I am not one of them."

"He's never come on to you? Said something? Maybe kissed you?"

Color swept into Bianca's face. Alessandra raised a fist in triumph.

"I knew it. I knew it! Tanner said I was crazy, but I said—"

"You and Tanner discussed this? You discussed me?"

"Don't get upset. We talked about it. Just a little. I mean, husbands and wives talk, Bianca. It's part of a relationship."

"I agree," Bianca said, in her best psychologist-as-clinician voice. "Talking is part of a relationship. Hurling insults back and forth is not."

Alessandra looked at her. "Insults?" She sighed. "Okay. Maybe I'm wrong. Maybe you're not interested in Chay. Maybe he's not interested in you. But you have to admit, he's gorgeous."

Bianca shrugged her shoulders. "If you like the type."

"I'd bet most women he meets like his type just fine."

"Perhaps. But I am not most women."

Alessandra gazed at her beautiful, brilliant, all-in-control-all-the-time sister and sighed again.

"No. You're not." She made a tsk-tsk sound, snatched the comb away and began smoothing it through Bianca's hair. "The bald look is out this year, B. Definitely out."

Bianca softened at the old childhood nickname.

"Thank you for that amazing information, A. I surely wouldn't have known it otherwise."

They smiled at each other in the mirror.

"So how was it?" Alessandra said.

"Mmm," Bianca said, tilting her head back as Alessandra worked the comb through her hair. "How was what?"

"The ride on the Harley."

"Are we back to that? It was all right."

"*Mamma mia!* Your first ride on a motorcycle, on a Harley, was just all right?"

"What do you want me to say? It was okay. Kind of loud. And not very comfortable."

"That's it? Loud? And uncomfortable?"

"What else could it have been?"

"I don't know. Fun. Exciting. Romantic."

Bianca pushed the comb away. "Okay. Enough. The sooner we get back to the table and order dinner, the sooner I can say goodbye to the lieutenant and to this inane conversation." She smoothed her hair, yanked it back to the nape of her neck, then groaned. "*Mannaggia.* What am I going to use to hold it back?"

"I guess you're just going to have to wear it loose," Alessandra said. She frowned as Bianca dug into her purse. "What are you doing?"

"Looking for another hair band. I almost always carry a spare… Aha! I have one."

"Where?"

"Right he—Alessandra! Why did you do that?"

"Why did I do what?" Alessandra said innocently, as if she hadn't just snatched the band from her sister's hand and tossed it into the trash.

"But I needed that!"

"What you need, B, is to learn how to deal with your emotions."

Bianca turned towards her sister, hands on her hips, eyes narrowed.

"Are you crazy? I'm a psychologist. What do you think that means? I deal with emotions every day."

"Other people's. Not yours. Or maybe I should say you don't deal very well with yours."

"All this because I didn't give you the answer you wanted about how it was to ride that motorcycle?"

"All this because your answer wasn't honest."

"Ridiculous!"

"I don't think so. There had to be more to it than noise and—what did you call it? Discomfort."

"The word I used was *uncomfortable*. And it was. The throb of the engine. The wind in my face. And the—the intimacy of it, sitting behind a man who's practically a stranger, your arms wrapped around him, your body leaning into his, your thighs spread to accommodate his hips…"

The bathroom door swung open. The sound of soft rock from the three-piece band that, it turned out, was a part of what drew patrons to *Piccola Italia* drifted into the room along with three giggling teenage girls.

Bianca stared at her sister, who was staring back her, wide-eyed.

Dio. She had said too much. Alessandra had a way of poking and prodding. She'd done it even when they were children.

It drove her crazy.

Bianca swung towards the mirror.

They'd grown up in the same house with the same parents—a father whose word meant little, a mother who adored him anyway—but somehow only she, not Alessandra, had benefitted from the lesson such an existence provided. And she had no idea why. Perhaps it was Alessandra's more even disposition. Her calmer temperament.

Whatever it was, Bianca had learned what her sister hadn't.

Yes, of course, people had emotional reactions to things, but what was the advantage in giving in to those emotions? Emotion only made you more vulnerable, and vulnerability was dangerous.

It left you open to pain, and nothing good could possibly come of pain.

The psychologist who'd worked with her—seeing a shrink was part of what you had to do to complete the grad program—had at first shaken his head at her attitude about what he called emotional self-concealment, but he had to admit it seemed to work for her in her professional capacity as a brand new clinician in a small, very successful practice.

The practice—five psychologists plus a psychiatrist-consultant they turned to when they they needed prescriptions written—dealt almost exclusively with clients others had failed to help. "Difficult cases," they were called, which was an understatement.

Her family didn't know any of that. Why tell them? Her sisters would go into lecture mode, her brothers into protective mode. There would be a BIG CONFRONTATION, caps all the way, and she'd end up telling them that she loved them all but she was an adult and they had to mind their own business.

As it was, she regretted telling Alessandra about the patient who'd somehow learned her private cellphone number and phoned her in Texas. Alessandra had been upset. She'd wanted to tell Tanner and everyone else what had happened, which was why Bianca made light of the incident, convinced her it wasn't worth mentioning—and never added that there'd been more than one call and that each call had been more disturbing than the last.

Anyway, she'd had her number changed so it wouldn't happen anymore.

Admittedly, some of her cases made her shudder. The guy who dreamed about his mother's death even though she was very much alive. The eighteen-year-old who'd served three years as a juvenile for murder and who'd stopped showing up for appointments with her as well as with his parole officer.

Her work could be tough. Draining. But she loved it, the challenge of listening without judging, and helping put torn lives back together.

"Someday," her shrink had said, "you might want to try to heal your own wounds," but he was wrong. She had no wounds. What she had was a logical approach to life. Those who didn't had no place in hers.

And that, she thought as she stared at herself in the mirror, brought her straight back to Chay Olivieri, a man whose life was all about emotion.

What else could you call it when he reveled in danger, risk, and adrenaline? She had to admit it did make him exciting, but quicksand was also exciting and no sane person would deliberately step into quicksand...

"'Scuse me. Could I get to the mirror?"

Bianca blinked. One of the teens was trying to peer over her shoulder.

"Oh. Oh, of course. Sorry."

She stepped back, ducked to the side so she could still get a glimpse of herself and made a face as she tried to flatten her hair.

"What you should do," the girl said, "is bend forward and run your hands through it."

Bianca raised her eyebrows.

"Your hair. You know. Fluff it. Get those waves even

looser. Wish I had hair like that. It looks great."

What her hair looked was awful. Wild. Untamed. Uncontrolled.

"No," Bianca said emphatically, trying to smooth it down again. "It doesn't."

"*Mannaggia*, B," Alessandra snorted. She grabbed he comb and dumped it into her purse. "If we don't get out there soon," she said, grasping her sister's hand and pulling her towards the door, "the guys will have given up hope, ordered pizza with garlic and anchovies, and we'll have to choose between pretending we like garlic and anchovies or just sitting there and stuffing our faces with bread."

The teens giggled. Bianca tried for a smile, and what choice did she have except to let Alessandra hurry her out the door?

Anyway, the evening was almost over. Supper would be quick. Chay wouldn't want to spend any more time in her company than she wanted to spend in his, and despite their so-called truce, she suspected things wouldn't be very comfortable for anybody. So they'd eat, make an attempt at polite conversation. Then they'd all say "goodnight"; the lieutenant would get on his Harley; she, her sister and Tanner would climb into the truck, and that would be the end of it.

The restaurant, already busy when she and the lieutenant had arrived, had crowded up. The place was evidently a weekend destination, probably because of that three-piece band on a raised platform in the rear of the room.

Music, Bianca thought disconsolately. Just what she

wasn't in the mood for.

And what had happened to their table? The lieutenant and her brother-in-law were no longer sitting where they'd left them. That space was now occupied by six women.

"Where—" Bianca started to say, but Alessandra interrupted.

"The guys are in a booth. See? Over there, near that big potted palm."

Bianca followed her sister's pointing finger and spotted Chay and Tanner seated across from each other in a leather booth that clearly had not been constructed to accommodate men who each stood six feet two inches and weighed in at what had to be two hundred muscle-hard pounds.

Alessandra laughed. "They look like giants trapped at a kids' table."

Bianca supposed it was an apt description.

But all she could really think about was how close she'd be sitting to Chay.

Her pulse beat stuttered.

And of how perfect a male specimen he was.

There was nothing new in the knowledge.

No matter how much he irritated her, she wasn't a fool.

The chiseled face. The deep green eyes with their thick fringe of dark lashes. The short, thick midnight-black hair. The long, sculpted body.

Any woman who didn't admire what she saw was kidding herself.

Now, for reasons that were beyond her comprehension,

looking at him almost stole her breath away.

Maybe it was how he was sitting, his arms folded over his chest because he really had nowhere else to put them, his body all but sprawled across the seat so he could gain some floor space for his long legs.

Maybe it was the intensity with which he was listening to Tanner, an intensity that radiated in the glitter of his eyes, the tilt of his smiling mouth.

Maybe it was something more basic than any of those things.

Maybe it was the memory of how it had felt to hold him on that bike...

"Here they are," Tanner said, smiling as he got to his feet. "They asked us to move from our table. Seems they had a larger group to seat...Well, anyway, we said this booth was fine." His smile broadened. "You know, ladies, there'll come a time when some smart guy is gonna figure out why women go to the bathroom in groups, what takes them so long once they get there, and he'll make himself a small fortune."

Alessandra slipped past her husband. It was a tight fit and she turned her face up to his, grinned and fluttered her lashes. Tanner brushed his mouth lightly over hers.

"Welcome back," he said softly. "I missed you."

Bianca looked away. The moment was too intimate, too tender to watch. Instead, she turned her attention to the lieutenant.

He'd stood up as soon as he saw her. And, unlike Tanner, he'd stepped into the aisle to give her room to get into the booth without their bodies coming in contact. She was grateful for that. Her thoughts were a maelstrom of confusion. The last thing she wanted was to feel him against her.

"Thank you," she said politely.

He nodded, but just as she started to edge into the booth, a harried voice said, "Sorry! Sorry! Coming through."

She barely had time to see the waiter barreling towards her, a huge tray laden with steaming plates in his hands.

Chay grabbed her arm and tugged her out of the waiter's path. She fell against him, his body hard against hers, his strong arms locking her to him.

A tremor swept through her.

She looked up and found herself staring into his eyes. They were fixed on hers and burned hot with emerald fire.

Her heart began to race.

And—and so did his. She could feel its swift beat under her hands, which had ended up spread over his chest.

She felt his hands spread over her back. Felt the quick, exciting response of his erection against her belly.

The sounds of the restaurant—the tinkle of silverware, the chatter of conversation, the music—faded. All she could hear was the quick, indrawn sound of Chay's breath.

And then it was over.

The world went back to spinning on its axis. The hum of conversation, the clink of china, the music… Everything was normal again.

Chay let go of her, stepped back, nodded politely and motioned her into the booth.

She searched for something intelligent to say, something that would erase whatever it was that had just happened, but her brain wouldn't work properly.

"Close call," was the best she could manage.

"Yeah."

Yeah? That was it? Had she misread that look in his eyes? Imagined the sudden race of his heart? The sharpness of his breath? Evidently she had, because he'd picked up his menu and was reading it as if it was the latest best seller.

Bianca reached for her own menu.

That was fine with her.

In fact, it was sensible, because her reactions as well as his hadn't come from his catching her in his arms. It had come from almost ending up wearing platters of pasta as adornments.

Amazing what your head could do with a simple incident.

"B? You okay?"

She looked up. Alessandra was staring across the table at her.

"Yes," she said quickly. "I'm fine. I'm just…What's good here? The pasta? Pizza? Anybody have any suggestions?"

"The zabaglione is fantastic," Tanner said, and Alessandra rolled her eyes and said that was just like him, to think of dessert first, and Tanner grinned, leaned in and kissed her, and said something about dessert always being the best part of anything.

Alessandra blushed and laughed.

And Chay… Chay made a sound, a muffled groan that

seemed to imply distress. Or maybe not, because when Bianca looked at him, his gaze was still on the menu.

Which was where hers should be, she told herself firmly, and though the letters swam before her eyes, looking at the menu was exactly what she did.

• • •

They decided to order drinks while they thought about what to have for dinner. Tanner stayed with Stone ale. Alessandra named something that made her husband sigh.

"Fruit salad in a glass," he said, "topped with a paper umbrella."

She poked him, he grinned and opened his menu so they could lean in and share it.

The waiter looked expectantly at Bianca. "Would you like something to drink, miss?"

Chay put his hand lightly on her arm before she could respond. "What Malbecs do you have?"

Bianca looked at him in surprise as the waiter rattled off several names.

"That one," Chay said. "The *Noemia de Patagonia*. The lady and I will have a bottle."

"You didn't have to do that," Bianca said quietly when the waiter was gone.

"No big thing." His eyes met hers. "I like something different every now and then."

"Eggplant lasagna," Tanner said, "and pasta carbonara.

And how about sharing an antipasto?"

Chay looked at Tanner. "What?"

"I said, we know what we're having. Eggplant lasagna for my veggie bride, the carbonara for me. How about you?"

Dammit, Chay thought. How about him, indeed?

Why had he said that to Bianca? That thing about wanting to try something different every now and then? It was a come-on line. She'd known it—he'd seen her eyes widen, the color sweep into her face when he'd spoken—and the last thing he was interested in was coming on to Bianca Bellini Wilde. All he'd wanted to do was order a wine she'd like by way of apologizing for having been such an asshole in the parking lot at the LZ.

And in the LZ itself.

He'd been rude.

Okay. He'd been deliberately unkind.

Truth was, no way would he have abandoned her in that lot, let her take a taxi even if he'd remembered the name of the restaurant they were now in. She was a walking, talking bundle of attitude, and she got under his skin every time, but he wasn't a man who'd ever treat a woman badly...

"Hey," Tanner said, "I know it's a huge decision, but what are two going to have for dinner?"

Chay looked at Bianca. From the expression on her face, she hadn't paid the menu any more attention than he had.

She shook her head. "I haven't...I'm not really very hungry."

"Cioppino," Chay said, because it was the first thing he

thought of. "For both of us."

That brought things back to normal. She sat up straighter and fixed him with what he was starting to think of as That Look.

"Lieutenant," she said briskly, "I am perfectly capable of choosing my own meal."

His eyes narrowed. "Then choose it."

"A steak. Small. No more than seven ounces. Done rare. Not raw. Pink, not red…" She looked around the table. Alessandra and Tanner were dutifully staring at their menus. Chay was staring at her.

Glowering was more like it.

She considered slapping him with her menu.

No! Never. Why would she even think of doing something so out of control? She smiled, though it wasn't easy to do, and closed her menu.

"On second thought," she said pleasantly, I'll have the *tagliata* with parmesan."

The Akechetas seemed to let out their breath.

Chay nodded. "Sliced steak. With cheese shaved over it."

"Good idea?" she said, smiling with all her teeth.

"Great idea," he said, smiling with all his.

And in the flurry of handing over their menus, and then the arrival of the wine and the drinks, the conversation eased into more normal channels, giving Chay the chance to glance at his watch and figure how much more time he'd have to spend before he could say good-night, hunt up Maguire and

Sanchez, find some women men could understand, and take them to bed where life could be reduced to basics. Hot sex. Mindless pleasure, and never mind how badly he'd handled things with the brunette a couple of hours ago. He was back from deployment, his mood was in the toilet, and a night with a woman who knew how to please a man would change it, not a night spent sparring with the prickly, pluperfect, pain in the ass Bianca Bellini Wilde who knew nothing about pleasing a man.

And never would.

• • •

The wine was excellent. The antipasto they'd eventually settled on was good. And if the food wasn't four-star, what in life was?

As for Bianca…

Alessandra was working hard at drawing her into conversation. At first, it didn't work. Then Alessandra told a joke, a god-awful joke, and after they all groaned, Bianca told it again, but with an ironic twist that actually made it funny.

Interesting.

The lady had a sense of humor. Wry, but that was fine with him. He'd never laughed at slip-on-the-banana peel jokes and, it seemed, neither did she.

And she had a brain. Well, he'd already figured that out, but once you got her off that high horse she rode, she could make interesting conversation.

So many of the women he met didn't, unless you

thought discussing the lives of pop stars in endless, boring, unbelievable detail was interesting.

Bianca had real interests, and a real life.

She didn't bring up any of that. Her sister did. Alessandra got her to admit that she was writing her PhD dissertation.

"What's it called again?"

"Alessandra. Nobody wants to hear—"

"I do," Chay said. "What's the title?"

Bianca sighed. "*Interpersonal Bonding Among Millennials in the Age of the Internet.*"

There was a beat of silence. Then Tanner raised his bottle of ale. "I'll drink to that."

Everyone laughed, even Bianca. "What can I tell you? I wanted to research something current."

"And she has a fancy job," Alessandra said proudly, "as a clinical psychologist at this mega-upscale private practice. East Side Associates," she added, rolling her eyes.

"Alessandra," Bianca said in a low voice, "really—"

"Where you help millennials form interpersonal relationships."

Bianca gave Chay a cool look.

"Actually, that's not at all what I do."

"No?"

"No. I help people with serious problems."

"Ah." Chay grinned. "Meaning, people in interpersonal relationships don't have real problems?"

Was he laughing at her or just laughing at life? Because

he was right, even if she had no intention of telling him so. The people she'd studied for her dissertation were lightweights compared with the real people she now dealt with day to day.

"Meaning," she said, "I don't talk about my patients." She said it more harshly than she'd intended, but she had the feeling she knew where Alessandra was taking this. "Professional ethics," she added quickly, hoping she was wrong about her sister.

Unfortunately, she wasn't.

"It's true," Alessandra said. "She never does—but I wish she'd talk about the one who called her when we were in Texas."

"Yeah," Tanner said. "I'm glad he never called you ag—What?" he said, when his wife dug her elbow into his ribs. "Oh." He cleared his throat. "Yeah. Alessandra told me what happened."

Bianca glared at Alessandra, who tried to look contrite—and failed.

"I'm sorry," Alessandra said. "And I didn't mention the call to anyone else." She looked at her husband. "When you love someone so much that it feels as if you're a part of him and he's a part of you…" She shook her head. "I was upset. And when I'm upset, I turn to Tanner."

"I hope you always will," Tanner said softly, taking his wife's hand and bringing it to his lips.

Chay cleared his throat.

"Would one of you like to clue me in on what the hell you're all talking about?"

Bianca hesitated. Then shrugged her shoulders. "I had

a call from a man. A patient."

"While you were away? Don't you have somebody who covers for you?"

"I do. The thing is, I'm not sure how he got my private cell number."

Chay frowned. "What do you mean?"

"Just that. I never give my personal number to patients."

"And the call from this guy was upsetting?"

Upsetting wasn't a good enough word to describe that call or the five that had followed, but Alessandra didn't know about them—and she wasn't going to.

"He was," Bianca said carefully, "a little distraught."

"Distraught," Chay repeated in a grim tone.

"Look, I really don't want to—"

"Does he have other personal information about you? Your address, maybe?"

"He had my cell number," Bianca said emphatically. "That's it."

She hoped that was it, but she wasn't going to say so. The conversation had already gone deeper than she wanted.

"Anyway," she said lightly, "the worst part was that I had to change my phone number. And I'd barely memorized the first one!"

Alessandra laughed. "Thanks to Siri, nobody has to memorize phone numbers anymore."

Everyone laughed, including Chay, but years in Special Ops had given his attitude a cynical spin.

A man who tracked down a woman's private phone

number wouldn't be that easy to get rid of. Not if he really was determined. Besides, the guy knew where she worked. And hadn't there been something in Bianca's voice when she talked about him? A hint of—not fear, exactly. Concern.

Maybe yes. Maybe no. After all, what did he know of shrinks?

Nothing. And it was going to stay that way. Professionally—he'd ignored a couple of suggestions by Captain Blake, his CO, that he might benefit from seeing one about this last deployment.

And personally?

Chay reached for his glass of wine and took a sip.

After tonight, anything to do with Bianca Wilde would be history.

• • •

The conversation veered to movies. Then to books. Turned out the Tigress was quite a reader.

Well, he got that. So was he. He was into sea stories. What his English 101 instructor back in his university days had referred to as classics. *Moby Dick. Twenty Years Before the Mast.* All the Horatio Hornblower novels.

Nobody knew that that he was into that stuff and nobody was going to, but he was.

And she knew wine.

She'd sipped the Malbec and when the taste of it bloomed on her tongue, she'd reacted physically, closing her eyes, smiling a secret little smile, and breathing a soft hum of appreciation.

Damned if he hadn't reacted physically too.

Not to the wine.

To the sight of her. The closed eyes. The Mona Lisa smile. The little sigh. He could imagine her making all those same moves in bed.

Why not?

She was prim and proper, but she had a great face and a great body.

She even had great hair.

It took him a while to realize she'd left it free. Once he did, he also realized that if she were his woman, he'd make sure she always wore it that way.

Her hair moved with her. That was a revelation in his world.

The women he knew sprayed their hair into submission. She didn't.

Her hair swung forward when she leaned over the table, swung to the side when she turned towards him. He wondered if it felt as silky as it looked. If one of those long, loose curls would cling to his finger if he caught hold of it

He wondered, too, what would happen if she undid the top button of her blouse. The top two buttons. A couple more than that.

And, dammit, he was drinking too much.

Except, he wasn't.

He was always careful, when he had the Harley out.

Tonight, he'd had ale at the LZ and half a glass of wine here. It took a lot more than that for wine or beer to get to him.

So what was making her look so good to him? He was tired. The endless flight home from Afghanistan took it out of you, that was for sure. And even last night, safe in his own bed, he hadn't slept well. He'd kept dreaming about that fucking mountain, that fucking kid, that fucking bomb…

Chay shot to his feet.

Everybody looked at him.

"What?" Tanner asked.

"Nothing. I mean…" He cleared his throat and looked at Bianca. "Let's dance."

She looked as surprised by his statement as he felt at having made it.

"Dance?" she said.

"Yeah. Dance."

"I don't want to dance."

"Sure you do."

"I just said—"

Tanner rose, grabbed Alessandra's hand and drew her up beside him. "Excellent plan, dude."

The Akechetas hurried off to the dance floor.

Chay looked down at Bianca. "Come on."

She gave him That Look. The one that said he'd had his fun for the night when he'd made her ride his Harley.

"Thanks, but no thanks."

He could have shrugged and sat down, but he was already standing. And he'd be damned if he was going to click his heels and obey words that seemed simple unless you were attuned to the dismissiveness implicit in them.

Chay reached for Bianca's hand. She tried to tug free, but his grip was like iron.

"We're in a restaurant," he said tightly. "There's a band playing. People are dancing, including your sister and my best friend, who are out to have a good time. No way am I going to let you spoil that for them."

"That's ridiculous! They're not the ones who suggested dancing. Even if they had, what has it do with us?"

She was right. His reasoning was ass-backwards, but he was already committed to getting her on that dance floor.

"It has what I say it has to do with us," he said, and if she'd laughed in his face for that burst of male chauvinist crap, he wouldn't have blamed her—but he didn't give her the chance to laugh. Instead, he pulled her to her feet, wrapped a proprietary arm around her waist, and led her to the dance floor.

Once there, he let go of her hand and faced her. She looked about as happy as somebody waiting for a root canal.

"I don't dance very well," she said stiffly.

"You did fine at the wedding."

"I did what had to be done."

"Yeah, well, this is what has to be done now." He sighed, decided to cut her a little slack. "Trust me," he said. "They're never going to invite me to be a contestant on *Dancing with the Stars*."

She almost smiled, which was probably the best he

could hope for.

They began dancing.

And, man, she was right.

He'd been so pissed off over being stuck with her at the wedding that he hadn't really paid attention to how she danced, but just as she'd said, she wasn't very good. She was stiff. Almost mechanical.

Other women shimmied. Flung their arms in the air.

She moved like a robot.

Why? Dancing was easy. This kind especially. There were no formal moves, no patterns to follow. You just let your body feel the rhythm.

Was that the problem? Was his always-sure-of-herself-not-actually-a-date date only comfortable when her brain was in charge?

Before he could figure out the answer, the music changed. Went from fast and hot to slow and hot. Something bluesy had sent the couples around them into each other's arms.

It sent his not-a-date date into a panic.

He saw it in her face. In her body language.

She was going to run.

And though he didn't know why, he was not going to let that happen.

"Bianca," he said, and when she looked up at him, her eyes wide and almost panicky, something deep inside him stirred. "Bianca," he said again, and he took her in his arms.

CHAPTER FIVE

THEY WERE DANCING.

At least that was the lieutenant called it.

She could think of more basic ways to describe what it was like to have his arms around her, his body tight against hers, to be moving in time to the music in the couple of feet of floor space they'd claimed as their own.

If only she'd moved fast enough to make it back to the booth.

Still, this was probably better than sitting next to him, trying to make small talk.

It had been okay when Alessandra was there.

Her sister knew her so well. She'd realized that making conversation wasn't one of her strengths. Well, date conversation, not that this was anywhere close to a date. Still, Alessandra had made things easier. She'd asked the right questions. About things that were easy to talk about. School.

Books. Her new practice. Stuff that had undoubtedly bored everyone else silly, the lieutenant for sure—but between the wine and Alessandra, she'd managed to hold up her end of things.

Or maybe she'd held it up too well.

Maybe she'd said too much.

Maybe she'd monopolized the conversation.

Maybe she'd made a fool of herself…

"Hey."

She looked up. He was smiling. The lieutenant. The gorgeous, sexy lieutenant and, yes, absolutely, she'd had too much wine.

Except, she hadn't.

One glass. That was all she'd had.

Maybe what she'd had too much of was him.

Too much handsome, virile, sexy male sitting for the last hour with his thigh pressed against hers, now with his arms wrapped around her, one big hand splayed over her back, the other down low at the base of her spine.

He felt wonderful. Hard. Warm. He smelled wonderful, too. Night. Man. Even leather, though he'd left his jacket in the booth.

Wonderful, she thought, and stepped on his toes.

"Sorry! I'm so sor—"

"My fault."

"There's no need to lie. I told you, I'm not a very good dan—"

"Stop apologizing. And stop watching yourself."

Stop watching herself? That was precisely what she was doing. What she always did in moments like this, but how did he know that?

"That's better," he said. "Come on. Lean into me. Feel the rhythm."

His voice was a little low. A lot sexy. Lean into him? It made her want to burrow into him, as ridiculous as that was.

"Better," he murmured. His breath stirred a tendril of her hair. "Much better. Just let the music take over."

No way. She never let anything take over. Success depended on control.

Still, if they weren't going to sit down, it was easier to move with him. To let him lead. It was just a dance, after all, and Chay Olivieri was a good dancer. A very good dancer. She remembered that from the wedding.

He was so big, so masculine, but he knew how to move.

He was also easy to look at.

Not only by her standards.

Other women had been eyeing him all night, but why wouldn't they? That face. That body. That everything, and why was she thinking about his looks again? What did his looks matter? Nothing about him mattered, except getting through the rest of the evening.

And yet—and yet, it felt right, being in his arms. She couldn't understand it. Well, she could. There were times things physical got in the way of things intellectual. It had never happened to her before, but she knew it was possible.

Okay. It had happened to her before. With him. That

kiss at the wedding…

Not that it meant anything. It was like—like having a hot dream about sex with a man you'd met.

Just because you had the dream didn't mean you wanted the reality.

The lights dimmed. Changed color, anyway. Blue lights to match blue music. A singer trying hard to sound like Adele.

Chay held Bianca closer.

She sighed. Let her head droop against his shoulder… and jerked back. "We should sit down," she said quickly.

"We should do exactly what we're doing," he said softly.

But that was the problem. Exactly what were they doing?

And then she stopped fighting and let him take over.

• • •

Eventually, the music stopped.

The lights came up. The dance floor emptied. And as Chay took her hand and led her across it, Bianca realized that the entire place had emptied.

Or damn near emptied.

Including their booth.

Tanner had left a note scrawled on a paper napkin.

Hey, dude. Got late. Didn't want to interrupt you guys. Dinner's on us. Will give you a call tomorrow.

Bianca stared at the note, then at Chay. "Did we miss dinner?"

He nodded. "Yeah. So it seems."

"But—how long were we on the dance floor?"

"Long enough," he said, trying to sound casual while he wondered how the time could have passed so quickly.

"What must they think?"

Chay didn't give a damn what Tanner and his wife thought. The real question was, what had *he* been thinking? When had dancing as a way of killing time become dancing to keep Bianca in his arms?

He could feel his head buzzing. With anger. With irritation. At himself. At whatever in hell he'd walked into tonight. His little dance partner liked to be in control of her life? Well, dammit, so did he. It was what he was all about. It was the trait that had gotten him off the reservation, into college, into the SEALs and then into STUD.

He knew who he was and what he was, and somehow tonight had turned all that on its head and he didn't like it, didn't like the woman who'd done it to him.

He dug bills out of his pocket and left them for the waiter as an additional tip, then grabbed his jacket.

"Let's go," he said, his tone brusque.

Bianca's purse had been lying under his jacket. She barely had time to snatch it before he locked his fingers around her wrist. It was not a gentle gesture; it was a commanding one.

"Hey."

He kept moving. He walked fast, his strides long, as he headed for the door.

"Hey," she said again.

He turned and looked at her. "Just keep moving."

Forget brusque. This was a growl. A snarl. Well, dammit, she felt like snarling, too. How had she been drawn into this mess? An evening in the company of a man with all the charm of a wildebeest. Dancing for what seemed like hours when she didn't like dancing. And now this. Abandoned by her sister, sniped at by the wildebeest who was stuck with her, or maybe wildebeests didn't snipe, maybe they were just unpleasant and unattractive, and why was Chay Olivieri the one but not the other? That would make life so much simpler.

They were at the door. He reached for her purse. They scuffled over it and, of course, Lieutenant God won.

"Give me that," she said, breathing hard, more from anger than from the little battle over the purse. What kind of man all but made love to a woman when they were dancing and treated her like an enemy combatant when they weren't?

"First put on my jacket."

He held it out. She shook her head.

"I don't want it."

"I'm not asking if you want it. You'll wear it until I get you to your hotel."

"I'll take a cab."

"No, you will not. I brought you here. I'll deliver you where you belong."

"I am not a package," she said, glaring up at him.

"You might as well be," he said, "for all the softness that's in you."

"I beg your pardon!"

"Beg all you like." He draped the jacket around her again and caught hold of her arm when she tried to push it off. "We've played things your way long enough. Now it's my turn."

"What are you talking about?" she sputtered.

She was looking at him as if he were crazy. Hell. Maybe he was. The truth was, he didn't know what he was talking about. He only knew that he was pissed. More than pissed. He was steaming, and he couldn't wait to be rid of her. And, yeah, while a tiny, still-logical part of his head was saying, *Dude, this isn't her fault,* the not-so-logical part insisted that it was.

He slapped open the door, pushed her outside ahead of him. She shivered. The night had turned chill. A salt-laden wind blew in from the sea.

"I want a taxi."

"I want to fly to the moon," he said. "Neither thing is going to happen."

He kept walking. And he was too big, too strong for her to stand her ground instead of getting dragged along behind him.

"Is deafness another of your qualities, Lieutenant? I said—"

"I brought you here. I'll take you home."

"Such a gentleman."

"Just pick up the pace, Wilde. The sooner we end this charade, the better."

What could she say to that when she agreed with it?

They reached the Harley. He handed her a helmet and put his on. Then he swung his leg across the saddle.

"Get on," he barked.

She gave him a look and climbed on behind him.

"Put your arms around me."

Not until hell froze over. Bianca looked at the bars on either side of her. She hadn't noticed them before. Surely a passenger could cling to them.

"I said—"

"I heard what you said, Lieutenant. Just start this horrible machine and take me to my hotel."

"Which is?"

She named it. He knew it. It was actually a motel, right on the beach and only about ten minutes away.

He turned the key.

"I'm warning you," he said. "You should put your arms around me."

"In your dreams," she said sweetly, and he gritted his teeth, turned on the engine, and they flew out of the parking lot.

He was right.

She knew it instantly. She needed to wrap her arms around him. Sitting up straight, clinging to the bars on either side of her didn't help take away the awful feeling that she was going to fly off the motorcycle. They were soaring through the night, flying past hills on one side and the Pacific on the other, going faster, much faster, than before.

"Damn you," she said, and she leaned in, wound her arms around him, felt his heat, his strength penetrate her skin, her muscles, her bones. "Damn you," she said again, and she did something daring, freed one arm so she could pound her

fist against his shoulder because this was impossible, impossible
for her thighs to tingle where they cupped his body, her nipples
to peak where they pressed into his back, and she loved it, the
feeling of speed, of flight, and the feel of him against her.

She wanted to throw back her head and laugh, or throw
back her head and weep because everything was upside down,
everything was terrifying and exciting and none of it made
sense, and suddenly he jerked the Harley hard to the left and
they were bouncing across sand, the Harley's headlight picking
out the shape of her motel, but he rode past it, down the beach,
along the hard-packed sand down where the waves rolled in
from across the world.

He stopped the bike under one of the palms and turned
it off.

The night became very still. All she could hear was the
sigh of the breeze through the palms, the whisper of the surf,
and the heavy thud, thud, thud of her heart.

 She let go of him and sat up straight. "The motel is
behind us."

"I know where it is."

"Then what are we doing all the way down here?"

"We need to talk."

"I don't think so."

"Get off the bike."

"Didn't you hear me? We'd don't have anything to talk
about."

He put down the kickstand. "Get off the bike, Bianca."

"*Mannaggia*! What is this nonsense, Lieutenant? You

do not give me—"

He slid off the Harley, dumped his helmet on the sand, wrapped his hands around her waist, lifted her from her seat and stood her in front of him.

"This has to stop."

His voice was low. Hard. Hard and…Her pulse rocketed. Hard and hot.

"I don't know what you—"

"Yes. You do. This fighting. This wanting. It stops. Right now. Tonight, goddamn it, it stops…."

He said something short and sharp, pulled her against him, and then his mouth was on hers.

She struggled. Or perhaps she only thought she did, because a heartbeat later, her mouth was open to his, her hands were in his hair, and she was sobbing his name.

Not *Lieutenant*. What she was sobbing was *Chay, Chay, Chay,* and it added to the frenzy building inside him.

This was what he'd needed. What he'd ached for. This, his tigress in his arms, the taste of her desire, of her surrender, sweet on his tongue.

"Tell me," he demanded. "Tell me you want this."

She knew what he meant. That other time he'd kissed her, she'd told him never to touch her again and he'd said he wouldn't until she begged for him to do it.

How could everything have changed so completely? She'd gone from hating him to wanting him in in one night. Just one night…

She couldn't think.

She could only feel. His mouth on hers. His breath whispering over her skin. The rasp of his teeth against her flesh. Pleasure shot through her, but this wasn't enough. She needed more than his kisses, more than his touch, and she whimpered with need, rubbed herself against him like a cat.

He said her name.

She loved the way it sounded coming from his mouth. She loved everything he was doing and when he pulled off her helmet, thrust his hands into her hair, let the silky strands twine around his fingers, she moaned with the electric feel of him caressing her.

He kissed her. Again. And again. His kisses were hard and deep; his tongue swept against hers. He tasted of wine and of himself, and she couldn't get enough of him.

"Bianca," he said. "Say the words."

She rose to him, clasped his face with her hands.

"Kiss me," she whispered. "I want you to kiss me. To touch me. Please. Please. Ple—""

She fell back with him against the trunk of a palm tree. He drank from her mouth, nipped her throat, kissed the pulse that beat wildly in its hollow.

He tugged her purse off her shoulder and let it fall to the sand. His jacket slipped from her shoulders and puddled at her feet.

His hands were at her blouse, working at the tiny buttons, his fingers too big, too clumsy, and finally he cursed and tore the blouse open.

He could see her by the soft light of the ivory moon

that rode high against the black, star-shot sky.

And, God, she was beautiful.

She had on a bra. White. Some pale color. It was plain. No lace. No silk. Nothing about it was sexy, but she didn't need a sexy bra.

She was sex itself.

She was the woman he wanted.

A woman he wanted more than any woman he'd ever been with, and now sure as hell wasn't the time to try and figure that out.

What it was time for was to taste her mouth. Her throat.

Her breasts.

He pushed the bra up.

Her hands rose to cover her breasts.

He caught her wrists, brought her hands to his mouth and kissed the palms.

Then he bent his head and closed his lips around one warm, erect nipple.

She cried out. Her body bucked against his. Her hips arched towards his. He groaned, gathered her breasts between his hands, kissed one and then the other, drew the eager tips into the heat of his mouth.

She tasted the way she smelled. Of flowers. Of the sea. And of cool forest mornings and hot prairie afternoons. She tasted of dreams he'd dreamed and dreams he'd lost, of dreams that had always been just beyond his reach.

She was sobbing. Saying his name. Pressing herself

against him.

Her teeth nipped at his jaw. At his lips. He gave her his tongue and she sucked it into her mouth.

Jesus.

Another minute, he was going to come.

Quickly, he reached for the waistband of her pants. A button popped; the zipper snagged. He cursed and she shoved his hands away and undid the zipper herself.

He pushed her pants and panties down her legs, knelt and tugged one of her feet free. Then he rose. Reached for his fly.

His hand shook as he undid it.

His erection sprang free, throbbing with life.

He put his hand between them. Between her thighs. She gasped. He groaned. She was hot. Wet. For him. For this, he thought, for what only he could give her, and he grasped her thigh, lifted it, brought her leg over his thigh.

"Hang on to me," he whispered.

He drove into her.

Deep, deep into her.

She screamed in ecstasy. Sank her teeth into his shoulder. He rocked into her. Harder. Deeper.

The world was spinning. And she was sobbing his name.

It was everything he had imagined because, yes, he had imagined this.

And it was more.

His name like a song on her lips. Her silken heat

clasping his swollen penis. Her scent, the scent of sex, in his nostrils.

He was close to the edge. Too close. He wanted her to come again. Wanted to feel the glovelike clasp of her around him as she fell off the edge of the world.

He slipped his hands under her ass. Lifted her off the ground. Her legs went around his hips and he drove into her again. And again. And this time, when she screamed, she screamed his name and he let go.

Emptied himself into her. Deep. So deep.

She slumped forward in his arms, her face buried in his shoulder.

He held her that way while his heartbeat steadied. While hers steadied. She was damp with sweat. She shivered, and he knew she must be chilled.

He held her tighter. Stroked his hand down her back.

She deserved more. And more was what he would give her. He'd take her to her room… Hell. No. Tanner and his wife were in this hotel. Where, then?

"Put me down."

He nodded, made soft, soothing sounds. He'd take her to his place. His small cottage up the beach. He never took women there. He'd never even considered doing it, but tonight…

"Lieutenant. Put me down."

Lieutenant?

The word penetrated his thoughts. Still holding her, he drew back. Not far. Just enough so he could see her face.

Hell.

Her face was pale. Her gaze was downturned.

Not good, he thought, dammit, not good.

"Bianca."

"Please. Put me down."

Her voice was a whisper. He could barely hear it. But whatever she was feeling, it wasn't the sweet afterglow of sex.

Slowly, he did as she'd asked. When her feet touched the sand, she raised her hands, placed them against his chest and pushed against it just enough to make it clear she wanted him to step back.

Okay. She needed some space. He got that. What had just happened... No finesse. No tenderness. Yes, he got it. The next time would be—

"Let go of me, please."

Shit. She was polite. Too polite. A stranger asking another stranger to pass the salt would have spoken with more emotion.

"Bianca?"

She looked down at herself. He heard the indrawn hiss of her breath. She took her hands from his chest, grabbed the waistband of her pants, stumbled a little as she jammed her foot back into them. When he tried to help, she jerked away.

"Baby—"

Her gaze flew to his. Her eyes flashed with cold fire. So much for the politeness of strangers.

"Don't."

"Honey. Baby. If you'd just listen—"

"*Honey? Baby?* What's the matter, Lieutenant? Did you forget my name already?"

Okay. She was upset. He'd been a little fast. Not just the way he'd taken her. The entire thing had been a little fast...

"Bianca." She was trying to button her blouse, but hell, that wasn't going to happen. He'd seen all those tiny buttons go flying. "Honey," he said, trying to help her tug the edges of the blouse together, "listen—"

She slapped his hands away.

"No," she said. "*You* listen! This was—what you just did was—"

Chay drew back. "What *I* did?"

"You're right. What we did. It was—it was awful."

Apparently, nobody was going to enjoy the afterglow tonight.

"Look," he said carefully, "I know it was fast. But—"

"Not fast enough." She bent down and picked up her purse. "Would you please step aside?"

"What in hell does that mean? 'Not fast enough.'"

"It means what it is. I thought you would never get to the end."

He felt his jaw tighten. "You made a lot of interesting noises for a woman waiting for something to end," he said coldly.

"You flatter yourself, Lieutenant."

His eyes narrowed. "I'm not deaf or dumb or blind, Ms. Wilde. When a woman comes with me inside her, when she comes twice, I'm aware of it."

"I guess if vibrators could talk, they'd make that same statement."

His smile tilted at one corner of his mouth. "Very nice. Charming, in fact. Anything else you want me to know about your sex life?"

Color swept into her face.

"Remember what I told you the last time you touched me? That it would never happen again?" Her chin lifted. Her mouth thinned. Her eyes glittered with rage. She looked angry and beautiful and for one crazy second he thought of hauling her into his arms and making a lie of the crap she was spouting. "What I'm telling you now is that you are never, ever to so much as speak to me again."

Chay folded his arms over his chest.

"And how, exactly, are you going to explain that to your sister?"

"I won't even try. Tanner has only another couple of days here. There's no reason for our paths to cross."

"What if he suggests dinner? A movie? What if he wants the four of to get together?"

"I'll say I have a cold. A headache." Her chin went up another notch, although how it could have gotten as high as it was struck him as impossible. "If you're afraid I'll tell him the truth, stop worrying. I am not about to cause problems for my sister and her husband."

"You mean you're not about to tell anybody I just fucked your brains out."

She slapped him. Hard. Really hard. The force of the

blow snapped his head back and he figured he'd be wearing her handprint for a couple of hours.

Yeah, but what the hell, he'd deserved it.

What he'd just said had been crude… Hell. Crude, but accurate. Because he damn well had fucked her brains out, which was precisely what she had done to him.

He'd never experienced anything like it.

Sex in a public place? Of course. With a woman he hardly knew? Damn right. Sex that was fast and furious? Hey, there were all kinds of ways to get off.

But sex that had driven every rational thought from his head?

No.

He'd never had sex quite like that, sex that, even now, made him think about silencing her with a kiss, about taking her down to the sand, about burying himself inside her because, despite what she said, it was what she'd want, what she'd sob for, what would drive away all the anger inside him, the emptiness, the pain…

His breath caught.

Was that the reason the sex with her had seemed to explode through him? Was it because of that kid on the mountain? Had he needed this to get the kid out of his head?

Made sense.

Maybe the sex hadn't been mind-blowing.

Maybe his need for it had been what made it seem that way.

Maybe it wasn't about this woman.

It couldn't have been about this woman.

All of a sudden what she said, what she'd laid down as law, that they never deal with each other again, made sense. The truth was, he wanted to forget the entire night and he wasn't going to waste any time getting started on making that happen.

"Get out of my way."

Chay stepped back, but he didn't step aside. Instead, he bent down, picked up his jacket and held it out to her. "You'll need this."

"Are you *pazzo*? I want nothing of yours!"

His gaze raked her from head to toe. "Really?"

She frowned and looked down at herself. He knew what she saw. A blouse hanging open. Pants that no longer had a working zipper.

She said something through her teeth, snatched the jacket from him and wrapped it around herself.

"I will ask Tanner to return it to you."

"Consider it a souvenir," he said as he mounted the Harley. "Go on. Walk to the hotel. There's a back entrance to the lobby. I'll wait until you're safely inside."

"I do not need you to do that."

There it was. That stilted speech. She was upset, and wasn't that just too damn bad?

"No," he said, "I'm sure you can take care of yourself, but I'm going to wait anyway. Consider it part of the services I provided this evening."

She spat a word at him. Then she turned on her heel, a small, stiffly erect figure oozing dignity with every stride as she marched up the beach to the hotel.

He waited until she opened the door and stepped inside. Then he turned the bike on and gunned the engine.

Of course this had been all about what had happened days ago on that fucking mountaintop. It had had nothing to do with Bianca Bellini Wilde.

But that didn't explain her part in it.

Shit.

The truth was, it really didn't explain his part either. Sex to shut the door on a bad memory? Yes. It had worked before. But sex like what he'd just experienced…

Chay rode the bike over the sand and onto the road.

Be honest, man.

It had been…different. It had turned him inside out. Left him feeling as if he could never get enough of the woman he'd held in his arms.

And that was ridiculous.

He upped the Harley's speed.

He knew exactly what to do. Go back to the LZ. Find a woman. There would be one. There always was. Somebody beautiful, hot and eager. Take her to wherever she was staying. Fuck her again and again until the Tigress wasn't even a blip in his mind.

It was a good plan. A great plan.

Except, when he reached the turnoff for the Landing Zone, he hurtled past it and headed straight for home.

CHAPTER SIX

5:10 p.m., a Friday evening in late June, Bianca's office on the Upper East Side of Manhattan

THE DAY HAD started with bright sunshine. The weatherman had predicted rain, but how often was the weatherman right?

Bianca hadn't been surprised that the skies remained clear.

Then, with amazing speed, clouds moved in until they covered the city like a thick gray blanket, so dense that a little while ago she'd had to turn on the lights in her office.

Now, as the first tentative patter of rain hit the window, she looked up from her desk, where she'd been making entries in the file open on her laptop. Could she finish up and get out of the office before the rain turned into a downpour? The subway was right at the corner.

Maybe.

Wait.

Bianca groaned.

Only one problem.

She had an appointment. A meeting. And it was two blocks from here, at the *Cuppa Joe's* on Madison Avenue.

And—she glanced at her watch. *Mannaggia!* She was going to be late.

Her fingers flew over the keys.

Patient shows lessening signs of anxiety. Recommend dosage change in meds—see attached note sent to Dr. Carlyle— and a decrease in sessions from two per week to one.

She read what she'd typed, read the note to Dr. Carlyle, the psychiatrist in the practice who would, as a medical doctor, review the request and authorize the prescription, and added a couple of words. Then she hit Save, followed by Close. The screen went blank and she shut her laptop, sat up straight and grimaced as she flexed her shoulders.

"You're too young for aches and pains."

Bianca swung towards the door and smiled at East Side Associates' temporary receptionist, Lacey Hilton. Lacey was a bright MBA student, working as a summer fill-in for the regular receptionist, who was on maternity leave.

"Tell that to my muscles," Bianca said. "They're reminding me that I haven't gone to the gym in a couple of days."

"Five."

"Five what?"

"Five days. You didn't go once this week."

"That's it," Bianca said, laughing. "Keep track and make me feel guilty."

Lacey grinned. "Hey, Doc, I'm just sayin'..."

"I'm not a 'doc.' Not yet."

"Yeah, but you will be."

Bianca sighed. "Assuming I ever complete my dissertation."

"My money's on you, Doc. Anyway, everybody's gone and I'm heading home—unless you need me to do something last minute."

"Thanks. I'm fine. You go ahead. Enjoy the weekend."

"You too. I hope you have some exciting plans."

"Very exciting," Bianca said dryly. "The laundry. A trip to the Union Square Greenmarket. A trip to Whole Foods. Maybe a quick stop at Bloomingdale's to look for a new towels."

"No hot date?"

"No," Bianca said, and she knew she'd said it too quickly because Lacey gave her a funny look. "No," she said, this time with a smile. "No time for dates, hot or otherwise."

Lacey nodded. "Dissertation before men," she said solemnly, clapping her hand to her heart. "I have the same attitude about my thesis."

"Exactly. Work first. Everything else second."

"But you're almost done with the research, right?"

Bianca nodded. "I'm close. In fact, I'm meeting with the last subject in my study this evening. In..." She shot a look at her watch. "In half an hour."

"Well, I won't keep you. Have a good weekend,

whatever you end up doing with it."

"You too."

Lacey held up her hand and turned away. Bianca could hear her heels tapping against the highly polished oak floor in the reception area, then the opening and closing of the door that led into the hall and to the elevators.

"Okay," she said briskly. It was time she left, too.

She reached under her desk, pulled out the zippered tote she used to carry things to and from her office, and began loading stuff into it.

How could she have forgotten tonight's meeting?

The answer was simple.

She'd wanted to forget it.

She was in the final stages of her research. That should have been cause for celebration. And, yes, in some ways it was.

In other ways…

Not so much.

The topic of her dissertation, *Interpersonal Bonding Among Millennials in the Age of the Internet*, hadn't worked out quite as she'd hoped.

She'd run into difficulties she hadn't anticipated.

Bianca had run carefully worded ads in the *New York Times* Personals section, the *Village Voice*, Craigslist, and in two university alumni quarterlies.

PhD candidate in psychology wishes to meet with users of online dating services for open and honest discussions of expectations and results. Privacy and anonymity assured.

Her adviser, Dr. Marilyn Epstein, had read it and

smiled.

"You sure about this, Bianca?"

"What do you mean? Do you think there's a better way to state the criteria?"

"What I think is that you're liable to be walking into a problem. You may find yourself dealing with women who'll take one look at you and hate you. As for the men… I wouldn't be surprised if they forget all about the science." Epstein had winked at her. "You might want to hire some big, strong, sexy hunk to go to the interviews with you and just sit nearby, watching you with smoldering eyes, making it crystal clear you're no competition to the women—and clear to the men exactly whose woman you are."

The doctor had chuckled. So had Bianca, but she'd immediately thought of Chay. The way he'd looked at her when they'd made love had left no doubt that she belonged to him.

Except, they hadn't made love. They'd had sex. And she'd only been his for as long as the sex had lasted.

Not that she'd wanted to belong to him. To any man. Surely not now, and surely never to a man like Chay.

Besides, she'd been certain Epstein had things wrong. This was a survey. She was a trained scientist. She'd made the parameters of her study clear, especially for those participants—ten women, ten men—she'd chosen for what she called Closing Interviews.

She'd been correct about all those things. Unfortunately, they were also beside the point.

A few of her meetings with the female subjects had

gone well.

Others had not.

One woman had taken a look at her, turned on her heel and walked out of the *Cuppa Joe's* on Madison Avenue, where Bianca had decided to hold the interviews.

Another had burst into tears. "Why would I want to talk about the misery of online dating with somebody who looks like you?"

A third had accused her of being a shill for a dating service.

"That's ridiculous," Bianca had said. "Why would I do that?"

"Why wouldn't you?" the woman had answered, ending the interview.

Score one for Dr. Edison. Bianca sighed as she checked the contents of her tote. Actually, score two, because she'd done as bad or worse with the male subjects.

So far, she'd interviewed nine of them.

Two had been informative and honest.

An astounding seven had found it difficult to believe that what she wanted from them was data, not hookups.

Men.

What was it that made them so arrogant? So sure of themselves? Even the ones who had nothing to be arrogant or sure about, not just the ones who did, not just the Chay Olivieris of this world...

And what was he doing in her head again? And what was that nonsense about him having something to be arrogant about?

Yes, he was good-looking. Yes, he could hold up his end of a conversation. And yes, he certainly knew how to dance.

Unfortunately, he was also a rat.

Bianca dug into her tote. She had a compact buried somewhere inside. There it was. She snapped it open and peered at herself in the mirror.

Good.

She looked professional. No makeup. Her hair was in its usual neat ponytail at the nape of her neck. Combined with a dark pantsuit plus sensible shoes—her usual outfit—the way she looked might keep tonight's interviewee—Noah? Yes. Noah—from reading things wrong.

That hadn't worked with seven other guys, but she still had hope, especially since Noah had come across as a low-key, quiet person in his responses to her questionnaire.

She needed, desperately, to end the research portion of her study and settle into writing her dissertation and preparing to defend it, and that kind of get-it-over-with attitude was not a good way to feel about the work she'd spent months planning and more months researching and collating.

She kept reminding herself that she had, in fact, gathered some useful data. Epstein had even suggested that once she had the dissertation written, it might be that rare paper that would pique interest outside the hallowed halls of academia.

"I know we're supposed to gag at the possibility some TV show or magazine might sit up and take notice of something we do," Dr. Epstein had said with a wink, "but a little commercial success never hurts."

Bianca scooped up a couple of pens and a small notebook, and she tucked them into the tote.

Yes. But what she did in this office, working with patients Epstein called *difficult*—though calling them individuals with possible sociopathic leanings might be closer to the truth—made her feel as if she were doing something of value. The work was often draining and sometimes disturbing, but always rewarding.

Almost always.

Her thoughts bounced to the patient who'd called her in Texas. Only Epstein, who was also the founder of East Side Associates, knew what those calls had involved, the litany of sick perversions her caller had whispered he was planning for her.

Not even Bianca's training had kept the horror of his words from making bile rise in her throat.

The man was out of her life now, someone else's worry. He'd have been locked away in an institution if it weren't for his family name, his money, his bristling denials—and the fact that his new therapist, a nationally famous psychiatrist, said he was responding well to treatment.

Still, the experience had left her jumpy. On edge. And she hated being like that.

Bianca rose from her desk and went to the closet. Maybe, with luck, she'd left an umbrella in it. Or a jacket. The rain had increased in intensity. She could hear it pelting against the window, and a couple of jagged streaks of lightning, accompanied by still-distant rolls of thunder, made it clear she wasn't going to reach *Cuppa Joe's* without getting wet.

Thud!

She spun around, heart racing—and breathed a sigh of relief. It was only the tote. It had fallen on its side.

Yes, she was definitely on edge.

Take what had happened last week. She'd answered two calls on her cellphone, said "Hello," and received no response. Just silence. Of course she'd had calls like those once or twice before. Everybody got them.

But because of Texas, when the third call came in, she'd rushed to her carrier's nearest store.

"They're just hang-ups," the guy at the store had said after checking her phone. "Well, not real hang-ups. You know, nobody actually hangs up a cellphone, but that's what we called them back in the day. Some jerk dials around, usually at random, and when he gets an answer, he hangs up. Disconnects."

Bianca had explained that she'd been the one who'd had to disconnect. The person who'd made the calls didn't.

"Kids," the guy said, rolling his eyes. "Little SOBs—pardon my language—with too much time on their hands. Look, if you want to change your number we'll do it, but…"

The "but" was exactly why she told him *thanks, but no thanks.*

Changing the number again meant notifying everybody she'd notified just a couple of months ago. That time, she'd told her family she'd had to change her number because the person who'd owned it before had turned out to be a guy with a bad financial history.

"I'm getting calls from all kinds of credit agencies," she'd said, and they'd all said yeah, getting a stranger's bad number was a hassle.

What excuse could she use now?

The same one wouldn't work twice. Even if it did, Alessandra wouldn't be fooled. She would know something was up and then, absolutely, she'd break her vow of silence and the Wildes and the Bellinis and Tanner would all be involved.

Everybody but Chay.

Bianca blinked.

Dio, she was thinking about him again! Ridiculous. She hadn't thought of him in weeks. Not since that night in California. Not once. Not for a minute. Not for a second. And she never would. Never, ever…

Thunder roared. A jagged spear of lightning illuminated the room. Bianca jerked back from the half-open closet so quickly that she bumped her head on the door.

"Dammit," she whispered.

No umbrella. No jacket. A storm of epic proportions outside. What the hell. She could stay here until it ended. All she had to do was call *Cuppa Joe's*. Ask one of the baristas if he'd please see whether there was a man sitting at the table in front, the one nearest the counter that held sugar and sweeteners, milk and cream. The man would be holding a copy of today's *New York Time*s. And if somebody like that was there, would the nice barista please hand the guy the phone and—

Another flash of lightning. Another roar of thunder.

The lights flickered. And Bianca held her breath.

East Side Associates had a small conference room. At the conclusion of her first week here, her new colleagues had thrown what they'd called a Welcoming Party on her behalf. All the associates, including the one she was replacing had shown up as well as some of their spouses and partners.

That part had turned out to be…interesting.

For starters, the guy she was replacing had smiled too broadly, pumped her hand too hard, and several glasses of wine later, he'd marched to where Bianca stood and informed her that if she thought she could fill his shoes, she was wrong.

"Choosing someone as inexperienced as you to take my place," he'd said, loudly enough to silence all other conversation, "is ridiculous!"

Dr. Epstein and the man's partner had taken him by the elbows and hurried him out the door.

"Sorry about that," Epstein had said.

"No, that's okay," Bianca replied, because what else could she have said?

It had been an insightful experience, if not a pleasant one.

There'd been other insightful moments that evening too, but nobody had ever said psychologists and psychiatrists lived trouble-free lives.

One associate's wife had taken Bianca aside and said brusquely that her husband liked to flirt and she hoped Bianca would not be foolish enough to take him seriously. The warning had been surprising, to say the least, because the man in question was in his eighties and about as flirtatious as a clam.

The husband of another associate had offered to refill Bianca's wineglass and as he did, he'd said—in the same conversational tone he'd used in suggesting more wine—that he and his wife had an "arrangement," and if she were so inclined, Bianca should feel free to give him a call sometime. Wink wink.

Bianca hadn't responded. What could she say to that, especially when what little she already knew of the wife suggested that the woman would have been astounded to hear that her husband believed they had any sort of *arrangement*?

Dr. Epstein had no spouse to put in an appearance. She was recently divorced, and she seemed surprised but pleased when her son showed up.

The son was nineteen, tall and gangly and shy.

"This is David," she'd told Bianca when she introduced them. "My only child." She'd beamed up at the young man. "I'm so proud of him! He's the man in our lives."

He was also the opposite of his gregarious mother, Bianca realized after a two-minute conversation. David mumbled when he spoke and looked down at his feet, and the most Bianca had been able to get him to say about himself was that he was a graduate student in mathematics, home on vacation. He left before the party ended, and it had touched her when Epstein took her aside and thanked her for being "so kind" to David.

"He has an IQ of 180," the doctor had confided. "And, as is the case with many who have such brilliant minds, his social skills aren't the best. He's especially tongue-tied with women, who are not often as gentle with him as you were, Bianca."

Mostly, though, the party had been a mix of pleasant chatter and funny anecdotes, including one about the time a storm had rolled in.

"A summer storm," someone said. "You know the kind. Lots of *Sturm und Drang*, and after maybe twenty minutes of the lights flickering on and off, all the power went out."

"I suppose we could have walked down the nine flights," someone else said, "but the maintenance guys kept assuring us the power would be coming back any minute. Plus, it turned out a couple of us had little stashes of gin and whiskey."

"Don't forget the crackers," someone else added to a round of laughter. "Anyway, by the time the power came back on, nobody really wanted to leave."

More laughter. Then Dr. Epstein said that the moral of the story was that it had taken that storm to nudge the building's management into finally modernizing the system.

Or maybe not, Bianca thought now, as the lights flickered again.

One thing was certain.

She had absolutely no wish to be trapped in the dark, alone. And she probably would be alone, considering that this was a summer Friday, meaning that all over Manhattan, people rushed to leave work as soon as they could to get the weekend started.

No raincoat. No umbrella. So what? This was June. Lightning and thunder couldn't change the fact that the rain, though heavy, would be warm.

Bianca shut the closet door, went to her desk, tossed her phone into her tote, grabbed it, and went quickly out of her office and into the reception area.

Was she mistaken, or were the overhead lights a bit dimmer than usual?

All the more reason to quicken her pace. Through reception. Out the door. Down the corridor to the elevators. *Brrr!* It was chilly out here. The lights might be playing games, but the air conditioning was working overtime.

She looked up at the station lights above the elevators. Both were on the lobby level. Bianca pressed the call button. Then she tilted back her head and watched the lights.

Nothing happened.

Neither elevator was moving.

She huffed out an impatient breath and poked the call button again.

Then she checked her watch.

Not good. It was almost a quarter of six.

"Come on," she muttered, hitting the call button with her fist. Yes! One car began moving. She could hear it groaning as it rose. Still, no matter how fast it got here, she was going to be late for her meeting with—with—

What was the name of tonight's subject? Something biblical. David. Daniel. Joseph. Noah. That was it. She was meeting with First Name, Noah; Last Name, Charles. Male.

Age thirty-four. Heterosexual. Never been married. Was signed onto three dating sites.

The photo he'd emailed along with his filled-out questionnaire showed a pleasant-looking man, skinny, shy smile, curly red hair. Not unattractive, but not someone you'd notice in a crowd the way you'd notice someone like Lieutenant Chay Olivieri—and where was that damn elevator? It paused at the third floor. And at the fourth.

It was ridiculous that she would think about the lieutenant. About that night. *Dio*. Why would she want to think about it? Sex with a man who was basically a stranger. Sex in a public place. No preliminaries. Not foreplay. It had been embarrassing. Humiliating.

Exciting. Oh, so incredibly exciting…

"Something wrong?" Alessandra had said the next day, and Bianca had said yes, unfortunately she'd have to cancel going on to the Flying Eagle because she'd had an email from New York and one of the other psychologists in her practice had fallen ill and they were desperately shorthanded.

Alessandra had looked at her in a way that said she didn't believe a word of the story, but she'd said that of course she and Tanner were disappointed and maybe another time…

To visit the Akecheta ranch? Definitely. To see Chay Olivieri? Not even if the end of the world was imminent.

No woman in her right mind would want to see the lieutenant again.

She was willing to admit he was probably a superb warrior. All that toned muscle. All that attitude. The sense of command. What was it he'd said about being part Lakota Sioux? Back in the Old West, women would probably have gone crazy for him.

Some probably still did.

Maybe most probably still did.

But an independent I-am-in-charge-of-myself female? No way.

Bianca glared at the elevator door, reached forward and pounded the call button. What was taking so long?

The lieutenant had the attitude that came of male privilege. Yes. Warrior privilege. Insisting she dance with him. Insisting she ride the Harley. Insisting they have sex...

Except, he hadn't insisted. All he'd done was kiss her.

And she'd responded by wrapping herself around him.

She'd loved everything he'd done. The possessive way he'd kissed her. The urgency of his need. The way he'd taken her, hard and deep and fast.

And then, afterward, the overwhelming sense of guilt. Of self-loathing.

Why?

Because, the scientist in her said crisply, *he's everything you dislike in a man. That's the reason you've spent six weeks lying to yourself, the reason you accused him of forcing himself on you when you knew it was a lie.*

What the scientist in her couldn't explain was why she'd wanted sex with him in the first place. It was a little late in life to develop a thing for bad boys.

Ding.

At last! The elevator had arrived.

"Finally," Bianca said on a long, grateful breath.

The doors slid open. She took a step forward.

And stopped.

The car was dark. Not unlighted. The overhead chandelier, part of the building's original nineteenth-century décor, was fully lit.

It was the car itself that was dark. How come she'd never noticed it before? It was because of the mahogany-paneled walls, another holdover from the past. The wood was so old, so highly polished, that it was almost black.

And why was the car empty? It had stopped at other floors.

Idiot. It's empty because whomever had pushed those call buttons had left the building.

And why was the car swaying?

It always sways. Remember? Lacey joked about it. She said standing in this car was kind of like standing on the deck of a ship. Stop procrastinating and get mov—

Flicker. Bzzz. Flicker.

Wait.

A bad storm. Lights that were all but typing out an SOS, and she was about to get into an elevator? Laughter burst from her lips. Okay. Shaky laughter, but laughter nevertheless. Only the heroine in a Grade B horror movie would do such a foolish thing.

Well, she was not the heroine in a movie, Grade B or otherwise. She might be foolish when it came to men, to one man, but she wasn't foolish when it came to weighing the facts and making a logical choice.

Quickly, she turned away from the elevator and headed for the fire stairs. Nine flights down was nothing. She worked out on a treadmill. Not every day, but so what? She could run, never mind walk, and walking down the stairs was what she'd be doing. It helped that she had on comfortable shoes. Black nubuck flats. Not sneakers, but almost as good as sneakers.

The door was directly ahead. *Fire Stairs,* the sign said. *To Be Used in Case of Emergency.*

Bianca grasped the doorknob, pulled the door open...

And the lights went out.

All of them.

The ones in the hall. In the stairwell. Even the always-on, always-dim nighttime lights that were lit 24/7 in all the offices.

The first slimy whisper of panic danced along her spine.

Easy.

She had to stay calm. She wasn't a child. She didn't believe in monsters or bogeymen. She wasn't afraid of being alone in a place where she couldn't see anything, not even the floor or the walls, not even her hand when she held it in front of her eyes.

She wasn't afraid...

But she was as good as blind.

And she was alone.

Wasn't she?

What if her patient, her former patient...

"Stupid," she said briskly.

She was stuck in a power failure. For all she knew, the power wasn't just down here, it was down in the entire city. Hadn't something like that happened to one of her half-sisters? Yes. To Jaimie. And Jaimie had gotten through it intact.

But, of course, Jamie hadn't been alone. She'd been with a strong, powerful man who'd been able to protect her...

Enough.

Light. She needed light. And... Bianca caught her breath. And she had light. Her smartphone. She'd downloaded an app that provided a steady beam of light if you needed it, and she surely needed it now.

She dug into the tote bag. Laptop. Keys. Kindle. Notebook. Pens. Comb. Why on earth did she carry so much garbage? Where was the...

There!

Her hand closed around the phone. She pulled it free of the tote. Felt for the Home button. Found it. She knew where the light app was. She'd read an article in the *Times*.

Place vital icons where you'll be able to locate them easily.

Yes. She'd done that. The light icon was the top left one on the screen.

Bianca pressed her thumb to the screen. Moved it around a little. And then, *yes*, the light came on. She pointed the beam at the stairs. Its field of illumination was narrow, but it was bright, more than adequate to get her down nine flights to the lobby.

The thing was to stay calm. She took a breath, exhaled, took another. Then she started down the stairs.

It seemed to take a long time until she reached the eighth floor, but that was okay. All she needed was steady progress—and for the light on her phone to hold out.

Seventh-floor landing. Good.

Sixth. Excellent.

Fifth, then fourth, then third. Perfect. She had to concentrate on the stairs, not on the sound of her footsteps, the hiss of her breath or the thud of her pulse. She'd left the silly heroine of a thousand and one overdone horror films way back on the ninth floor.

Besides, in real life, there were no Freddy Kruegers.

But there were Jeffrey Dahmers and Ted Bundys. There were men like her former patient, but he was in treatment. Wasn't he? And if he was, why would he have made those recent so-called hang-ups? If he'd made them. But really, wasn't it a logical assumption that he had?

"Stop it," she said briskly.

Another set of stairs completed. Only one more to go. And then, hurray! The lobby floor. All she had to do was grasp the doorknob, like this, pull the door open, like this. Dammit. The door was heavy. She'd have to tug hard to open it fully. The best she could do at first was to crack it an inch at a time…

A long, ululating scream burst from Bianca's throat. Or it would have if she had not gone mute with terror.

Quickly, she shut the door. Swung the phone down towards the floor. The light from it had barely reached the shadows in the lobby, but she'd seen something.

Someone.

A man was standing in the corner next to the main entrance. Tucked into the corner, hiding. A man who was tall and thin and ohGodohGodohGod...

Bianca drew back. Plastered her shoulders against the wall. A dozen urban myths, a dozen newspaper headlines sprang to full blood-soaked life in her mind. All those, plus an image of her former patient, a man who was tall and thin...

The man in the corner hadn't seen her yet, or surely he'd have been on her by now. *Grazie a Dio* that she'd only been able to open the heavy door a couple of inches.

What now? The door had no lock. If he hadn't seen her, she could get away. Race up the stairs. But if he had seen her, if he was waiting her out...

She was trembling.

What if she opened the door again, no wider than before, and said—and said, *Hello? Is someone there?*

Brilliant, Absolutely brilliant. Someone *was* there, that was the point, hiding in the corner, and someone hiding in a dark and empty building wasn't about to say, *Why, yes. There's someone here.*

Bianca took a steadying breath.

She could do better than this. She had years of training. She'd read dozens of textbooks and scholarly articles. She'd sat through endless lectures given by the best people in her field. What she had to do was figure out, fast, the best way to approach a criminal or someone criminally insane.

And then Chay was in her head again. Chay, repeating what he'd said when she'd balked at riding his Harley.

The best way to deal with fear is to face it.

Yes. That was the only way—but it wouldn't hurt to have some kind of weapon.

Carefully, never taking her eyes from the man in the corner, Bianca switched her cellphone to her left hand and dipped her right hand into the tote. The keys. The keys... She had them! There was a pocketknife on the keychain. Calling it a knife was pretty much a joke. It was a tiny thing that folded up into nothing. Scissors. Nail file. Knife. No blade was more than an inch and a half, two inches long, but the guy in the corner didn't know that.

She just had to make the first move. Make it count.

Whoever was waiting for her had his own agenda.

Now, she had hers.

Dio. If her heart beat any faster, it would leap out of her chest.

The best way to deal with fear is to face it.

She moved forward, her steps purposeful. Phone in one hand. Joker of a knife in the other. Fumbled with the doorknob with the hand that held the phone.

The door opened.

The phone fell to the floor.

She almost cried.

Now the light was useless. Worse than useless. The beam was pointed straight up, illuminating her, not the man, but the door was open. He had to know she was there, meaning it was too late to change tactics.

The best way to deal with fear is to face it.

"Step forward," she said. "Whoever you are." Amazing. She sounded strong. Authoritative. If only she felt that way. "Do you hear me? Step forward and identify yourself. I'm going to count to five and then—"

Blink.

The overhead lights blazed on.

Bianca stared into the corner. Then her knees gave out and she sank to the floor.

She'd been talking to a janitor's mop and pail.

Laughter erupted from her throat. "A mop," she said shakily. "And a pail."

She laughed until she was breathless, until the wild laughter became sobs of relief. At last, she swiped her hands over her eyes, picked up her phone, rose to her feet and almost ran to the front door. She could hardly wait to get the hell out of this building, leave what had moments ago felt like a prison or maybe the set for an old Hitchcock movie.

Was it still raining?

Yes. Standing on this side of the door that led to the street, she could hear it beating down.

She'd be soaked by the time she got to *Cuppa Joe's*, and what she needed was a drink, not a latte, but the latte was going to have to do unless the man she was supposed to meet tonight had given up and gone home. She'd have to check. That was the courteous, the professional thing to do, but if she was lucky, Noah had built himself an ark and left.

She really didn't want to interview anybody tonight, and she certainly didn't want to interview a man who might have the wrong idea of what the meeting was all about.

The only man she'd want to see tonight was the one who had just given her the courage to deal with reality and not only was he thousands of miles away, there wasn't the slightest possibility he'd want to see her.

Which was all for the best. Nothing about her was right for him, nothing about him was right for her, and it was time to get moving.

She pulled open the door and stepped out onto the sidewalk.

The rain was coming down as if some gigantic hand had turned on a celestial faucet. She was soaked in a heartbeat, but the downpour felt wonderful, a magical, mystical cleansing after the nightmare of the last half hour.

Bianca lifted her face to the rain, opened her arms and whirled in a little circle. There were people on the street and they probably thought she'd lost her mind, but for the first time in her life she didn't give a damn what strangers …

"Baby?"

Her heart leaped into her throat. She stood still, then swung towards the sound of that low, familiar voice.

The lieutenant, her lieutenant, was running towards her.

"Chay," she said, and flew straight into his arms.

CHAPTER SEVEN

SHE WAS WET.

A brilliant assessment, Olivieri.

Of course she was wet. She was soaked, but why wouldn't she be?

The rain was as heavy as anything he'd seen during a monsoon-season stint in Pakistan. The unlucky pedestrians caught in the storm were keeping close to the side of the building in a mostly useless effort to avoid the worst of the downpour.

Not Bianca.

The lady who was self-conscious on a dance floor had been dancing in the middle of the sidewalk.

At first, he'd had trouble believing his eyes. Maybe it wasn't her. Maybe it was a lookalike. But the closer he'd come, the more he knew that the sweet curves under the water-drenched clothing could belong only to one woman. He hadn't really seen her naked that night on the beach, but the feel of her against him was stamped on his memory.

Finding her dancing in the rain had only been his first surprise.

The second?

She'd flung herself into his arms.

All during the flight here, he'd tried to imagine how she'd react to seeing him. This—Bianca in his embrace—hadn't even made the list.

Telling him to take a long hike on a short bridge kept emerging as a logical winner.

That was why he hadn't called to tell her he was coming. Well, that and the fact that he didn't have her number. Okay. That and the fact that six weeks had gone by, six very long weeks, and he'd have bet not even Miss Manners or Emily Post could tell a man what to say if he phoned a woman he'd made love with and never seen again.

Hi, how've you been and, by the way, I need to ask you a question…

"Inadequate" didn't come close.

She was shaking. Why? The rain was pouring down, but it was a warm rain. Maybe not warm enough for her, he decided, and he started to step back so he could peel off his jacket and wrap her in it.

But she clung to him.

He liked it. A lot. Enough to keep holding her a little longer. But the rain was relentless and finally he clasped her shoulders and eased her away.

"Wait," he said. "Let me take off my jacket."

He got the jacket off. It was denim, too heavy for a hot summer day but right for tossing into his carry-on, and he'd been glad he had it when the skies opened up just as he'd reached his hotel. The outside of the jacket was wet but the rain hadn't penetrated the fabric. He wrapped her in the jacket, helped get her arms into the sleeves, then closed all the buttons right up to the collar even as she protested.

"You'll get soaked."

"Heck, no problem. I can skip showering tonight." She laughed, but she was still shaking so he gathered her into his arms again. It took a couple of minutes, but finally she stopped trembling. "Better now?"

She nodded. "Much. Thank you."

He hesitated. The last thing he wanted to do was make her feel awkward about that little rain dance.

"When I came along," he said, "you looked as if you were thinking about joining my people."

She tilted her head back and stared up at him. "What?"

"That rain dance." He smiled. "Not that the Sioux are much into rain dances. That's pretty much a southwestern Indian thing, but you were doing a good job. In fact, now I'm wondering—does Manhattan have you to thank for this downpour?"

She blushed, but that was okay because she also gave a quick little laugh.

"I was celebrating. The power went off in my building and I was the only one left."

"In the entire building?"

"Uh-huh. As far as I know, yes. I was stuck there, alone in the dark on the ninth floor and—and—" She paused. He could see a question forming in her eyes. "What are you doing here?"

Half a dozen answers ran through his mind. In the end, he decided the honest one was best.

"I came to see you."

Now she looked surprised. Well, why wouldn't she? They'd had sex six weeks ago and hadn't exchanged a word since.

"You came to see me?"

"Yes."

She was still in his arms, but he could sense walls going up around her, and for the first time it occurred to him that what he hadn't felt comfortable asking over the phone wasn't going to be any easier to ask now, especially while they stood on a busy street in a rainstorm.

"Look," he said, "how about getting get out of the rain before we discuss this? We can grab a taxi. My hotel is only—"

"Your hotel?"

Uh-oh. Talk about walls going up…

One quick step and she stood free of his embrace.

"It's been nice seeing you again, Lieutenant, but I don't have time for chatchit."

Chatchit. He remembered that quirk of hers, the way her English got twisted when she was upset.

It was not a good sign.

"Bianca. Honey—"

Her eyes narrowed. Her chin rose. She gave him one of those I-am-the-queen looks he remembered all too well.

The only thing that ruined it was the rain dripping from the tip of her nose.

"I am sure an invitation to your room works with all of your women, Lieutenant, but I assure you, it does not work with me. Goodbye."

She turned and started to walk uptown. He cursed and went after her.

"Wait a minute," he said, catching her by the arm. "Wait just one damn minute…What are you doing?"

"Your jacket," she said, as she worked at the buttons.

Chay grabbed her hands in his. "Forget the jacket. Add it to your collection."

Her cheeks turned pink. "A true gentleman. Thank you for the reminder."

"Bianca. I came three thousand miles to see you. The least you could do is give me an hour of your time."

"Do not tell me you ran out of available females back home."

Now it was his eyes that narrowed. Maybe he hadn't put on a stellar performance the last time they'd seen each other, but he deserved better than this.

"Trust me, baby," he said coldly. "I didn't come all this distance to get laid. "

She flinched. Okay. It had been a stupid thing to say— and the truth was, he hadn't meant to reduce that night on the beach to a four-letter word. He'd never once thought about it that way. And, dammit, he thought about it all the time.

"I came to talk," he said. "Just talk."

"I cannot imagine about what."

"Give me an hour and you'll find out."

She stared at him. He was drenched. He couldn't have been any wetter if he'd just stepped out of a shower. The only difference would be that he'd be naked then—although he was amazing to look at even with clothes, considering how the rain made his pale blue T-shirt cling to his shoulders and torso, delineating what she knew were ridges of taut muscle. She could still remember spreading her hands over his chest, feeling the race of his heart beneath her fingertips.

Heat swept through her.

She imagined getting into a taxi. Going to his hotel with him. Walking into his room. The anonymity of a hotel room, a hotel bed…

Bianca! Are you insane?

She took a quick step back. "Sorry," she said in a way that made it clear she wasn't sorry at all. "I don't have an hour."

"I'll settle for thirty minutes."

"I have an appointment."

"Cancel it."

If she hadn't been so wet and uncomfortable, she'd have laughed. How could a man be so sure that any demand he made would be met?

"I can't cancel it. And I'm already very late. So good-bye and—"

"Did you get your period?"

Her mouth dropped open. "What?"

Jesus. Chay ran his hands through his wet hair. On a scale of ten, he was somewhere around a minus five, but it was too late to change things, to work up to the question that had plagued him for the last few weeks or even to rephrase it.

"I said, did I get you pregnant? I never used a condom that night. It's the first time in my entire life I forgot all about condoms and—" Someone walking past inadvertently poked him with an umbrella. Chay shot the guy a furious glance, took Bianca's arm and tugged her closer. "We can't discuss this here. I'll get a cab. My hotel. Your apartment. I don't care which. You pick it."

Bianca couldn't think straight.

The lieutenant had come all this way to find out if he'd made her pregnant? Impossible. She knew what kind of man he was, she knew all she needed to know about men who lived for risk. Her father had, pretending to be one man with her mother and a different one entirely with the other wife and family he'd kept a secret.

Men like that were not the kind to worry about anyone but themselves.

And yet—and yet here Chay was, a continent's width from where he lived, asking her if—

"I've been going crazy," he said in a low voice. "Just, you know, wondering. I told myself you'd contact me if you were pregnant and then I thought, no, maybe you wouldn't. After a while, I decided there was only one way to get the answer." A muscle knotted high in his cheek. "I need to know."

He looked—desperate. The woman in her was amazed. Didn't most men walk away from chance encounters without second thoughts? The psychologist in her was curious. There had to be more to this than met the eye.

But there was nothing the least bit professional in their relationship, if you could call a one-night stand a relationship, and all she owed him was an answer.

"You can stop worrying, Lieutenant. You did not make me pregnant."

He nodded. "Yeah." He puffed out a long breath. "Okay."

"But—but thank you for asking."

"You're welcome."

They stared at each other. Then the slightest of smiles tilted across his mouth.

"I have to tell you, this is the strangest conversation I've ever had, especially when you add in the fact that we're standing here and nearly drowning."

"*Si.*" She tried a smile, but she wasn't sure it worked. "I mean, yes. Me, too."

"Which is why we should go somewhere and talk."

"We just did. Talk."

"Look, it's late. And we're beginning to look like flood survivors. How about a drink? A meal? A cup of coffee?"

"*Mannaggia!* Coffee!"

"Fine. I passed a coffee shop on the next—"

"No. You don't understand. When you said 'coffee,' it reminded me... Really. I have an appointment."

His eyes met hers. "Cancel it."

This time, his voice was soft. Rough. Sexy, just as she'd remembered it. Heat swept through her as it had a few minutes ago, and wasn't that ridiculous? The way she'd reacted to him that night in Santa Barbara had been an aberration.

He wasn't her type, and one decent instinct did not turn a rogue into a gentleman.

"I can't. As it is, I've kept him waiting."

"Him? You mean you have a date?"

Her eyebrows rose. He sounded as if she'd said she was on her way to Mars. So much for his being a gentleman.

"Is it that so difficult to believe?"

"No. I didn't mean…"

She stuck out her hand. "Thank you for—for your concern, Lieutenant, but I assure you, you have nothing to worry about."

He looked at her hand. Looked at her face. Enough, she decided, and she spun away from him and started for the corner.

The light was red. Red lights had never stopped Sicilians nor did they stop New Yorkers. But there was traffic coming, so she tapped her foot and waited.

She wasn't just late, she was unforgivably late.

That wasn't all that was unforgivable.

The way she'd run into the lieutenant's arms. As if she were a maiden fleeing a dragon, and he were a knight come to rescue her.

Dammit, why didn't the light change?

If her feelings about him had softened those final minutes she'd been trapped in the dark, it was only because remembering what he'd said about facing fear had been effective. In a sense, he'd helped her. And then there he was, just outside the door. Was it any wonder she'd lost perspective and rushed to—

The light changed to green.

Bianca stepped off the curb.

A horn blared.

Chay's hand closed on her wrist. He dragged her back as a truck hurtled by.

"Goddammit," he growled, "you want to get wherever in hell you're going in an ambulance?"

"I told you, I'm late."

She hurried forward. He did, too, one hand still clamped around her wrist.

"How come this guy you're in such a rush to see didn't meet you at your office?"

"He didn't meet me at my office because he doesn't have the address."

"What do you mean, he doesn't have the address?"

"I mean exactly what I said. He doesn't…" She shot him a sideways glance. "Come to think of it, neither did you." Her eyes widened. "You did not ask Tanner for—"

"I did not, no."

"Why are you mimicking me?"

"I am not mimick…" His grip on her tightened. "Watch out for that puddle."

"I am perfectly capable of avoiding puddles on my own," she said, and silently cursed herself when she stomped straight through it. "You still have not told me how you got my address."

"I remembered the name of the place. East Side Associates."

"I did not tell you that."

"No, you did not. Alessandra did. At dinner that night. Did you know that your speech changes when you're upset?"

"I am not upset and my speech does not change."

"Maybe *upset's* the wrong word. It changes when you get emotional."

" And I do not get emotional, either." She stopped walking and turned towards him. "We are here."

"We are where?"

"What I meant was, *I* am here. I am where I am meeting someone."

"A man."

"A man, yes. Please let go of my wrist."

Chay looked around him. They were standing outside a coffee shop. *Cuppa Joe's.* The place he'd passed getting to her office building. It looked like a thousand other coffee shops, but it had one saving grace—an awning that extended the length of the window and ended over the door.

He drew Bianca under that awning, out of the rain.

"Who is he?"

"That is none of your business."

"Why would you meet him here instead of giving him

your address?"

"Because."

"That's a ten-year-old's answer."

Her head came up. "It is my answer."

"How many times have you gone out with this guy?"

"I do not see any reason to continue this discussion."

"You want a reason?" He stepped closer to her, so close she could feel the heat coming off his body. "Here's one. I find it odd that a man you're dating wouldn't pick you up at your office."

"I told you. He does not have—"

"The address. Right. Odder still." His eyes focused on hers. "How many times have you and this loser gone out?"

"He is not a loser."

"How many times?"

"Thr—four."

"Thr—four." Chay folded his arms over his chest. "Interesting number. What's his name?"

"*Dio!* None of this is your—" She sighed. The best way to get rid of him was to answer his questions, but, dammit, what was the man's name? A biblical name. "Jos…Noah."

"Josnoah." His mouth twisted. "Unusual."

Bianca tossed her head. "An old family name. Now, if there is nothing else—"

"You don't really remember his name."

"Nonsense."

"Because you've never met this guy before. He isn't your date. He's part of your study."

"My…" She blinked. "What do you know of my study?"

"Only what you said at the restaurant. That you were studying online dating."

"My sister said that, and why would you remember such a thing?"

Why, indeed? Why had he remembered everything about her, about that night? God knew he'd seen enough women since then to wipe out those memories.

Well, he'd seen them, yeah, but he hadn't *been* with them. Not in bed. Not even in spirit or whatever you wanted to call it.

He'd spent his time thinking about this woman and that night.

And that was when he'd realized that there might have been consequences.

He'd thought of calling, but he couldn't come up with an easy way of saying *Hi, this is Chay Olivieri, and I just wanted to find out if maybe I knocked you up.* Better to do that in person. And then, after he knew the answer, surely he could get the Tigress out of his head.

So far, he thought grimly, that part of his plan didn't seem to be going too well.

"Just answer the question. Is this guy a subject in your study?"

"Lieutenant. Please let go of me."

Chay focused on her face. Her wet, makeup-free, lovely face.

"Ask me nicely." He caught hold of her chin. "Say, 'Chay,

please let go of me.'"

"That is precisely what…" She blushed. Jesus, he loved that blush, that rush of rosy pink into her cheeks. "This is not a game, Lieutenant."

"No, it's not. Just ask me nicely and I'll let go."

Her eyes gleamed. He wanted to laugh. Or maybe he wanted to kiss her. In truth, it wasn't a tough decision to make and he lowered his head, brought his mouth to hers and kissed her. It was a light kiss, barely the whisper of his lips over hers, but it put a knot in his belly. And it did something to her, too. He saw it in her face, heard it on a swift little intake of air.

"Ask me," he said softly.

She touched the tip of her tongue to the center of her bottom lip. He fought the urge to kiss her again.

"Chay," she whispered.

"Good. Excellent." The hell with fighting urges. He bent to her, kissed her again. This time, her lips parted on a sigh. "Is he a date? Or is he research?"

"I told you. It is none of your—"

One more kiss, a little longer, a little more intense than the last.

"Research," she breathed, and he had to struggle against the desire to pump his fist in the air.

"I'll wait for you, Tigress."

"Who?"

He smiled and smoothed a wet curl from her temple.

"I'll explain later."

"No," she said again. "There is no reason for you to

wait." She stepped back. "Goodbye, Lieutenant."

He clasped her shoulders. Turned her around. Opened the door to the coffee shop and stepped aside.

"You're late," he said, and the next thing she knew, she was standing inside *Cuppa Joe's*.

And freezing.

It was summer, this was Manhattan, and of course the AC was on. Normally, that would have been perfect—but she was wet, wetter than wet, if that was possible, and the last thing she needed was to be blasted with icy air.

At least she wouldn't have to stay.

A quick look around the shop assured her that though some of the tables were filled, the one she'd specified to Noah as their meeting place was empty.

Well, it would be.

According to her cellphone, when she pulled it from the tote and checked the time, it was—*mannaggia*—twenty of seven!

Okay. She'd have to text Noah an apology, but really, she was glad he'd given up and left. She wasn't in the mood to sit through tonight. The only thing she wanted was to go home, take a hot shower and try to figure out why being with the lieutenant—with Chay—seemed to turn all her convictions inside out—

"Bianca?"

No, she thought, please, no...

"Bianca. You're here!"

She turned towards the voice and her heart sank. Noah

had not given up. Not unless there was another tall, thin man with curly red hair and a copy of the *New York Times* tucked under his arm who would recognize her from the site she'd set up for her study.

She took a breath, plastered on a smile and went towards him.

"Noah," she said, and stuck out her hand. He took it and clasped it in both of his. His grip was surprisingly strong; his palms were clammy and she tried not to recoil. "I'm terribly sorry I'm late. The storm…"

He smiled.

Not only clammy hands. His teeth were an unpleasant shade of yellow. Well, she wasn't here to make personal judgments on anyone.

"I understand, Bianca. I knew you were surely as eager to meet as I was, and that it was the weather that had delayed you."

His answer sent a prickle over her skin. And he still had hold of her hand.

"Your photo on the study website is great, but it doesn't do you justice."

Uh-oh. Prickle number two. Smiling, she tugged her hand free of his.

"Since it's already so late," she said politely, "let's sit right down and get started."

She started towards what she thought of as the Interview Table. Noah cupped her elbow and led her away from it.

"Why don't we sit someplace a bit more private?" he said, drawing her to a corner table. Smiling, he tossed the newspaper aside and pulled out a chair. "Bianca?"

Uh-oh, indeed.

Is this a date or research? She could hear Chay's voice in her head.

Noah seemed to have the answer to that question. The wrong answer. Not even the male subjects who'd come on to her had moved this fast or this definitively. She'd have to regain control of the situation quickly or the time she spent here tonight would be wasted.

"Thanks," she said pleasantly, "but I'm going to get us some coffee."

"I'll do that. A double espresso for me—and a café latte for you A grande, with an extra shot of espresso and skim milk." He winked. "And one sugar."

She stared at him. "How did you know that?"

Noah laughed. Truly laughed. *Ha ha ha.*

It was not a comforting sound.

"That's my secret. You just sit down, Bianca, and I'll take care of everything."

"It's Ms. Wilde."

She felt foolish as soon as she'd spoken. She'd given up the Bellini-Wilde thing months ago, once she'd decided it was occasionally confusing and often sounded too formal. For this study, she'd wanted to keep things as relaxed as possible, and she'd told all the other subjects she'd met with to call her by her first name.

Now, she really had to regain control, but hurting Noah's feelings would be counterproductive. It was too late remedy that now. The best she could do was keep moving forward.

"Okay," she said brightly. "One double espresso coming right up."

She almost flew to the counter. Only one barista was on duty, and he gave a low whistle.

"Man," he said, "how long were you out in that rain?"

"I know. Pretty bad, huh?"

"Pretty wet. You want something to dry off?" He reached under the counter, came up with a big stack of heavy-duty paper towels. "Be my guest."

"Thanks," she said, grabbing the towels and blotting her hair, her face, her jacket.

Chay's jacket.

She ducked her head, tucked her nose inside the collar. The denim smelled like summer rain and like him.

Had he really come all this way to make sure she wasn't pregnant? It was such an amazing thing to do…

"…BWW?"

She blinked and looked at the barista. He was a nice-looking guy, but she'd never seen a *Cuppa Joe's* barista who wasn't nice-looking.

"Sorry. Did you ask me something?"

"I said BBW are your initials, right? The ones I've printed on, what, a dozen cups? You're a café latte grande. Extra shot of espresso. Skim milk. One sugar. Yes?"

"Yes. That's nice. That you remember." Bianca handed over her credit card. "And a double espresso for my, uh, for my friend."

"Part of the job—although in your case…" The barista shook his head. "All these dudes," he said in a quiet voice, "and a pretty lady like you still hasn't found the right one?"

"These are business meetings," she said quickly, and after the words left her mouth, she blushed. "Serious business meetings."

"Whatever you say, BBW. But this dude tonight? Do yourself a favor. He's an N-G."

"An N-G?"

"A No Go. My advice is lose him, fast."

Bianca glanced over her shoulder. Noah was seated at the table, arms folded, looking sullen.

The barista grinned. "Hey, bartenders and baristas, right? Scholars of the human condition."

"Thanks for the advice," Bianca said. "I just might take it."

• • •

When she was little and complained about anything, especially about her father never making it home to Sicily for birthdays and holidays, Bianca's mother would either smile or scowl, depending on her mood, and say—in Sicilian, of course—that nobody ever said life would be easy.

Dio. Mama had spoken the truth.

Life was certainly not easy tonight.

Bianca had gone through her set list of questions. At first, Noah's responses had been clipped. He'd sounded like a spoiled child. *Yes. No. I don't remember.* So she'd instituted a short break by changing the subject. She'd asked him about his job—he was an actuary—and where he'd grown up. Little by little, his attitude had thawed. By the time she took the conversation back to the survey, he wasn't just talking, he was talking at endless length.

She imagined the little digital recorder she'd placed on the table gasping for breath.

She wished she could hurry him along. His answers struck her as mostly lies, and when he smiled, the flash of his discolored teeth was unsettling. Yellow was definitely not her favorite color, especially when it came to people's mouths. Added to that, she was chilly. Cold, actually. She'd blotted away a lot of the water in her hair, and Chay's jacket was warm, almost as if it still held the heat of his body, but her clothes were stuck to her, and walking through that puddle had left her feet wet.

Ten minutes into what should have been a two-minute reply to her final question, Bianca glanced at her watch.

"You're not listening," Noah said.

She looked up. He was smiling again, showing all those teeth.

"I am," she said pleasantly. "You were talking about your first date. In high school. I was just going through things, making sure we've touched on all the topics." She smiled, too, even though she didn't much feel like smiling. "And we have!"

She reached for the recorder and thumbed it off. "So, Noah, thank you very much for your time and—"

"I'm not finished."

Bianca shoved back her chair and reached for her empty coffee container. "Really, I have all the data I need. I can always contact you if—"

Noah's hand clamped down on hers.

"I said, I'm not finished."

"Noah," Bianca said calmly, "let go of my hand."

"There's lots more I want to tell you, Bianca."

"Ms. Wilde." This time, she didn't give a damn if she hurt his feelings or not.

"Surely we're on a first name basis."

"Noah. Our interview is over. I'm leaving now. Please let go of—"

She gasped as his hand tightened painfully around hers.

"You're right. You *are* leaving now. With me."

"Noah," she said, her tone firm, "let go of my hand."

"Didn't you hear me, Bianca? We're leaving here together. I know that's what you want to do."

Her heartbeat skittered. The man across from her had undergone a frightening transformation. His eyes gleamed with manic determination. His breathing was rapid. The fingers that clasped hers felt like a vise. They were in a public place, which might be her salvation, but if he was undergoing a psychotic episode, anything was possible.

"Noah," Bianca said quietly, "you need to let go of me."

"What I need is you. Don't you understand?" He leaned towards her. She could smell his breath, a mixture of coffee, decay and desperation. "I don't want to hurt you. I don't want to hurt anybody—"

"Baby?"

The voice was deep. Rough. Sexy.

And blessedly welcome.

Bianca looked up. Chay was standing just behind her, looking big and imposing and beautiful.

He smiled. At least, his lips curved up at the corners, but she knew she would never forget the tightly banked fury in his eyes.

"Honey," he said, "I know we said we'd meet outside, but that awning is the size of a bandage and the rain…"

Say something, she told herself, but what could you say when you'd needed a miracle and a miracle materialized?

Chay laughed. "Just look at you, baby. So surprised to see me that you're speechless."

He bent to her, wrapped his hand around the nape of her neck, tilted her face up to his and kissed her.

It was a kiss of ownership. Of possession.

Of salvation, she thought wildly as the hand holding hers fell away.

Chay raised his head and looked at Noah

"A friend of yours, honey?"

"A—a professional acquaintance."

He nodded. Smiled again. "Baby? Why don't you wait for me at the door?"

Once, a long time ago on the cliffs in Sicily, Bianca had almost stepped on a viper. The snake had reacted instantly; she remembered the coiled tension in its body, the reality of its cold, flat eyes.

She thought of that now, looking at Chay.

"Chay," she said in a low voice, "don't—"

Noah's chair groaned in protest as he shoved back from the table. His face was a pasty white.

"It's okay," he said as he rose to his feet. "Actually, I was just—"

Chay grasped his shoulder. Noah squealed and sank back in his seat.

Good, Chay thought grimly, although what he really wanted was to put his fist in this skinny bastard's face and lay him out.

He'd stood under the leaky awning, watching the scene inside *Cuppa Joe's* unfold. Two minutes in, he knew he'd have realized the meeting was business even if Bianca hadn't told him it was.

For openers, it was impossible to see the guy talking with her as her type. Bianca would go for some intense-looking, pipe-smoking academic nerd all turned out in tweed. This guy was wearing his pants hiked up above his waist, his white socks showed below his cuffs, and even at a distance Chay could see that his teeth needed more than a tube of toothpaste could provide.

But there was more to his assessment than that.

The body language was all wrong.

He could tell.

There was that sensing thing of his, the ability to pick up on something happening that shouldn't be happening. Plus, the same as Tanner, the same as all STUD operatives, Chay was a sniper. A highly trained sniper.

What it added up to was that he was good, hell, he was outstanding at reading body language. That was partly how he'd known the boy on that mountaintop was a killer and, Jesus, he hadn't wanted to think about that now.

He was focused on what was happening inside that coffee shop and what he saw was more than a meeting of strangers.

He saw a man wanting a woman who didn't want him.

Every gesture the guy made was off.

Hanging onto her hand. Leading her to one table when she'd obviously been headed towards another. A couple of minutes of conversation and then the folded-arms, petulant-child bit.

All of it had given him a bad feeling, but there wasn't much he could do except watch as the situation played out, so he'd stood under an awning that wasn't deep enough to cover his broad shoulders, rain dripping down his neck, hands tucked in the back pockets of his jeans, trying to be patient.

Until he saw Bianca making it clear she was ready to leave and the guy grabbing her hand and saying something that made her stiffen and attempt to pull away.

After that, instincts honed on endless mountaintops, in endless deserts, in jungles that stank of rot had taken over.

Chay had made his move.

So, yeah, he wanted to hurt the man cringing in his grasp, but what he wanted didn't matter.

This mission had only one objective, and that was to get Bianca out of here.

But there could be a secondary mission.

Yellow Teeth needed a meaningful warning. Something subtle.

In the way of true New Yorkers, the few patrons in the shop were carefully looking everywhere but at them. Still, Chay could sense they were fully aware of what was going down. Only the barista was watching and Chay had to give the guy credit because he'd looked as if he were moving towards the end of the counter, maybe to step out from behind it and give Bianca some help.

"Sir," Yellow Teeth said, "I have no idea why you—"

Chay tightened his grasp.

"Bianca," he said, never taking his eyes from the guy he had pinned to the chair, "please, wait for me at the door." She didn't move. Jesus, was she going to argue about this, too? "Honey. Just do it, okay?"

A couple of long seconds went by. Then she pushed back her chair and picked up her tote.

"Don't hurt him," she said softly.

"We're just going to have a little chat. A minute, no more. I promise."

She nodded and got to her feet.

"Noah," she said, very calmly. "You need help."

Chay almost rolled his eyes. Did she have to get the last word in? Dumb question. Of course she did. Saying what she was thinking no matter the situation, hanging tough, was who she was.

Caring about people was who she was, too.

The Tigress had more than balls and intellect and beauty.

She had a heart.

He watched her make her way through the shop. As soon as she got to the door, he leaned over the table and looked deep into Yellow Teeth's tiny, terrified eyes.

"You so much as think of my woman again, even mention her name, you really will need help, pal, because I'll take you apart. Piece by piece. Understand?"

Bianca's aggressor shrank back in his seat. "I didn't mean any—"

"Did I ask you for an explanation?"

The guy was sweating. Trembling. Chay leaned closer.

"Say her name, think of her, you're finished. Got it?"

"Y—y—yes."

"Say *yessir. I understand, sir.*"

"Yessir. I understand, sir."

"Good." Chay straightened up. He looked around the little café. Nobody would meet his eyes. Hell, he thought, and he dug into his pocket, pulled out a couple of twenties, strolled to the counter, flashed what he hoped was a smile at the barista and started to tuck the bills into the tip jar.

The barista stopped him. "Keep it."

Chay looked at the guy. He had the kind of perfect face women probably loved.

"You keep the money," the barista repeated. "I'm just glad you showed up."

"You were going to help her," Chay said.

The barista nodded. "She's really something."

"Damn right she is. Thanks for being ready to step in. And just for the record..." He flashed a quick, hard smile. "You might want to remember that she's all mine."

Another nod from the barista. "Hey, man, anybody could see that."

Chay leaned in, shook the guy's hand. Then he tucked the twenties into the tip jar anyway.

Bianca was waiting for him at the door.

"Ready to leave, honey?" he said softly. And even though he knew he didn't have to keep the deception going any longer, he lowered his head and brushed his lips lightly over hers.

She tasted delicious. She felt the same. Soft. Feminine. Perfect.

But it wouldn't last, he thought, as he led her out into the rain. She'd been scared in that coffee shop, but she'd regained her composure fast.

Chay suspected she'd give up being compliant just as fast.

And she did.

The light turned red as they reached the corner. They stopped on the curb, and she used that as her chance to ease out of his encircling arm.

"Thank you for your help, Lieutenant."

The good news was that color had returned to her face.

The bad was that she sounded exactly as she had that night at the Landing Zone. And, really, were they back to her calling him lieutenant?

Okay. They'd play it her way for a while.

"You're welcome."

"But just so you understand… I didn't need your help."

He raised his eyebrows. A couple of seconds went by. Then she blushed.

"Very well. Having you appear was—it was—"

"Helpful?" he said, his tone polite.

Some of her rigidity faded. "Okay. You showed up at an opportune time, but I'm sure I could have handled things if I'd had another few minutes. That man is sick. I'm sure he needs—"

"Help?"

"You can joke all you like. But when someone is ill—"

"He could have hurt you," Chay said harshly.

"We were in a public place."

"Oh, well, that's a relief. Sickos never hurt anybody in public places."

Bianca searched for a response, but what, really, could she say? She hadn't thought herself in any danger.

Well, maybe that "you belong with me" stuff had upped the game a little, but—

"Did his voice seem familiar?"

"What?"

"His voice," Chay said. "Could he have been your Texas caller?"

She stared at him. "My Texas… No. My Texas caller was one of my patients."

"Right. I forgot that."

But he had forgotten nothing else. It seemed as if he had memorized that night in Santa Barbara. She had too. Not the things they'd discussed. The other part of it. The part that had taken place on the beach…

"How many calls did you get?"

"How many… Five. Six. But they were from my patient."

"You sure the calls were from only the one guy?"

"I'm sure. Besides, it would have been unlikely that two sick men would call me during the same time period."

"Nothing is unlikely when it comes to crazies."

"That's a harsh word, Lieutenant."

"It's a harsh world, Doc."

"I am not yet a—"

"Anyway, you're probably right. The odds on you getting calls from two loonies within the same time span are probably zero to none. Still, don't they teach you how to protect yourself from nutcases in shrink school?"

"That's not an appropriate way to describe someone with issues. Or to describe my training."

"Live and learn," he said mildly. "The light's green." They stepped off the curb. "Watch out for that puddle."

"What puddle?"

"*That* puddle," he said. He grabbed her elbow and tried to steer her around it, but it was too late.

Rainwater sloshed over her shoes.

That made twice.

She knew it. He knew it. And though he didn't say a word, she could almost hear him laughing.

Merda, she thought, and then, just because it seemed more appropriate, what she thought was *Shit, shit, shit!*

That was what her day had turned into. Shit. The power failure. Her pathetic fear. Getting drenched in the rain. And now this, the absolute zero data she'd gotten from what was to have been her final interview.

She'd have to find some way to incorporate the incident into her study results. As an anomaly? Yes, but the last thing she wanted was to end up taking part of her dissertation down a new path.

And why was she leaving out the most improbable of the day's occurrences? The lieutenant, turning up in the city to ask her if she was—if she was—

"You could have phoned."

She spoke before she thought. It took her by surprise. Not him. He simply clasped her arm a little more tightly and said, "Curb."

Dio. Did he think she needed an early warning system?

"I see it! Just answer my question. Why did you not simply phone and ask me if—and ask me if—"

"If you were pregnant?" He shrugged. "It didn't seem an appropriate conversation starter."

Was he trying to be amusing? She couldn't tell.

"I would have informed you if—if—"

"I don't think so. You can't even say the words now." He came to an abrupt stop on the sidewalk and swung her towards him. "Is it so awful? The thought of you carrying my child?"

His eyes bored into hers. The dark green irises seemed bottomless. All at once, she had the feeling that she could tumble into their depths and if she did, she would never find her way out.

He was waiting for an answer, and she had none.

What saved her was another roar of thunder.

The storm had doubled back. In an instant, before the thunder had finished echoing overhead, they were standing in a downpour.

Chay cursed, threaded his fingers through hers and ran to the curb.

"Taxi," he shouted, raising his hand.

He had the New Yorker-hailing-a-cab gesture right, but there was no way a cab would stop. Taxis and rain didn't go together. Either the vehicles magically disappeared from the streets or the drivers ignored the desperate souls trying to flag them down...

A cab slipped out of the steady stream of traffic and set off a barrage of angry horns as it slid through two lines of vehicles and pulled up beside them.

Amazing. Even wet, the lieutenant commanded attention.

"Get in," Chay said as he yanked open the door. When

she hesitated, he all but pushed her inside, climbed in after her and pulled the door shut. "You want to keep arguing? Fine. We'll argue, but I'm not in the mood to drown while we do." He leaned forward. "Four-forty-four Thompson."

Bianca stared at him. "That's my address."

"I hope so," he said calmly, "because another thing I'm not in the mood for is dropping in on a stranger."

The cab pulled away from the curb, made a turn at the next intersection, then joined the river of traffic heading downtown on Fifth Avenue.

"But," Bianca said, or tried to say except her teeth were starting to chatter. She was freezing, not just wet now but drenched, and at the mercy of the taxi's air-conditioning system.

Chay muttered something short and succinct, and rapped on the partition.

"Driver? Turn off that AC."

The cabbie started to say something. Then he glanced in the mirror, caught a look at Chay, and quickly complied.

"I—I—I'm f—f—fine," Bianca said.

Chay put his arm around her and gathered her against him.

"Yes," he said. "I can tell."

His arm was hard and comforting around her and after a minute, she let out a long sigh, lay her head against his shoulder and gave up fighting the inevitable.

He was big.

Strong.

Determined.

He was intent on protecting her whether she wanted his protection or not.

He was—she knew the appropriate term—a classic alpha male, which was just an academic's way of saying that Chay Olivieri was really a classic bad boy, and she wasn't into bad boys, not as a woman, not as a psychologist.

A little tremor raced through her and it had nothing to do with being wet or cold.

It had to do with admitting—but absolutely, positively only to herself—that what she might be into was him.

CHAPTER EIGHT

CHAY HADN'T SPENT a lot of time in New York.

Big cities, big buildings and lots of people crowded against each other—that kind of living wasn't his thing. Still, he'd made enough trips to the Big Apple to have gotten the hang of urban survival.

Walk briskly. Never stroll.

Avoid eye contact unless you meant business.

Attitude was everything.

So was an aura that said: *Don't fuck with me, Jack. Not unless you want to pay the price.*

All that made sense.

Lions didn't survive the Serengeti by being pussycats.

Still, knowing how to survive in a city didn't mean understanding why anybody would willingly choose to live in one.

He thought about that as he and Bianca stepped onto

the sidewalk in front of the four-story brick building where she lived in SoHo.

As neighborhoods went, SoHo was one of the easiest to take. Not much grass or blue sky or trees, but the buildings were mostly old and, he had to admit, interesting. There was lots of cobblestone, lots of out-of-the-ordinary little restaurants, bars and shops. True, most of those places were almost painfully trendy, but Chay had to admit they were an improvement over the big, glitzy places farther uptown.

The buildings on Bianca's street were mostly four and five story jobs. Still, they made him feel penned in. Maybe it came of growing up in the vastness of the Dakotas. Maybe it came of spending most of his working life—the missions, anyway—in the open.

Maybe it was because of what had happened in the coffee shop, or the phone calls Bianca had dealt with, or even that power outage. He hadn't said anything about it to her and he wouldn't, but even that had made him wary.

Whatever the reason, being in a place he didn't know, hemmed in by buildings, traffic and people, made him vaguely uneasy.

Fortunately, he knew what to do about that feeling.

You found yourself in a place that was new to you, you checked it out. Identified visual landmarks. Made a mental note of egress and access routes. Observed and quantified whatever creatures shared your space.

He was living proof that survival often depended on such things. It certainly had a couple of months ago, on that mountaintop on the other side of the world.

When Bianca started towards the brick steps that led into her building, he caught her hand, then put his arm around her.

"Give me a minute," he said.

She started to tell him that standing in the rain and looking around as if they were tourists was crazy—until she realized the lieutenant looked nothing like a tourist.

He looked like—like a warrior scoping out new terrain.

She probably wouldn't have said that aloud—it sounded foolish, even pretentious. But that was the only way to describe what he was doing.

And as strange as it sounded, that tough, hard-lined awareness made her feel…

Safe.

So did the powerful arm holding her close.

The ugly truth was that she hadn't really felt safe for a long time. Not since the ugly phone calls in Texas and then the so-called hang-ups of a couple of weeks ago. She certainly hadn't felt safe today when the power went off. And what had gone on at *Cuppa Joe's* with Noah…

No. She hadn't felt terribly safe lately. And that was senseless, when there were logical explanations for everything that had happened.

A patient whose mental illness had taken him over the edge.

Kids fooling around with randomly dialed numbers.

An electrical system that clearly had not been upgraded

despite the claim that it had.

A study subject with delusions.

Random happenings, all of them. The scientist in her knew that. Wasn't that one of the laws of the universe? If anything could happen, it usually did.

But the woman in her said to hell with science. Too many bad things had happened at almost the same time. If it was silly for them to make her feel edgy, well, so be it.

So be it, too, that a man she hardly knew could provide her with the comfort she so pathetically needed, especially since he wasn't a knight come to the rescue—he was a guy who was after a replay of what they'd done on a beach three thousand miles away, six long weeks ago...

Except, that was unfair.

Okay. Maybe he hoped to get lucky a second time.

He was male, after all.

But his motives in coming to see her had been honorable. Such an old-fashioned word and yet so appropriate.

And so rare.

She'd been with other men. Not a lot, it was true, but she wasn't an inexperienced virgin. And though she'd always taken responsibility for herself sexually—she was on the pill—and the few men she'd slept with had been decent guys, she couldn't imagine one of them spending so much as a minute wondering if he'd accidentally gotten her pregnant.

She couldn't image having sex with any one of them, either, now that Chay had shown her what sex could be like...

"Okay."

For one awful moment, she thought she might have said what she'd been thinking, but when she looked up at him, she breathed a sigh of relief.

He had no idea what had been bouncing around in her head and that was how it was going to stay.

He smiled. *Dio*, why did that smile turn her inside out?

"If we stay out here any longer, we're gonna grow gills. How about we go dry off?"

"An excellent plan," Bianca said briskly. "Hot coffee. Stacks of towels. And then you can head to your hotel."

"Fine," he said—and she told herself that the twinge of disappointment she felt when he didn't object was simply the result of exhaustion.

It had been a long day, and one she knew she would not forget.

• • •

Three wide brick steps led to the building's front door—a door that opened without a key.

Chay frowned. This wasn't a city in which doors should open without keys. Come to think of it, there wasn't a city in the world where that should happen.

Would the rest of Bianca's living arrangements be as unsafe?

Almost, he thought grimly as she led him through a small vestibule to another door. This one, at least, was locked, but the lock was pretty much a joke, and besides, anyone could walk straight through that front door and be waiting right here for an unwary tenant.

For Bianca.

A staircase loomed ahead.

"I'm four flights up," she said.

It was an apology as much as a warning.

Yeah, well, he was going to owe her an apology too.

Her plan to get rid of him after a pot of coffee and a handful of dry towels just wasn't going to happen.

He had every intention of sticking around for a while. What had happened at *Cuppa Joe's* had shaken her, but it worried the crap out of him. Sure, he'd scared the nut job, but enough to make a lasting impression? That was the thing about crazies. You could never be sure of how they were going to behave even five minutes later.

Besides, he thought as he followed her up the stairs, he didn't want to leave. Not yet. He knew it sounded weird, but he felt as if he was just getting to know her. Yes, they'd had sex, but he'd never had a real look at the woman who lived inside that prickly exterior.

He had tonight.

And he liked what he saw.

He'd never thought much about liking a woman before, which made this kind of interesting.

Not that his thoughts were entirely Snow White pure.

He could still remember having sex with her, in lush detail. And, yeah, something new in the way of a memory of those moments would be nice.

If nothing else, he liked looking at her. She was beautiful. Natural. What you saw was what you got.

Right now, he was getting was a great view of what was an extremely nice ass. Part of it, anyway, the part not covered by his denim jacket.

Only a dead man wouldn't notice, and even though he hadn't been deployed for weeks, he was far from being dead.

An extremely nice ass. And long legs. And great hip action.

And, thank God, they'd finally reached the fourth-floor landing.

Bianca paused just long enough that he wondered what she'd do if he wrapped an arm around her waist and pulled her back against him so she could feel what going up the stairs behind her had accomplished.

Slap his face, maybe, he thought, and he choked back a laugh.

"What?" she said.

Chay turned the laugh into a cough. "Must be coming down with a cold," he said, "from being out in the rain so long."

She clucked her tongue as she marched to the end of the hall.

"One does not acquire a cold from being out in the rain."

He watched her unzip the bag she carried and dig into it. And through it. And into it again. If she was searching for her keys, it looked as if it might take a while.

He leaned against the wall and folded his arms over

his chest.

"Really," he said.

"Really."

"One does not acquire a cold from being out in the rain?"

"No. One does—" She looked up. "Have I said something amusing?"

What she'd said, though not in so many words, was that she was nervous. That maybe it had just occurred to her they were about to be alone in her apartment. That maybe she was as aware of him as he was of her.

"Lieutenant?"

"Doctor?"

"I told you. I am not a doctor. Not yet."

"Yeah. Well, I'm not a lieutenant. Not when I'm dressed in civvies and on a date with a woman."

Color surged into her face. "We are not on a date."

He nodded. "You're right. We're not. Well, we're just going to have to do something to remedy that situation."

She opened her mouth and shut it again. He wanted to bend down and kiss that mouth. That soft, sweet mouth.

How come he couldn't stop thinking about that soft, sweet mouth?

Yes, he'd come east for serious reasons, to find out if she was okay and to apologize for the way he'd behaved. Not for having sex with her. For the way he'd acted afterwards. She'd been upset, and instead of trying to calm her, he'd let his ego get between him and common sense.

The thing was, he'd never had a woman want to get away from him after sex.

Just the opposite.

Most of his sexual encounters involved him trying to be polite even as the lady in question tried to get him to go for an encore. Well, yeah. Sometimes he'd go for an encore, but never after a session of hard, fast, unexpected sex. Times like those, he got his rocks off, so did the woman, and that was it.

Sex with a stranger had its benefits.

Other times, in bed, he'd roll over, hold the woman he'd just fucked for the requisite ten, fifteen minutes and then he'd get up, get dressed, get out. Okay. Not that abruptly. A quick kiss, a promise he'd be in touch, and he was gone.

And he would call. Usually. A couple of times until the relationship—and, man, what a terrible word that was—grew stale or the warning bells began to ring.

But he'd never been on the receiving end of what was basically a *Thanks, but no thanks* situation.

This had been a first.

Ever since, it had bothered him.

Why hadn't the sex been as incredible for her as it had been for him?

Had he remembered it wrong? Had he prettied up the memory for himself? Had what he'd experienced been a hallucination?

Or had she lied about what she'd felt that night? Jesus. It was driving him up the wall…

And she was still pawing through that stand-in for a

suitcase she carried. Chay rolled his eyes.

"Give me that thing," he said, grabbing the bag's handles.

"That thing," she said, trying and failing to hang onto it, "is my tote."

"Is that what you call it? I thought it was a portable closet. How can you possibly lug all this stuff around?"

"Give it to me, Lieutenant. You will never be able to find—"

Chay dug into the tote and pulled out a set of keys.

"Which key?"

She glared at him. "Give them to me. You will never figure it out."

He gave the keys a quick look, chose one and stabbed it into the lock.

The door swung open.

"Ridiculous," he muttered.

Bianca looked at her living room. It was small and barely furnished, but calling it ridiculous was overkill.

"I like it," she said stiffly. "And since I am the one who lives here—"

"Not your apartment. What's ridiculous is no lock on the downstairs front door. A lock on the inner one that a kid could open with a paper clip. The same kind of lock on this door, and to make things worse, an entire army of muggers and thieves could come up behind you while you spend eternity digging for your keys in—that—"

"It is a tote bag." Indignation glittered in her eyes. "And

if you escorted me home so you could insult me, Lieutenant—"

"I escorted you home to make sure you got here in one piece."

"Which I did."

"And to tell you I behaved like an asshole that night in California."

He hadn't intended to say it quite that way. From the look of her, she hadn't expected to hear it.

"Oh."

The Tigress at a loss for words. Amazing.

"Oh," she said again. "Well then, I accept your—"

"Could we have this conversation after I check out your apartment?"

"For what?"

"I don't know for what. Errant phone calls. Looney Tunes patients. Just stand here while I take a fast look, okay?"

He dropped the tote on the floor.

She huffed out a breath, folded her arms, waited impatiently while he moved quickly through the dollhouse-size living room, bedroom, kitchen and bath. In truth, she was glad he was doing it. Surely his diligence was unnecessary, but she had to admit that it was comforting.

"Okay." He came back to her, put his palm against the door and slammed it shut. "And you're got it wrong. I'm not apologizing for making love to you."

Bianca slapped her hands on her hips. "I should have known better than to think you would behave like a gentleman."

"I wasn't one. Not that night. And that suited you just

fine."

His hand was still splayed against the door; she was trapped between his raised arm and the wall. Close. Too close. He was all heat and masculinity, and she didn't like the feeling it gave her.

"You know nothing about what suits me. And what happened on that beach had nothing to do with making love. It was sex."

"I don't give a damn what you call it. It was fantastic. Why won't you admit that?"

"Such a huge ego, Lieutenant. Did you have to buy two seats on the plane?"

He almost laughed, but laughter wouldn't help this conversation.

"How about honesty, not ego? We had one hell of a night."

"We had five minutes."

His eyes narrowed. "It was a lot longer than that."

"It is time you left."

"It is time you were honest. " His hands closed on her shoulders. "Look me in the eye and tell me that what we did that night wasn't special."

"Why must you say such things?"

He took a deep breath. "Because I need to hear you admit the truth. That I'm not the only one who can't forget." His voice turned low. Urgent. Rough. "All these weeks, remembering the taste of you. The feel of you…"

Her cheeks flamed. Her mouth was trembling. And,

hell, were those tears glittering in her eyes?

"Bianca." Chay put his hand under her chin and gently lifted her face to his. "Tell me that what happened shook you as much as it shook me."

"Why are you doing this?" she whispered.

"Because, goddammit, because I can't get you out of my head." She tried to look away from him, but he wouldn't let her. "I'm a fool in a lot of ways, baby, but I know what we felt that night. I just don't know why you won't admit it— and why you didn't let me make it better, let me take you to a bed, a real bed where I could have made love to you."

"You just wanted to—to make me lose myself again."

The tears he'd seen in her eyes rolled down her face, and he felt his heart turn over.

"I wanted you to lose yourself in me," he said softly. "In my kisses. My caresses. Was that so wrong?"

She stared into his eyes.

He waited, and realized he was holding his breath. The next move had to be hers.

And just when he thought all was lost, she sighed.

"Chay," she said brokenly. "Chay…"

She rose to him. Kissed him.

And then she was in his arms.

CHAPTER NINE

HE KEPT HIS head just long enough to turn the pathetic lock on the door.

Then he carried her to the bedroom.

It was a room he wouldn't have expected until he'd gotten to know her. Crazy as it seemed, he had gotten to know her tonight.

The walls were pink, as soft and delicate a shade as the inside of a seashell. The furniture was the shade of pale bamboo. Everything else was the color of cream. The curtains at the windows. The duvet on the bed. The throw pillows. Framed pictures were clustered on one wall. Family. A meadow of Texas bluebells. A house on a cliff.

There was more to see, to learn about her, but right now she was all that mattered. Bianca, in his arms, her mouth warm and supple against his.

He lowered her slowly to her feet, right beside the bed.

She looked up at him and everything he'd wanted to see was in her eyes.

Desire. Need.

Him.

Still, he had to hear the words.

"Tell me what you want," he said softly.

"You," she whispered without any hesitation. "I've wanted you for weeks and weeks and wee—"

Her admission, the words he'd been desperate to hear, beat through his blood. He kissed her, his hands in her wet, tangled hair, kissed her until the taste of her was a part of him.

Then, slowly, he began to undress her.

He unbuttoned her denim jacket. *His* denim jacket. Slid it from her shoulders, from her arms, and let it drop to the floor.

There were buttons on the jacket of her linen suit, too, and undoing them was more difficult because they were small and his fingers were big. She would have helped him, but he caught her hands, brought them to his lips and kissed the palms.

"Let me," he said, and the rough heat in his voice almost made her knees buckle.

Her jacket fell beside his.

There were more buttons on her blouse, more indescribably small buttons. By the time had them undone, his hands were shaking.

Her pants had yet another button, but it was easy to undo and then—mercifully—he saw a zipper. He pulled the tab down slowly, slowly. As much as he wanted her, he also wanted to prolong these moments. She had never yet taken her eyes from his face and he loved seeing the hunger building inside her.

Hunger and... Was that trepidation? Was she afraid of him?

He caught her face in his hands. "Baby," he said urgently, "don't be afraid. I'd never—"

She rose on her toes and pressed her mouth to his. "Chay." Her voice shook. "Don't make me wait."

Excitement spiked in his blood.

To hell with his determined need to be as gentle and slow as he had been rough and fast the last time.

She wanted him the same way he wanted her. The realization was almost more than he could take.

He pulled her pants down. She stepped out of her shoes, those eminently sensible flats.

All that separated them now was her bra. White again, but with a pattern of tiny pink flowers. And her panties, white with those same pink flowers.

He fumbled with the bra. He, the man who'd opened more bras than he could count since he'd turned sixteen, and she batted his hands away, reached behind her and undid the hook herself.

The bra fell to her feet and he groaned at the sight of her breasts. Small. Uptilted. The color of cream tipped with pale pink nipples and, God, he had to taste them, tongue them...

She cried out, and the world spun.

He said her name, sucked one nipple into his mouth and she cried out again, sobbed his name and, Jesus, could a man come from this? Only this?

He had to get inside her.

Now.

He was moving too fast. All his self-made promises to take her slowly were vanishing the way he'd seen a late-spring Dakota snow vanish under the golden heat of the sun.

He said her name. All but tore off those white panties with the little flowers all over them, toed off his mocs, stripped away his shirt, his jeans, his boxers.

Then he was on the bed with her in his arms.

He kissed her mouth. Her throat. Her breasts.

She moaned and shifted against him.

Her hands were on his face. In his hair. They spread over his shoulders, his chest, his back.

His heart was racing. His mind was blank. And then he remembered and he said "Wait," and started to fumble for his jeans, but she said, "No, it's all right. I'm on the pill," and he almost wept with relief because the thought of having anything between her silken walls and his dick was more than he could take.

He kissed her belly.

Parted her thighs.

Knelt between them.

The world stood still.

"Bianca," he said.

His voice was raw with command.

She looked up at him. His jaw was taut, his eyes almost black. She could feel the urgency in him, hot and sharp as electricity surging through a wire.

"Watch me," he said. "I want to see you watch me."

She raised her hips. Sighed his name, and he groaned and rocked into her.

Filled her.

She sobbed and arched towards him.

He rocked into her again. Deep. Fast. Taking for himself what he had to have. Giving to her what she needed.

Quickly, much too quickly, he felt it happening. The tightening in his groin. In his balls. The realization that he was coming apart even though it was too soon, too soon…

Her muscles contracted around him.

She cried out, and he put his hands under her ass, lifted her to him, felt her coming, heard her saying his name again and again and again.

He drove deep. One final time. She screamed, bit his shoulder.

And the whirlwind swept them away.

• • •

Time passed.

Seconds. Minutes. Hours.

An eternity.

Bianca didn't know. Didn't care. Nothing mattered but Chay.

He was on top of her, his face buried in her throat, his arms still around her. He was hard and hot and heavy; she could feel him pressing her into the mattress and that was fine.

It was wonderful.

She was where she'd dreamed of being.

There was no sense in denying it now.

The only question was… What happened next?

Instinct told her he wasn't a man who'd stay for breakfast.

He lived hard. Lived in the present. Tomorrow didn't exist for someone like him. He would take one day, one experience at a time. She knew that. She even understood it.

How else could he deal with the existence he'd chosen? Half the time, he was a guy who knew the right wine to order; the other half, he risked his life doing things he couldn't talk about, in places most people couldn't locate on a map.

She knew that much from Alessandra.

Tanner had settled down.

Maybe Tanner was the exception to the rule.

Chay would never settle down. Live a normal life.

And really, that was none of her business.

This was a fling. A weekend at most. Maybe not even that. For all she knew, he was flying back to California tonight—and what did it matter? She certainly wasn't looking for anything permanent. Not now, not for the foreseeable future, not with a man who would surely see a suit and a desk as a prison…

"Hey." Chay's voice was low. Husky. He lifted his head,

gave her a long, slow kiss, then rolled onto his side. "Are you okay?"

"Yes," she said quickly. "I'm fine."

"You sure?" He smiled as he propped his head on his hand and looked at her. "Are you cold? We never did get around to drying off." He leaned towards her, brushed his mouth over hers, stroked his free hand lightly over her throat, then her breasts. "Are you sure you're all right, sweetheart?"

"Yes. Really, I'm fine."

"I'd say you were perfect." He gathered her close, kissed her again. "For a minute there, you looked so serious. Want to tell me what you were thinking?"

What she'd been thinking were the dumbest possible things. Postcoital blues? No, not blues. Postcoital nonsense. If the term didn't exist, it should.

"Baby?"

Bianca touched the tip of her finger to his chin.

"Lots of different things."

"For instance."

"Well, I was wondering where you got this dimple."

He laughed softly. "It's a cleft."

"It's a dimple," she said, "and where did you get it?"

He paused, but so briefly that she figured maybe she'd imagined it.

"From my father."

"And this?" She ran her finger lightly over the bump in his nose. "I bet you weren't born with it."

"Nope. That bump is strictly man-made."

"From what? Unless you can't tell me," she said, fluttering her lashes. "You know, if it was on some secret mission."

He grinned, caught her finger and brought it to his lips.

"It was quite a mission, all right. But not secret."

"No?"

"No." He nipped her fingertip, then soothed the tiny bite with a kiss. "High school. Championship game. Fourth quarter. Tanner was supposed to pass to Roger Raintree, but he saw damn near the whole defensive line coming at him, so he threw to me instead."

"Football!"

"Uh-huh." He smiled. "The great American pastime."

"Tanner was—what is it called? The quarterback?"

"Yup. I played tight end. Anyway, he sent that ball sailing over the heads of everybody, straight to me."

"And you scored a goal."

"A touchdown. Yes, I did—but on the way to the end zone, I met up with a guy from the Plains Pirates—the opposing team—who weighed seven hundred pounds."

Bianca laughed. "Why do I think you're exaggerating?"

"Okay. Six hundred pounds. Anyway, it didn't matter. The important thing was that we won."

"And you were...?"

"A Dakota Grizzly. Very imaginative, right?"

"You should have been called a wolf. Because that's what you are. Big and smart and beautiful."

His eyebrows rose. She blushed and buried her face

against his chest. He rolled her gently onto her back.

"I like that," he said. "Big. And smart. But beautiful? I think you're looking at the wrong guy."

"Beautiful," she said emphatically.

Chay kissed her. Slowly. Tenderly, but with growing passion. She parted her lips, let him in, touched the tip of her tongue to his, and he gave a soft, sexy growl.

"Do you have any idea how it feels to have you in my arms?" he murmured. He kissed the hollow of her throat, kissed his way to her breasts, licked and then sucked on her nipples.

She could feel herself melting. Little sounds rose in her throat. Her breathing quickened. They'd just made love. How could she want him again?

There was no question that he wanted her.

He was hard again. Hard as a rock.

She put her hand between them and touched him.

He groaned.

"Do you like that?" she whispered.

He gave a broken laugh. "Too much. Unless you want this to end before it really begins."

She loved hearing him say that. Feeling him surge against her hand.

"Baby," he said in a warning whisper, and he caught her hand. Both her hands. Pinned them to the bed on either side of her hips. "My turn." He shifted down over her body. Kissed her navel. Her belly. His breath was warm against her skin. "Do you like when I do this?"

Her answer was a sweet, sexy moan.

"That's good," he said on a soft laugh. "It's absolutely the right answer." His hand slipped between her thighs. "And this?" he said, all the laughter gone. "Do you like me to do this, too?"

His mouth followed his hand.

She reached down to stop him. "No," she said quickly, "Chay…"

"I want to taste you," he said, and her protest became a soft, keening cry as he put his face against her. His mouth on her clitoris.

Bianca cried out.

The room tilted.

Nobody had ever done this to her before. She'd never wanted anybody to do this to her before. It was—it was too intimate. Too intense.

Too everything.

She'd read descriptions, even viewed educational films, but, *Dio*, the reality of it, of Chay's mouth, his tongue, his teeth…

"Come for me, honey," he whispered.

His voice cajoled. Commanded. He was not giving her a choice—and she didn't want one. She wanted this. What he was doing. What he was making her feel.

A cry broke from her throat.

She arched off the bed. Came on a hot rush of blurred colors only she could see, a swell of music only she could hear.

And when she said Chay's name, he rose up and thrust into her, and the world ceased to exist.

• • •

Bianca came awake to darkness shot through with ivory moonlight.

The clock radio read four a.m.

And the bed beside her was empty.

She sat up, switched on the lamp that stood on the nightstand.

His clothes were gone too.

Except for the indentation on the pillow beside hers, her lieutenant might never have been there.

Her throat constricted.

She'd been right. Chay wasn't a man who'd hang around for breakfast.

She told herself that was okay. That she'd known what to expect. That she had no right to feel lost—but she did.

She did.

Her eyes burned with unshed tears and for a heartbeat, she almost gave in to it, the feeling of pain, of emptiness.

No.

She had grown up watching her mother do that. Weep each time her husband left. Weep as she waited for him to return. Shout and scream and curse because his promises that the next time he would stay, the next time he would not be gone so long, were only that. Promises, ones he never kept.

At least Chay had made no promises.

What he'd done was make love to her.

And it had been magic.

Bianca rose from the bed, plucked her robe from the chair where she always kept it, pulled it on and tied the sash. She needed the bathroom and then some coffee—or maybe a glass of wine to make her stop thinking, keep her from slipping into self-pity.

She'd slept with Chay because she'd wanted to, wanted *him* more than anything she'd ever wanted in her life, and she'd known how this would end from the start.

Barefoot, she padded into the bathroom. Peed. Flushed. Washed her hands and headed for the kitchen…

The overhead light was on.

Her heart leaped.

It was on because Chay was sitting at the table, his hands wrapped around a steaming mug, wearing a low-slung towel and nothing else. His clothes were there, too, draped over the backs of her kitchen chairs so they could dry.

"Chay?"

He swung towards her. Then he smiled, put down the mug and got to his feet.

"I made coffee," he said. "Want some?"

She walked straight to him, wound her arms around his neck, tilted her head back and laughed.

"What I want," she said, "is you."

CHAPTER TEN

HE MADE PERFECT coffee.

She, it turned out, made perfect scrambled eggs.

Chay was at the kitchen table. His chest was still bare, but he'd pulled on his now-dry jeans and he was sitting back, his long legs stretched out, his feet crossed at the ankles and his arms folded over his chest as he watched Bianca poke through the refrigerator in a search for something or other.

He hadn't really paid attention to what she'd said she was looking for.

He'd been too busy looking at her.

Perfect coffee. Perfect eggs

Or maybe it was simply being here that was perfect. Having breakfast with a beautiful woman, enjoying the sight of her as the sun rose over the city.

And, damn, she was one lovely sight.

All that tousled golden hair loose on her shoulders,

the totally non-sexy dark blue terrycloth robe made sexy by the fact that he knew what lay beneath it—knew it intimately. The delicate fullness of her breasts, the flatness of her belly, the sweet essence his tongue coaxed from between her thighs.

Hell.

He shifted his weight in the chair.

They'd made love twice during the night and again this morning, but his body was telling him he'd be happy for a repeat performance.

He couldn't seem to get enough of his Tigress. And it turned out he'd given her the right nickname. He'd dubbed her that because of her determination. Her toughness. And now, to his unabashed delight, he'd discovered that she was also a tigress when it came to sex.

When she'd walked into the kitchen an hour ago, he'd felt a momentary wariness. She'd seemed surprised to see him.

Had she hoped he'd have left by now?

He had no intention of going anywhere. Not just yet.

Then the look in her eyes had changed. He'd tried to read it, but he couldn't. So he'd risen to his feet, wondering which Bianca was he going to see—the Tigress who'd gone wild in his arms, or the one who was determined to keep tight control over her world.

Coward that he was, he'd opted for caution. *Want some coffee?* he'd asked.

And she'd smiled, gone straight into his arms and said that what she wanted was him.

Those simple words had been enough to make him

hard.

Seconds later, they were on the living room sofa because the bedroom was too far away.

Yes, and the sofa was too short.

But it didn't matter. Not once he was buried inside her, her legs wrapped around his hips, her cries of passion, the slap of their bodies against each other rising into the predawn silence until she sobbed his name and he collapsed against her.

Damn.

Chay shifted his weight again.

He'd had sex with a lot of women. And—why be modest?—he'd never needed much recovery time between sessions, but this... This was a new experience. This nonstop need, not just for sex but for her. Even just sitting here, being in the same room with her, watching her do something as ridiculously mundane as peer into the refrigerator—

The fine hairs rose on the nape of his neck.

Domesticity was not his thing. It was most definitely not his thing. Neither was confusing good sex—okay, great sex—with anything but what it was.

Sex.

Although he knew women preferred the term "making love."

He used the words, too. Why not? They were interchangeable. Okay. Maybe one meant something more casual and the other meant taking your time, slowing things down.

What he'd never considered was that it meant more

than that. That maybe it meant letting yourself feel more than the obvious things as you touched a woman. As you kissed her, caressed her, moved inside her until her response was, hell, until *your* response was beyond anything you'd ever known.

Until you couldn't stop thinking about her. Wanting her.

And, dammit, there was a way to get past that.

Chay kicked back his chair and rose to his feet. The kitchen was not much bigger than a walk-in closet. He crossed it in two quick strides, clasped Bianca's shoulders and whirled her towards him. He'd startled her; he saw it in her eyes.

"What?" she said, and then, as her gaze swept over his face, she took a quick indrawn breath. "Chay?"

She never finished speaking his name.

His mouth captured hers.

He swept the robe from her shoulders. Lifted her. Sat her on the kitchen counter. Something clattered to the floor. Silverware. The napkin holder. He didn't know. Didn't care. All that mattered was the kiss, the heat and savagery of it; all that mattered was unzipping his jeans, sliding his hand between her thighs and, God, and finding her hot and slick and ready, so ready.

And then he was inside her. Hard inside her. Thrusting deep. Deeper. Deep enough so there was no way to know where he ended and she began.

She grabbed his shoulders. Then she pressed her palms against the countertop and her head fell back. Her body arched like a bow.

His hands dropped over hers.

"Now," he groaned, "now, now…"

She came on one long, glorious cry as he emptied himself into her.

And he thought, *Jesus, what have I done?*

His arms went around her. He gathered her in, one hand in the center of her back, the other cupping her head.

"Baby," he whispered, "honey, I'm sorry. God, I'm sorry. I never meant to—"

She jerked back. Clasped his face between her hands. Her eyes were the color of blue flame.

"I thought I was going to die," she said breathlessly. A look he knew he would never forget lit her entire face. "And oh, Chayton, what a glorious death it would have been."

He stared at her. He wanted to say something, to tell her that he—that he—

He kissed her instead. Cradled her in his arms. And faced the slowly dawning truth.

No matter how many times he made love with his Tigress, it was never going to be enough to drive her from his head.

Or from his heart.

• • •

They showered.

Dried each other off and fooled around doing it, and then Chay wrapped Bianca in an oversized bath towel, swept her into his arms and whirled her around in a tight circle. A very tight circle, because of the size of her bathroom.

"Stop," she pleaded. "You're making my head spin."

"I'll take that as a compliment, Ms. Wilde."

"There's that ego of yours again, Lieutenant."

He grinned and she giggled, and the sound of that giggle shot through him. Who would have imagined his I-Am-in-Complete-Control queen of the universe giggling? Who would have imagined all the fire inside her?

He kissed her, and she sighed and leaned her head against his shoulder.

"I should be doing Saturday chores," she said after a couple of minutes.

He pressed a kiss to her temple. "For instance?"

"Mmm. Grocery shopping. Straightening up."

He drew back and looped his hands at the base of her spine.

"Huh. Standing up, you look pretty straight to me."

She punched him lightly in the biceps. "Cleaning up. You know what I mean."

He smiled and dropped a kiss on the tip of her nose. "Tell you what. We'll go out. Have breakfast."

"We already had breakfast."

"Hey, what can I tell you? Exercise builds a man's appetite." She blushed. God, he loved that blush. "You've worn me out," he said, pressing his lips to her throat. "And if you want to wear me out again, I'll require fuel."

Her smile was the smile of a very contented tigress.

"That's exactly what I want," she said softly, touching her finger to his lips.

"See?" He caught her hand and kissed the palm. "So, breakfast first. Then we'll take care of those other things."

"Groceries? Straightening up? You?"

"Me. I have a secret plan."

She tilted her head and smiled. "You do, huh?"

"The woman doubts me," he said, trying his best to scowl. "Damn right I do."

"And your plan is…?"

"After breakfast, we'll go to my hotel. Groceries? I'll phone for room service. Straightening up? I guarantee that someone will have already done all the straightening you could ask for. How's that sound?"

Bianca smiled. "It sounds decadent," she said. "And absolutely perfect."

There it was. That word again. *Perfect.* Her using it this time, not him.

The hairs on the back of his neck did that stand-up routine again. Before he could think about it too long, he gave her a quick kiss, set her on her feet and got to his.

"Go on, honey. Get dressed. Then we'll find a place where we can get eggs, waffles, pancakes, sausage, bacon, bagels, biscuits…"

She laughed.

He grinned, spun her in the direction of the bedroom and stepped over to the sink.

Bianca had given him a toothbrush. He squeezed a

ribbon of paste onto the bristles and began brushing.

Man, he needed a shave. As it was, he'd left red marks on her breasts and her thighs. When he'd tried to apologize for his dark stubble, she'd stopped him.

"I love the feel of it against me," she'd said softly, and a weird kind of feeling had swept through him as he thought of how those light abrasions marked her as his.

Chay frowned at his reflection, spat into the sink, turned on the water and cupped his hand under the flow.

What was with him? So many crazy thoughts in his head… But why question it? He was happy, happier than he'd been since he'd come back from that last deployment. Happier than he could recall ever being.

His Tigress was happy, too. He could hear doors and drawers opening and closing in her bedroom. She was singing, too, something in Italian. Her voice was sweet and warm and—

She screamed.

It was the kind of scream that almost stopped his heart.

Chay ran into the bedroom.

Bianca was standing in front of the dresser. The top right-hand drawer was pulled out. She was staring into it, trembling, her hands clapped over her mouth.

"Baby? What happened?"

She nodded at the open drawer.

Something in the drawer. Okay. A big bug was his first thought. Women didn't do well with big bugs. Or a mouse. Hell, this was an old building; this was New York City…

Chay froze.

The drawer held neatly folded bras. And neatly folded panties.

And something else.

A condom. A used condom. He could tell by the slightly bulbous shape of it. A used condom that the thoughtful user had knotted so the contents wouldn't spill.

If anyone had ever asked him if a man could really go blind with rage, he'd have laughed and said no. But he was blind now. Blind, and crazed with rage.

His hands knotted into fists. His pulse roared in his ears.

And then he heard Bianca, and the little sounds she was making. Not sobs. Not cries. Not anything he'd ever heard before except from the throat of a wounded animal back in the Dakotas.

He reached for her, tried to gather her against him, but her body was rigid. "Bianca," he said, and he pulled her to him, wrapped his arms around her, held her to him with a ferocity born of fury and desperation.

"Ohmygod," she whispered, "ohmygod," and that she was speaking in English somehow only made the reality of what had been waiting for her in that drawer more potent.

He knew, he *knew* that some sick piece of shit had done this to terrify her.

"Shh," he said, rocking her in his arms. "Shh. Come on, baby. Take some deep breaths. That's it. That's the way. Just breathe."

He scooped her up, carried her to the bed, sat on the

edge of it with her in his lap. She was shaking so hard he could feel it, and breathing like a runner at the end of a hard race.

He held her close. Stroked her hair. Kissed her forehead, her eyelids, her lips.

"It's okay," he crooned. "Honey. Sweetheart. It's okay."

After a few minutes, she gave an enormous shudder. Her breathing slowed, then steadied.

"Good girl," Chay whispered.

"That was—it was a condom?"

He nodded. "Yes."

Another shudder. "You need to know that I have no idea—"

"No," he said quickly. "I didn't think you did."

She sat up in his arms and looked directly at him. "I have never had a man here, Chayton. Not in my apartment, and certainly not in my bed."

Chayton. It was the second time she'd called him that. It was years since anyone had used his full first name. And what she'd said, about never having a man in her bed... What kind of scum was he that he even noticed those things at a moment like this?

"I know that," he said softly.

She nodded. "Who would—who would do such a thing?"

A lunatic. A maniac. A freak straight out of a nightmare.

"I don't know," Chay said. "But I'm going to find out."

She nodded again. She was too compliant. Was she

going into shock?

"Bianca. Do you have brandy in the house?"

"Brandy?"

"Brandy. Liquor. Whiskey."

"A bottle of wine. I think. In the back of the refrigerator. The last time Alessandra was here…"

Chay eased her from his lap and stood up. She grabbed his hand.

"Where are you going?"

 "I'm going to get you a drink."

"No! I will come with you."

He helped her up. Kept his arm tightly around her, led her to the kitchen and sat her down.

The wine, a half-bottle of white, was tucked behind a quart of milk. He poured her an inch of it, then thought about it and almost topped the glass. He squatted before her, but her hands shook when she reached for the glass.

"Let me," he said, holding the glass to her lips.

She took a couple of sips. Then she turned her face away.

"I feel as if I am going to be sick," she whispered.

Chay set the glass aside and gathered her into his arms again. He held her for a long time. A very long time. Then he drew back and cupped her face in his hands.

"I'm going to call the cops, honey."

She nodded.

"They're going to ask you questions…"

"They can ask whatever they have to ask."

He stroked a strand of hair back from her forehead. "I'll be with you all the time. Okay?"

She looked at him. Her face was still pale. Her eyes were damp. But she managed a quick smile.

"Okay."

• • •

The police came.

A pair of them, one who Chay figured was too young to be on the job, the other too old to give a crap about anything but his retirement.

Not that it mattered.

It took no time at all before it became obvious that they'd decided this was a nasty joke—and that maybe Chay was the joker.

He took them into the bedroom. They peered into the drawer, exchanged a *What the fuck?* look, and headed back to the kitchen where Bianca was waiting.

"So. Missus... Wilde?"

Bianca looked at the duo.

"You have any idea who might have done this?"

She shook her head. "No."

The older cop scratched his jaw. "An unhappy boyfriend?"

"No."

"A boyfriend with, you know, a grudge?"

"No. I do not have a boyfriend."

Both cops looked at Chay. He was standing next to Bianca's chair. Her hand was clasped tightly in his.

"What she means," Chay said, "is that I'm her boyfriend. There's no one else."

The young cop nodded. "You spent last evening with Ms. Wilde?"

"Yes."

"Here, I mean."

"Yes."

"The night too?"

Chay's jaw tightened, but he'd been trained in interrogation techniques. Not this kind, no, but the same principles applied.

"Yes."

"So you were, ah, intimate?"

To hell with the principles of interrogation.

"That has nothing to do with the situation," Chay said coldly.

The younger cop glanced at the older one. The older one shrugged.

"That's a condom in that drawer, Mister. If you spent the night—"

"It's *lieutenant*," Chay said, even more coldly. "And before you ask, I'm not in the habit of leaving calling cards."

Both officers nodded. "And your former boyfriend?" the older one said.

"She told you," Chay snapped. "There is no former boyfriend."

"Maybe the lady would prefer to answer questions with you out of the room, Mis—Lieutenant."

"No," Bianca said quickly. "Chayton. Don't leave me."

Chay looked at the cops. "Are you done?" They nodded and Chay brought Bianca's hand to his lips. "Just let me see the officers out, honey. I promise, I'll be right back."

He strode through the kitchen, through the tiny hallway and to the door. The policemen hurried after him.

"The thing is," the older one said, "there's not a lot we can do."

Chay nodded. "I understand."

"If the lady says there haven't been any other guys here—"

"If she says it," Chay said flatly, "it's because it's true."

"Yeah. I didn't mean…" The officer heaved a sigh. "No sign of a break-in. No other men in her life. I mean, you know, we can file a report. Hand this to the detectives, they'd maybe come by, check things out, but…There's not really anything to go on, you know what I mean?"

Chay knew exactly what the cop meant. In a city with more than its share of killers, thieves and gangbangers, a condom lying in a drawer, filled with what appeared to be semen, wasn't going to be high on anyone's priority list.

"What about a DNA test?"

"Sure." The younger cop shrugged. "Problem is, we've got hundreds of DNA samples waiting to be tested. Rapes, murders…"

Chay got the message. Compared to rapes and murders,

this would almost be a joke.

"I understand," he said as he shook hands with each man. "Thanks for coming so quickly."

Both cops nodded. "You might want to see to it the lady changes the lock on this door."

"Yeah. I'll take care of it."

The policemen left. Chay closed the door and turned the lock.

What now? His head was spinning. If this were Santa Barbara, if he were at Camp Condor, there were things, effective things, he could do. He could get a DNA test run—he had contacts he could turn to and the units had access to the most up-to-date resources.

He could get a look at the medical records of the patient who'd harassed Bianca a couple of months back, do a background check on the nut who'd been a problem at *Cuppa Joe's* yesterday, accomplish both things without the nonsense of court orders. Computers were wonderful things, if you had the right skills. And if you didn't have those skills, guys like Declan Sanchez did.

But this wasn't Santa Barbara.

Okay. There were things he could tap into long distance...

A phone rang. Not his, which was in the pocket of his jeans. Bianca's, in the kitchen.

It rang again.

A funny feeling came over him, that sense that something wasn't right, and he held up his hand as he reached her.

"Baby," he said, "wait…"

But she already had the phone at her ear.

"Hello?"

"Bianca. Give me the phone."

"Hello?" she said again.

The phone shook in her hand. Chay rushed to her, grabbed the phone and put it to his ear.

"Who is this?" he snarled.

Soft laughter, and the whisper of a male voice.

"Did she like my little gift?"

"Listen, you sick bastard…"

"I hope she didn't give it away to those two fine representatives of the law."

Chay hit the disconnect button. Then he all but lifted Bianca to her feet. His face gave nothing away; his tone was brisk.

"Pack some clothes," he said.

"Who was that? Chayton? Who was on the phone?"

"Bianca." Chay gripped her shoulders. "Listen to me. Pack whatever you think you're going to need for a few days."

"Chay. Please, what's happening?"

He pulled her to him. Kissed her hard and deep.

"Do you trust me?"

Tears were on her cheeks. He wiped them away with his thumbs.

"Yes," she said. "With all my heart."

"Then let me take care of you. Will you do that, honey?

For me?"

Her eyes searched his. Then she took his hand, brought it to her lips and kissed it.

Twenty minutes later, they were in a taxi heading for his hotel.

CHAPTER ELEVEN

CHAY'S HOTEL WAS just off Central Park.

His room was almost the size of his entire place on the beach back in Santa Barbara.

Well, okay, maybe not.

But it was big, with a separate sitting area, a picture-postcard view of Manhattan from the floor-to-ceiling windows, a bed that could have slept his whole unit on bivouac, and a bathroom that was all granite, stainless steel and glass.

Aidan Maguire, one of the guys in his unit, had a sister who was a travel agent. When Aidan found out Chay was heading to New York for a couple of days, he'd offered to call her and let her put the wheels in motion.

"She's three years older than I am and she owes me," he'd said with a grin, "considering all that I tolerated from her when we were growing up. No, seriously, dude, she's great at this shit. She'll get you one hell of a room at a price that'll make your jaw drop. I promise, you'll come back spoiled."

The niceties of a room had never mattered much to Chay.

When he was growing up, his home had been a falling-down trailer where you froze in the winter and boiled in the summer. College had been an improvement, but living arrangements went on the back burner when he made it into the SEALs and then into STUD.

Running water, soap and a roof over your head were luxuries.

Most often, all you needed was a place to put your head that was out of the line of fire.

He figured Bianca was accustomed to luxury.

Her Manhattan apartment was fairly conventional, but he'd been to El Sueño, the Wilde ranch. He knew she'd grown up in Italy, but if the Bellini branch of the family had lived a life comparable to the Wilde branch, he'd have bet she wouldn't have been comfortable in the kind of cheap hotel he'd probably have ended up with on his own.

Now, as he inserted his key card into the lock on this hotel room door, he reminded himself to send flowers to Aidan's sister when he got back to California.

Not that the room seemed to matter to Bianca. She hadn't said a word since they'd left her apartment, and it worried him. Still, he figured that a pleasant room, with flowers on a little table in front of the windows, handsome furniture, and high ceilings, might be good for her.

Maybe all of those things would help mask the image

that had to be lodged in her head, as it was in his.

The open drawer. The neatly stacked bras and panties. The condom.

The condom was in his pocket now, encased in a plastic baggie.

He closed the door, locked it, tossed the key card on a table.

Then he opened the wall-length closet. It contained a safe, and now he squatted before it, set a combination, hustled the baggie inside and shut the safe door.

If Bianca had noticed what he'd done, she gave no indication.

In fact, she gave no indication of anything.

She was still standing where he'd left her, her arms at her sides, everything about her tightly contained and unmoving. He knew only the ways to handle guys who were back from a mission gone bad and seemed to be falling into darkness. Some you left alone. Others you cracked jokes with, the kind of jokes that only men who'd faced death and worse could handle.

Still others you treated as if nothing had happened.

It was the method he figured he'd try first.

So he walked briskly to the windows and drew open the blinds.

"Some view, huh?"

She nodded.

"The room's not bad, either. Just look at that bed. It's the size of a football field. And wait until you see the bathroom. A double sink. A tub that's got to be three feet deep, and a shower big enough for a party." *Hell. He sounded like an advertising brochure.* "All in all, it's not much to look at, I admit, but it'll have to do."

Now he sounded like a bad late-night comedian.

No matter. She didn't smile. She didn't even nod. As far as he could tell, she might not even have heard him.

"So," he said in that same brisk voice, "let's get you settled. I'll put your stuff away in one of the draw—" *Crap! He was an idiot.* "—in the closet. Then we'll order something to eat. How's that sound?"

Still nothing.

"What would you like? Breakfast? Early lunch? What's that ridiculous word for it? *Brunch.* What jerk came up with a word like that? Sounds like something you'd plan for a party of three-year-olds." Silence. "Coffee, then. And we don't even have to wait for room service. There's this little tray—see it over there? It's got everything we need. A coffeepot. Little packets of coffee. Containers of cream and sugar and—" And now he was babbling. Chay took a long breath, then puffed it out. "Honey. Look, I know this isn't easy, but—"

"Why?" She spoke in a shaky whisper. "Why would someone do these things to me?"

Good question, he thought grimly. Hell, she was the shrink. If she couldn't figure it out, how could he? Although the truth was, he didn't care about the why. It was the who that mattered.

"I don't know," he said. "But we're going to find out."

"Whoever it is, he is sick."

The twenty-first century excuse for everything. For war. For torture. For abusing puppies and mugging old ladies. People were sick. Maybe so, but what had become of responsibility?

But he knew better than to argue with her. Not at a time like this.

"Sick or not, baby, we need to figure out who might want to hurt you."

She looked at him as he walked towards her. "I have tried. And tried. I cannot think of anyone who would want to—to frighten me like this."

They'd moved beyond the *frighten* stage. Chay could sense it. The crazy who'd been satisfied with scaring Bianca at a distance was changing the rules. Whoever it was needed to get closer to her, and he'd moved the game up a notch.

What Chay had to do was stop the game and make sure the guy would never play it again.

Bur for now—for now, all that mattered was getting his Bianca back.

The question was, how?

The answer was instinctive.

Chay gathered her gently in his arms.

"You're safe now," he said softly. "You're safe with me."

A quick little dip of her head. It was a start.

He drew her even closer, stroked her cheek, dropped kisses on her hair.

"Tomorrow we'll come up with a plan."

"We will?"

He nodded. "Yes. I have some ideas already."

Ideas he'd bet she'd veto, but he was the guy with the final vote.

"You do?"

"I do." He tilted her face up, smiled into her eyes. "But we're not going to talk about that now. I'm too tired." He turned his smile into a grin. "For some reason, I didn't get much sleep last night."

For a second or two, she didn't respond. Then she offered a hesitant smile and he felt as if he'd won the lottery.

"Thank you," she whispered.

"For what?"

"For everything. For being so kind and so patient with me."

"Me? Patient? You'll have to put that in writing so I can show it to my unit."

A tiny, very tiny laugh. Not just the lottery. The Powerball lottery.

"Chayton?"

"I'm here, sweetheart."

"I feel so useless."

"You? Never."

She sighed. "I am a trained clinician. I am supposed to know how to deal with such a thing as this."

"And you have been dealing with it. You handled those telephone calls you got in Texas. And that asshole yesterday... You were great." He gave it a few seconds. If he could get a little information now, why not get it? "What was his name? That guy at *Cuppa Joe's*."

"Noah."

"Noah what?"

"Collins? Clinton." She sighed. "I can look in my... Why? Surely you don't think—"

"What I think," Chay said, clasping her face between his hands, "is that anything is possible in this world. That's Life Lesson Number One."

"Noah clearly has problems, but his personality is not that of a man who would—who would invade a woman's space in such a personal way."

Bullshit, Chay thought, but this wasn't the time to tell her that.

"Honey. We're going to order in some food. And coffee. We can discuss this later. Tonight. Or tomorrow morning."

"I don't know what we'll discuss. I don't know. I can't think of anyone who would do these things."

"Still, someone did. And we're going to find out who."

"How?"

They were heading into a conversation he wanted to avoid until she was stronger.

"You have access to your files on your laptop? Patient records? Whatever notes you've taken about the participants in your study?"

She nodded. "Of course."

"Excellent. We'll go through all of it."

"No."

"What do you mean, no?"

"I can't open my files to you. To anyone. It would be

unethical."

Shit. "Bianca," he said calmly, "the odds are good we'll find the answers we need in those files."

Bianca stepped back. Her chin lifted.

"What I have is privileged information between clinician and patient. As for the study—I promised all who participated anonymity."

"I'm not going to take out an ad and make their names and their problems public, honey."

"Still, such a thing would be wrong."

The good news was that she was back. No more stilted English. No more awful silence. No more emptiness in those beautiful eyes.

The bad news was that she was as intractable as ever. Or as determined as ever, depending on your point of view.

His point of view was that if getting into those files meant grabbing her laptop and breaking into it while she hammered him with her fists, that was what he would do.

But there was time. Not much, but some. She was with him, she was safe, and she needed enough breathing room to recover from what had happened a little while ago in her apartment. She was better, but she was like a guy crossing a mountain gorge on a shaky rope bridge.

Go slow. Go steady. One false move and you might fall.

It wasn't just that he wanted to make sure she was okay before she set foot on that bridge; it was that she—she was important to him.

Important? That wasn't really the right word.

She meant everything to him. Everything, in a way no woman ever had before.

A chill danced along his spine.

"Time to order lunch," he said, because thinking about food was a lot safer topic than what was tiptoeing through his head.

• • •

He ordered whatever he thought might tempt her. No rhyme or reason. Just whatever seemed like comfort food.

French toast. Omelets. A couple of small steaks. Soups. Chicken salad.

Rice pudding.

Bianca laughed when she peeked into one of the covered serving bowls and saw the rice pudding.

"Universal comfort food," she said.

Her laugh was what comforted him. It was the final assurance that his woman was beside him and in the world again.

They ate at the table next to the window.

He was determined they would only talk about upbeat, noncontroversial things. Movies? Yeah, but he wasn't much for movies. Travel? The last place he'd been wasn't high on anybody's let's-talk-about-interesting-places list.

Anyway, what he really wanted to talk about was her.

He wanted to know more about her. Everything about her. How she'd grown up. If she missed Sicily. All he knew was that she'd been raised there, which didn't make much sense, considering that her old man was a four-star general and her family's Texas ranch was the size of a small kingdom.

And the double surname. What was with that? What little he'd gleaned about the Bellini-Wilde thing had come from listening to Tanner and from the conversation that had swirled around him when Alessandra had been kidnapped and the entire clan had descended on Camp Condor.

"You have a big family," he said, when they were eating their French toast. "All those Wildes and Bellinis…"

She smiled. "Three half-brothers. Three half-sisters. Two full brothers and one full sister."

"And the Wilde part of it is John Hamilton Wilde. General John Hamilton Wilde. Your father."

Her chin lifted. "My father by blood, not by choice."

Chay laughed. "Trust me, honey. Lots of us have fathers we'd never have wanted if we'd had a choice."

"Yours too?"

"Mine too," he said, but he sure as hell wasn't going there. He swallowed the last bite of steak and reached for his coffee. "And you and Alessandra were born in Italy?"

"In Sicily, yes. Alessandra and our two brothers."

"Didn't the general want to raise you in Texas with the rest of his children?"

Bianca stared at him. "Tanner did not tell you?"

"Tell me what?"

She sighed. "It is a complicated story."

There it was. That little touch of English formality in

her speech. Chay reached across the table for her hand.

"Honey. If it upsets you—"

"My father—*our* father—never told his American children about us and he never told us about them." She took a breath. "He married the mother of my half-sisters while he was still married to our mother. "

It took a few seconds for it to sink in. When it did, Chay could hardly believe what he'd just heard.

"You mean—you mean he's a bigamist?"

"I mean," Bianca said, each syllable encased in ice, "he is a disreputable, lying, cheating *pezzo di merda*."

Whatever that was, Chay knew it was not good.

A couple of seconds went by. Then he snorted.

"Excuse me," she said, even more coldly, "but what is so amusing?"

Chay snorted again, and then, despite his best efforts, laughter burst from his throat.

"The four-star general who wears starched shirts and, I'm fucking certain, starched shorts is a bigamist?"

Bianca's eyes narrowed. "It is not funny."

"We were on a base one time," Chay said, "and he was inspecting the troops. And he pulled a guy out of line because his shirt was wrinkled. 'Have you no respect for your image as an American soldier?' he said. Something like that, anyway. And all the time—all the time... Honey. I'm sorry. I know the fact that he's such a whatever-you-called-him isn't funny to you, but—"

"I called him *uno pezzo di merda*. A piece of shit. And,

no, nothing about him is funny to—to—"

Bianca bit her lip. Then she burst into laughter, but it didn't last long enough for him not to see tears forming in her eyes.

Chay got up, went around the table, knelt beside her and drew her into his arms.

She sighed, looped her arms around his neck and slid from her chair to the floor so he could hold her.

"He was the world's worst father," she said, "and I'm still coming to terms with that."

"Sorry, baby. If we're giving out medals for the world's worst, my old man wins."

She leaned back in his arms. "Impossible."

"Okay. My old man is a close second. How's that?" He kissed her. Lightly. Gently. "And, trust me, I'm still coming to terms with that myself."

"What was he like? Your father?"

"You don't want to know."

"You're wrong. I want to know everything about you, Lieutenant. And just remember—I outrank you by way of my father, so I have the right to demand that you tell me what I want to know."

Chay laughed. "That's it. Hate the old man, but pull rank on me anyway."

She smiled. "Absolutely."

"Okay. What do you want to know?"

"You and Tanner grew up in the same town?"

"We grew up on the same reservation."

"You were best friends."

"Asshole buddies." Chay grinned. "Though not by today's terms."

Bianca smiled. "Blood brothers."

"Yeah. Literally. We did that cut-your-palms, let-your-blood-mingle thing when we were eleven or twelve."

"And Tanner's mother died when he was in his teens."

Chay's grin faded. "My mom outlasted his, but not by much."

Bianca's gaze swept over her lover's face. The conversation had taken a swift downward turn.

"Chayton," she said softly, "I was joking when I said you had to tell me all about your childhood. If you don't want to talk about this…"

He never did. Nobody but Tanner knew anything about him that dated back before he'd joined the SEALs and then STUD, but he wanted Bianca to know more.

Suddenly, he wanted her to know the worst.

She might run once she did, but he had to take the chance.

"My father was white," he said. "That's where I get the green eyes and the cleft chin. Thank God, that seems to be all of him that I have. He met my mother at a bar in Pierre. A month later, she was pregnant. Her old man—my grandfather—was tough. He confronted my father and demanded that he marry my mother." Chay shrugged. "Seven months after that, I popped into the world."

His tone was light, almost carefree, but Bianca knew

there was nothing light or carefree about his story.

"And that's why you were concerned you'd made me pregnant," she said gently.

"Yes. No. Maybe. The thing is, a man should be responsible for his actions."

Bianca ran the tip of her index finger down his nose.

"Well, your father was."

"The hell he was. He married my mother with the proverbial shotgun pointed at his head. The truth is, my grandfather should have stayed out of the situation."

"Because?"

"Because he died when I was a baby, and with nobody riding his ass, my father reverted to the piece of shit he was. He drank. He whored. He left us alone for months at a time. I hardly recognized him until I was five or six. He just wasn't there often enough to make a lasting impression." Chay's mouth twisted. "But he remedied that quick enough."

"Why do I get the feeling he didn't remedy it in a good way?"

"He had what my mother insisted on calling fast hands. What that meant was that he was good at beating her. And me. The one good thing that happened was that as I got older, she got less of it. I became his favorite target. I took it. What else could I do? I took it and took it, and then I began telling myself a day would come when I wouldn't take it anymore."

Bianca's throat constricted. "And," she said softly, "you were right and that day finally came."

Chay nodded. "He'd been gone for months. I was

seventeen, just naïve enough to start to think he was out of our lives for good."

"But he wasn't."

Chay leaned his forehead against hers

"Coach called me into his office after school."

"The Grizzlies coach."

Why did the fact that she'd remembered the name of his high school football team make him so happy?

"Yup. Coach Reed. He told me the University of Colorado was interested in me. That they'd sent him a letter. Well, me and Tanner—which made it even better because we were tight. We hunted together. Fished together. He'd pledged himself to the Sun Dance, but it took another couple of years before I did too."

"What's the Sun Dance?"

"A very old Sioux ceremony. You fast, cleanse your body, and kind of open your mind. Then the elders hook you up to a pole and you dance around it until you pull free or collapse. Sounds barbaric, I guess, but it's a very spiritual experience."

"I noticed two scars on your chest. Are they from the dance?"

He nodded. Hesitated. And said, in a voice so low she could hardly hear him, "I danced after I almost killed my father."

He heard her swift intake of breath, felt the sudden stillness in her. But she stayed right where she was. In his lap. In his arms.

"If you almost killed him," his Tigress said, very calmly,

"then he must have needed killing."

So he told her everything.

The years of beatings. Of incredible brutality. Of the ugly competition, the one-sided fiery jealousy that was his father's indulgence.

"He used to work odd jobs on nearby ranches, but most ranchers had given up hiring him years before—they couldn't count on him showing up. He used to saddle-break horses, too, but they stopped using him for that because he whipped the horses that didn't learn as fast as he wanted. Once I was old enough, I got jobs doing the same things. Odd jobs. Mending fences. Saddle-breaking horses, but without whipping the crap out of them. I worked hard and I got most of the jobs I went after."

"You were a good kid," Bianca said softly.

"Not according to my old man. By then, he was spending more time living with us, mostly because he had no income. People knew he was a mean drunk and nobody wanted to have him around. But he blamed me. He said it was because I badmouthed him, that I lied and cheated him out of work."

"And he took his anger out on you?"

Chay nodded. "It was bad, but I told myself I just had to stick it out. Another year and I'd be gone. College was only a dream because I didn't have the money, but I figured on enlisting in the service." He paused. "Then that scholarship letter arrived and changed everything."

"I can imagine." She smiled. "It meant you could get away."

"Yes. But that wasn't the change I meant."

"No?"

"No," Chay said. "I came home all excited that day. My father was sitting in the door of our trailer, waiting for me. One look at his face and I knew it was going to be bad. I could see the rage in his eyes, smell the booze on his breath. And I could see two other things. He had his belt wrapped around the knuckles of his right hand. I'd felt the bite of it before—it was wide and heavy, and it had brass studs embedded in the leather."

Bianca's eyes locked onto his. "Oh, Chayton," she whispered.

"The second thing I saw was the letter. Coach had forwarded a copy to him." Chay gave a bitter laugh. "Talk about mistakes…"

"What happened?"

"My father stood up. He spat on the letter and tossed it at my feet. He said he'd played football too. And that I was—I was shit compared to him, and how had I cheated my way into a scholarship offer? I should have kept my mouth shut—but I didn't. I got angry. I told him I'd never cheated on anybody or anything in my life."

"Don't, sweetheart," Bianca said softly, and she pressed a light kiss to his lips.

"He came at me. He slammed me in the face and I went down. 'Get up,' he said, and I got up. He put me down again. I got up. He kept hitting me and I kept getting up and then I heard my mother screaming. 'Stay down, Chayton,' she said, 'for God's sake, stay down.' But I got up and she came running down the steps and I saw her and he spun around and punched her in the face and she went down, unconscious, and I—I went crazy."

Bianca wrapped her arms around her lover. She felt his hot tears on her throat.

"This last deployment, I killed a boy. I had to kill him. He had a bomb and he was going to blow up my men. I know I did the right thing, but for a second I saw me, just a little bigger than that kid, my heart filled with a fury someone older and supposedly wiser had put there, and I knew that the kid was also filled with a fury someone older and supposedly wiser had created…"

Bianca kissed him.

And kissed him.

Chay whispered her name and then she was all around him and he was driving deep into her, and there was nothing but the two of them in the entire universe.

• • •

Hours later, as they lay in each other's arms with the moon shining through the windows, Chay remembered something Bianca had said.

She had called him "sweetheart."

He was a grown man.

He'd known a lot of women.

None had ever called him that. He'd have bolted if one had.

But he wasn't bolting tonight.

He was gathering Bianca as close to him as he possibly could, until he felt her heart beating against his.

Until he drifted to sleep with his woman in his arms.

CHAPTER TWELVE

THEY WENT OUT for dinner.

Chay had figured Bianca could use a change of scene, a touch of normalcy after the last two days.

And, he had to admit, his plan wasn't entirely altruistic.

They'd made love, but they hadn't had a date. Not unless you counted the night in Santa Barbara, and he damn well wasn't going to count that.

Aidan's travel agent sister had given him a list of restaurants.

"A bunch of places," she'd said happily. "Everything from where you can get the best pizza to where you can dine *très elegant* while getting the feel of New York."

Chay hadn't had the heart to tell her that elegant wasn't his style, but he'd saved the list and while Bianca dried her hair, he looked it over, read the thumbnail descriptions Aidan's sister had provided next to each, and picked one that sounded intriguing.

He phoned.

The maître d' was pleasant, polite—and very sorry to say that they were fully booked.

"I'm sorry, Mister—Mister—"

"It's Lieutenant. Lieutenant Olivieri. And hey, I understand. Talk about last minute…"

"Lieutenant? You're in the service?"

"Right. Look, I don't suppose you could recommend—"

"Isn't this amazing. Lieutenant Olivieri? My assistant just this second slipped me a note to tell me that we've had a cancellation. For a prime table, right next to the water. Sound good?"

Chay laughed. "Sounds great."

"Eight o'clock, Lieutenant?"

"That's fine. Thank you."

"No, Lieutenant. Thank *you*. See you at eight, sir."

"At eight," Chay said, and disconnected.

Bianca sneaked under his arm. "Look at that smile! Something nice just happen?"

Chay swung her towards him. "We just snagged a table at a restaurant Aidan's sister says we'll love."

Bianca raised her eyebrows. "Aidan's sister?"

"A guy in my unit. The sister's a travel agent."

"What's this restaurant called?"

"The *Boathouse*. It's on the lake in Central Park."

"Oh, I've wanted to go there! It's supposed to be so pretty."

"Pretty like you," Chay said, linking his hands at the base of her spine.

"Prettier. It's on a lake, remember? They say there are ducks in the water. And turtles. And frogs, too."

"Ducks and turtles and frogs?" Chay's expression turned serious. "Well, that might change things. I mean there's you—and then there are those frogs... Ouch!"

"You deserved that slug, Lieutenant. Actually, you deserve even more."

Chay gathered her in. "Damn right I do," he said softly.

It was good that their reservation wasn't until eight, because they were very busy for the next fifteen or twenty minutes.

• • •

There was an entrance to the park a block from their hotel, and the concierge told them that the restaurant was perhaps a five or ten minute walk from the entrance.

Chay started to ask the doorman to call a cab, but Bianca stopped him.

"It's a beautiful night," she said. "Let's walk."

They walked slowly, his arm around her, her head tilted against his shoulder.

There were other couples in the park. Bianca looked at the women and wondered if they felt as happy as she did—and then she wondered how she could be happy after the ugliness of the morning...

"Rule for the evening," Chay said softly. "Only good thoughts permitted."

She looked up at him and smiled. "You have a lot of rules, Lieutenant."

"That's one of the privileges of being an officer."

He was teasing her, and she knew it.

But the strange thing was that she didn't mind his having rules. She'd didn't mind handing over control to him.

It was what happened when you started to care for someone. To fall for someone, Bianca thought, and the sudden realization burned its way into her heart.

• • •

The maître d' greeted Chay like an old friend.

"Thanks again," Chay said.

The guy grinned. "I have a brother in the Marines."

Chay grinned back at him. "I'll try not to hold that against you."

Their table was, just as the maître d' had said, at the railing overlooking the water. He seated them. The busboy filled their water glasses, brought them a basket of warm breads, a little dish of butter, and two menus.

They left the menus untouched.

They were too busy looking at each other.

Chay kept thinking how happy Bianca looked.

And how happy he felt.

He loved watching her, loved listening to her, loved

being with her. He couldn't remember ever feeling this content.

And complete.

That was how she made him feel. Complete.

He told her things he'd never told anyone else. Little things, even foolish things. Like how a course he hadn't wanted to take and a professor he hadn't liked introduced him to a new world.

"I discovered books. Until my freshman year in college and English 101, pretty much the only reading I'd ever done was—"

"*Playboy.*" She laughed at his look of surprise. "I grew up with two brothers, remember? Besides, why waste time on a book when you could be outdoors, getting into trouble?"

Chay reached for her hand and wove his fingers through hers.

"I'm gonna have to keep that in mind. That you're an expert on guy behavior."

I'm not, she almost said. *I'm not an expert on men at all. I'm certainly not any kind of expert about this—about wanting to spend the whole day and night with a man, wanting to be able to reach out and touch him, wanting not just to be in his bed but in his arms...*

"Sweetheart? Where'd you go just now?"

"I was—I was wondering what happened in English 101 that changed your mind about books. Did you fell in love with a special one the way I fell in love with *Mary Poppins*?"

"Who?"

She laughed. "Never mind. Just tell me more about that

English course."

"Well, I walked in and there was this guy at the front of the room. A stereotypical academic nerd."

"Watch what you say about us nerds, Lieutenant."

"No offense, Doc." Chay grinned. "Besides, you're not a stereotypical anything."

That made her smile.

"I'm not?"

"You're not. In fact, you're one surprise after another."

"Is that good or bad?"

He hesitated. Something changed in the way he was looking at her.

"It's perfect," he said in a low voice. "You're perfect. One hundred and ten percent perfect."

Chay could hear his heart beating. What would happen if he pushed back his chair, went around the table to Bianca, asked her to say to hell with dinner...

A hand holding a printed sheet of paper appeared under his nose.

"Did you want to see the wine list, sir?"

"The wine list," Chay said carefully. He looked up at the hovering waiter and reminded himself that throttling another human being for asking a polite question wasn't something most people would find appropriate. "Just bring us a bottle of—Sweetheart? Malbec? A chardonnay? Something else?"

"Anything," Bianca said, "anything is fine."

He smiled at her answer and handed the list back to the waiter.

"You heard the lady. Bring us a bottle of something you think we'll like."

"But, sir…"

"A red. Your choice. Okay? It'll be fine, whatever it is."

The waiter smiled. He and the wine list vanished.

Chay leaned forward and took Bianca's hand again. "This is our very first date."

Her lips curved in a smile. "I know."

"And here we are, talking about me and how I'd never read a book and enjoyed it until I was eighteen. What I mean is, here we are, me boring you to death."

"No! You're not boring me at all. I want to know all about you. I mean…" She blushed. "I mean, tell me more about that professor in English 101."

Chay smiled and ran his thumb lightly over her palm.

"You are a very determined woman, Ms. Wilde."

"Like a dog with a bone, Lieutenant. That's what my brothers say. So, what book did your professor assign? He did assign one, didn't he?"

"Yes. *The Red Badge of Courage.* Do you know it?"

She nodded. "By Stephen Crane. It takes place during the American Civil War. It's about a man—a boy, actually—who goes into battle without any idea of what war is all about, and how the reality of it changes him."

"I read the first chapter and I was hooked."

"Were you like that boy? When you went into your first battle?"

A muscle knotted in his jaw. "I wasn't quite that naïve,

no. I don't think you can be in today's world. Still, the first taste of combat is always a shock. It's nothing like what you expect it to be, no matter what training you've had. It's ten times more brutal, ten times more terrifying…"

"And it's exhilarating."

Chay stared at her. "How can you know that?"

"It isn't difficult to figure out," she said softly. "Men who are drawn to certain professions love the risk that goes with those professions. Policemen. Firefighters. Warriors. Especially warriors, who believe in duty. In honor. In each other."

Chay gave a little laugh. "Crap. Do I sound as pretentious as that?"

"No. Oh, no, Chayton. You don't sound pretentious at all. You sound brave and caring and I love that about you, I—"

Bianca's eyes widened. Color swept into her face and she fell silent.

Chay—Chay looked stunned.

Why wouldn't he? She couldn't believe she'd said such a stupid thing. Thinking she might be falling for him wasn't the same as knowing she'd fallen for him. And she hadn't. She was a long, long way from that. From loving him…

"Bianca?" Chay's voice was low and rough.

She looked at him, looked away. "So," she said quickly, "did you always want to be in the service?"

He didn't answer.

"Because I always wanted to be a doctor. Well, a medical doctor. We had a cat when we were little, my sister and I, and I drove that poor creature crazy, bandaging its tail, trying to listen to its heartbeat…" She dragged in breath. "Chayton. Please. Do not look at me that way."

He started to speak and she reached over the table and put her fingers against his lips.

"There is no need to say anything," she said quickly. "I meant—I only meant that I admire you. As a warrior. I sometimes still have a problem with my English. You know that."

It was true.

He did know that.

And just because somebody said they loved something about you didn't mean they were saying they loved you. Why would a woman like this love a man like him? Why would he *want* her to love him?

She wouldn't. And he wouldn't want her to. No way. No way ever would he want…

"A bottle of our finest zinfandel, sir. I thought it would be best. This way, no matter what you order…"

The waiter's voice trailed off. No wonder, Chay thought. There was enough tension at the table to cut with a knife.

"Fine," he said briskly. "An excellent choice. Go ahead. Open it and pour. No, that's okay. I don't need to taste it…" *Jesus!* "So," he said, flashing a smile at Bianca, "what about you? Any, ah, any college class change your life?"

She swallowed hard. "Yes," she said, and he could almost see her reaching for the lifeline he'd thrown her. "I, uh, I thought, you know, when I was a little girl… What I said, about wanting to grow up to be a doctor… Actually, I wanted to be a surgeon."

"A surgeon," he said brightly, as if she'd just announced that she'd solved the mystery of how the universe began.

She launched into a story about a pre-med course. And a field trip to a hospital. An operating room, and an appendectomy, and how she'd passed out even before the surgeon made the incision.

Chay laughed where he was expected to laugh. He hoped he did, anyway, because he heard only bits of what she said. Mostly, he watched her. Her eyes. Her mouth. Her little gestures.

His woman.

His beautiful, down-to-earth, smart, scarily wonderful woman.

When was the last time he'd thought of a woman as his?

The answer came in a heartbeat

Never.

Never. Not once in his thirty-two years had he thought that way. Had he wanted to think that way. Had he imagined thinking that way.

He knew what he had to do.

Get to his feet. Dump some bills on the table, hustle her into a cab, get her back to the hotel and phone Aidan Maguire. Or Declan Sanchez. Or any of the other guys in his unit, tell them he had a woman in New York who needed protection...

Or take her to the hotel, to their room, away from lights and people, gather her into his arms, kiss her until she sighed his name and then tell her that what he should have told her this morning, that she was everything to him…

"Madam. Sir. Are you ready to order? We have some specials this evening… Or perhaps you have questions about our menu. I'll be happy to answer any you might have."

Chay opened the menu. Stared at it. The letters seemed to dance on the heavy paper. He looked at Bianca. She'd opened her menu, too, but judging by the expression on her face, she was nowhere near ready to order.

Bianca and menus.

He'd almost forgotten what that was like. Her almost-compulsive, drive-everybody-crazy attention to menu details.

Yes, but tonight that would be a good thing.

She'd come up with something, take five minutes to ask questions, another five to question the answers to the questions, and that was fine.

It was Bianca.

And it would give him time to get his head together.

"Bianca," he said briskly, "what would you like?"

At first he thought she hadn't heard him. Then she closed the menu, folded her hands neatly on top of it and raised her face to his.

"You order for me, Chayton," she said softly. "I know I'll be happy with anything you choose."

Chay looked at her. This made it twice. First, the wine. But that might have been because she was still embarrassed by what she'd said. What she'd seemed to say.

Now, this.

His Bianca. Ceding control. Trusting him. Trusting

herself to him.

Later, he'd think back and realize that he should have known his life would never be the same again.

• • •

After dinner, they walked to a little place she knew on Fifth Avenue.

The night was still soft and warm, and since this was New York, the evening was just beginning.

Bianca wanted to sit at a sidewalk table.

Reality intruded when Chay realized that it was the last place he wanted to sit.

It was too exposed.

His time in those faraway mountains had taught him all about survival. So had the experiences of today. But he couldn't bring himself to tell her that or deny her such a simple pleasure, so they sat outside, drank coffee and shared a slice of New York cheesecake.

Once again, they talked about everything and anything, from music—she was a secret Frank Sinatra fan, which made him roll his eyes—to which was the more exciting sport, American football or European football. She told him about the cliffs in Sicily and how she'd loved climbing down them to the sea, and he told her that the sea had always been important to him, too, and somehow he found himself telling her about all those sea stories, *Moby Dick*, the Hornblower novels…

But Chay began to feel uneasy.

He felt the change coming over him, that almost subliminal contact with what was happening around them.

"… always wanted a dog," Bianca was saying, "but Mama said dogs were too much…"

"Honey?" Chay pushed back his chair and got to his feet. "It's getting late. We should head back."

His Bianca was smart. Too smart. "What's wrong?"

"Nothing," he said.

He could tell that she didn't believe him, but, thank God, she didn't argue. She stood up and he put his arm around her and they walked swiftly in the direction of their hotel. They were almost there when he tugged her into the doorway of a closed shop.

"Chayton?" she whispered. "Please. What's the matter?"

He hesitated, but she had the right to know, especially since he was going to step away from her to do a quick surveillance.

"Someone's following us."

She dug her fingers into his arm. "Who?"

"I don't know who. I only know that somebody's— Bianca. I want you to stand right here."

"No! Chay. Don't—"

"Baby. I'm not going anywhere. I just want to take a fast look around, okay?"

He knew that was the last thing she wanted him to do, but she swallowed hard and whispered, "Okay."

He gave her a quick kiss. She clung to him and he hated to let go of her, but he really didn't have a choice. If there was the slightest chance he could get a look at whoever was stalking her...

Another quick kiss.

Then he stepped forward in the doorway, just enough so he had a clear view of the sidewalk.

Slowly, he scanned the scene before him. He missed the high-powered binoculars he'd have been using were he on deployment, but with a field of vision so reduced, his own eyes would probably be sufficient.

Nobody seemed suspicious.

Lots of people walking. Walking slowly. That was unusual by New York standards, but it was a warm Saturday night and, for the most part, nobody would be in a hurry. Cars and taxis moved briskly beyond the sidewalk. He didn't pay them more than cursory attention.

You didn't follow walkers from a moving vehicle.

His tension eased.

He must have been wrong. He was, once in a while. His ability to sense something before others did sometimes suffered from sensory overload. And this was definitely the place for sensory overload. The beep of horns. The rumble of car engines. The omnipresent background sounds of people walking and talking and laughing...

There!

Chay's pulse quickened.

A tall figure. Thin. A mop of unruly brown hair that could easily be red in the proper lighting...

And then the figure was gone. Swallowed up by a

clump of laughing pedestrians and there wasn't a goddamned thing he could do about it without leaving Bianca alone.

No way was he about to let that happen.

One last look. Then he stepped back.

"Whom did you see?"

Her voice was steady, but he could hear the faint whisper of fear in it along with that telltale grammatical stiffness.

He slipped his arm around her shoulders. "Nobody," he replied, and, hell, it wasn't a lie. He *hadn't* seen anyone, not clearly enough to identify. The man he'd glimpsed could have been the guy from *Cuppa Joe's* as easily as it could have been somebody else.

"Honey," he said gently, as they moved out of the doorway and began walking, "I'm going to be blunt. We need to talk."

"Talk?"

He nodded. "I know how you feel about discussing your patients, but there's no other way to go about this."

"You really believe the man doing this is someone I'm treating? Because I don't. The only one, the only possible one it could be, is a former patient, the one I told you about, and he's in treatment. His doctor would surely know if he was causing this problem."

Causing this problem.

She had an interesting way of defining the word *problem*, but Chay figured debating that wouldn't be helpful.

"When was the last time you were in touch with this

guy's doctor?"

Bianca thought back. "Weeks," she finally said.

Chay nodded as they stood on the corner and waited for the light to go green.

"I want you to contact him again. Find out if anything has changed." They stepped off the curb. "And it's possible, isn't it, that a patient you wouldn't connect with this kind of behavior is responsible for it anyway?"

She hesitated. "Anything's possible, I guess."

They stepped onto the sidewalk. The hotel was just ahead and Chay picked up their pace, knowing he'd feel better once he had her safely inside. He'd considered—and discarded—the idea of not returning here. Of checking them into a different hotel.

If someone was tailing them, that might be the prudent course of action.

On the other hand, if, in fact, they were being followed, going someplace else would alert the follower that he'd been made.

Besides, Chay already knew the layout of this place. Like lots of other crisis-hardened cops and soldiers, he'd automatically asked for a room with certain characteristics when he'd checked in: he didn't want to be next to the elevators or the fire stairs, or even next to an ice machine because the sound of the machine could dull other sounds that might be more important.

He felt comfortable staying here for the night—but they'd be out by tomorrow. He already knew where they'd be heading, just as he knew it wouldn't be a good idea to drop that information on Bianca tonight.

"So," he said as they neared the hotel, "I want you to phone that doctor tomorrow."

"Tomorrow's Sunday. I don't know if he'll be available."

"Make him available. Tell him this is urgent. And while you're doing that, I'll take a look at your files."

Bianca didn't answer for what seemed a very long time.

"The most I'll agree to," she finally said, "is that I'll go through them and look for indicators of personality disorders that might lead to such erratic behavior."

Jesus H. Christ! Somebody had ugly plans for his woman and she was talking psychobabble. Yeah. Okay. Maybe that helped her deal with it.

He knew what would help him, and there was no reason to share that kind of thing with her.

"That's good," he said, lying through his teeth.

The doorman smiled as he opened the front doors. Chay nodded at him, led Bianca to the elevators, stabbed the call button. Then he turned and took a long, hard look around the lobby. Nobody looked out of place. Still, when the elevator doors opened, he hurried her inside the car.

She gave a little shudder as the car rose.

"What?" Chay said.

"Nothing. Just me, suddenly remembering yesterday, the blackout in my office building." She made a little sound that might have qualified as a laugh. "Would you believe that the lights had already dimmed and still I came this close to getting in the elevator?"

She held up her hand, thumb and forefinger an inch apart. An alarm bell went off in his head. That blackout. He'd been concerned about that blackout yesterday, but he hadn't followed through...

"Good thing you didn't," he said, with what he hoped was casual ease, and he lowered his head and kissed her fingers.

When they reached their room, he stepped in front of her as he inserted the key card in the lock.

The door swung open and he breathed a sigh of relief. The room was just as they'd left it, except the maid had been there to turn down the duvet and leave chocolates on the pillows.

Chay closed the door and locked it. Then he took Bianca in his arms.

"Bianca."

She smiled up at him. It was a very diverting smile, diverting enough so he knew he had maybe two minutes before his blood rushed from his brain to his dick.

"Chayton?" she said softly

"One last thing, honey. I'm good with you checking those files." Back to lying time. "I'll be satisfied with a list of your patients' names."

"Chay. We've been through this."

"Names. Nothing else. I just want to run them through a program that'll throw up an alert if anyone you're seeing has had a felony arrest."

"You have such a program?"

No, he did not. But he sure as hell knew somebody who did. Or at least he knew somebody who could write the program if he had to.

"Lots of people have such a program," he said carelessly.

She sighed. "I'll think about it."

He nodded. She could think about it all she liked. Things would be easier if she agreed, but life wasn't about things being easy, it was about taking action.

He had a plan. And a plan was what they needed. It was how you approached a mission—and finding the man who was stalking his Bianca was a mission.

And Chay knew, without question, that it might very well be the most important mission of his life.

• • •

He took her to bed.

They made slow, easy love. Lots of deep kisses, lots of touching, lots of tasting and then a long, incredible climb to the stars

After, she lay in his arms.

"I am," she said dreamily, "sated and happy."

He chuckled, nosed a strand of hair from the side of her throat and kissed the tender flesh.

"*Sated*. A shrink word if ever I heard one."

She sighed and traced her hand over his shoulder.

"Chayton?"

"Uh-huh."

"This tattoo." Her fingers danced over the small, elegant bird in flight. "A hawk?"

"A falcon."

She replaced her fingers with her lips. "It's beautiful," she said against his warm golden skin.

Chay gathered her closer. "He's been with me a long time. Ever since that Sun Dance."

"Is he a vision figure?"

Chay rolled her onto her back and grinned as he bent over her. "Have you been doing a little Indian research?"

She blushed. "No. Yes. All right. I did a little reading after—after that night."

"The night on the beach." His kissed her. "Sweetheart. If I could take back—"

"No," she said quickly. "It was—it was an amazing night. I was just so, you know, so shocked at what I'd done…"

He kissed her again. "I couldn't stop thinking about that night. About you."

"Mmm." She reached up, stroked her hand through his thick, dark hair. "So is the falcon a vision figure?"

"Yes. And no. I did have a vision, and it involved a falcon." Chay smiled. "But that wasn't a complete surprise, because of my name."

"Chayton?"

He nodded. "It means 'falcon' in Lakota."

"It's a wonderful name. It's just right for you."

"It was my grandfather's gift to me. He chose it when I was born. My mother said he told her he hoped I would grow up to be as brave and strong as a falcon."

Bianca smiled. "He must have been very wise."

"He was old-school. A man of another time, you know? I'm sorry I never got to know him."

"But he's part of you. Not only did he name you, you grew up to be the man he'd wished you would be."

"That's a good way to think of it. But…" Chay lowered his mouth to hers. Touched the tip of his tongue to the seam of her lips. "But," he said in a low voice, "as much as I care for his memory, I have to be honest."

"About what?" she whispered, her breath catching as he tongued her nipple.

"I have no desire to have grandpa in this bed."

She giggled. "No?"

"No," Chay said, and he gathered her in his arms and eased her on top of him.

His erection pressed into her.

She moaned and, God, he loved that sound. Loved this. The wet heat of her surrounding him in.

"Take me in all the way," he whispered. "Take me deep, sweetheart."

"Chayton? Oh God. Chayton…"

She slid down his hard, hot length. Her lashes swept her cheeks. Her head fell back.

"Yes," he said thickly, "like that. Like that…"

He clasped her hips, helped her rise. And fall.

Rise. And fall.

Until the rhythm was hers, the pace was hers, and they

lost themselves in each other as she rode him into the darkness of the night.

CHAPTER THIRTEEN

CHAY SLEPT FITFULLY.

His dreams were filled with broken images. Bianca, dancing in the rain. The tall guy, Noah, trying to restrain her at *Cuppa Joe's*. The condom. The malevolent phone call. The man on the street last night.

He had endless questions with no answers, and a plan that needed implementation. Lying in bed with Bianca nestled against him was wonderful, but it wasn't going to change what some bastard was trying to do to her.

At four in the morning, he eased his arm from around her shoulders. She sighed and stirred a little and he held very still. He didn't want to wake her until he had to. Once he had everything in place, she'd be less likely to give him a hard time.

At least he hoped so.

Carefully, he rose from the bed, found his smartphone, pulled on his jeans and made his way quietly to the sitting area. An ornate screen partially separated it from the rest of the room. He sat in the love seat that stood before the screen, turned on his phone and punched in a number. It rang once. Twice. Four times, and just when Chay figured that he was going to end up talking to voice mail, a male voice barked out a harsh "Yeah?"

Chay gave a soft laugh. "Hello to you, too, Sunshine."

"Listen, whoever this is, I'm not in the mood for… Olivieri?"

"Good morning, Sanchez."

"Man, you have any idea what time it is?"

"One in the a.m. your time. Don't tell me you've turned into a believer in that early-to-bed-early-to-rise thing. No way that will make you wise."

"Very funny. Anyway, I was up. I'm just, you know, kind of…busy."

"Declan?" a soft voice said in the background.

Chay bit back a groan. "Dude. My apologies."

"No. It's okay. Just let me…" Sanchez's voice grew muffled. "Okay," he said a few seconds later. "What's doing? Hey, man. Aren't you in New York?"

"Yeah. That's where I am. And I need a couple of favors."

Declan Sanchez laughed. "I didn't figure you were callin' to say hello. What can I do for you?"

Chay took a long breath. "I need some computer magic."

"For instance?"

"Would you be able to see if somebody's put a GPS app into a smartphone?"

"You mean, find out if the phone contains tracing software? So whoever loaded it in could follow the movements of the phone's owner? Sure. No big deal."

"And if I gave you a list of names and told you I needed deep background checks on all of them—"

"No problem."

"Or maybe you'd have to tap into a laptop, get the names that way."

"Yeah, yeah."

"Really deep checks. Medical records. Criminal records. Whatever."

"Chay. My man. We're talking child's play here."

"Great."

"Am I gonna do this long distance? Or are you bringing me the hardware?"

"I'm bringing it, and that takes me to favor number two. Is your brother still flying for the opposition?"

"Is he still a Marine pilot, you mean?" Sanchez chuckled. "Trust me, bro. Liam's in for life."

"Any chance he can pull some strings and get me a ride back home?"

"What, you run out of frequent-flier miles?"

Chay laughed. "Yeah, right." He hesitated. "I'd like to avoid leaving names in some commercial airline's database."

"Dude?" Sanchez's tone turned crisp. "You okay? I mean, you want to tell me what's goin' down?"

Chay got to his feet and paced to the window. The lights of the city glowed like a galaxy of stars against the still-dark sky.

"I'll explain everything when I see you. For now, if Liam can come up with something."

"I'll get right on it."

"That's great. And Dec—one last thing."

"Yeah?"

"There'll be two of us. Me...and a woman."

Sanchez grunted. "I can hardly wait to hear the details. Whatever it is, good luck, bro."

"Thanks," Chay said, and ended the call.

Okay. Excellent. Progress, at last. There were few things as bad as knowing you needed to put a plan into action and not being able to do it. Now, in a single call, he'd implemented steps one and two. A way to get to the coast without leaving footsteps—he had little doubt that Sanchez and his brother would be able to come up with something. And the assurance that he'd be able to get the information he needed from Bianca with or without her cooperation.

Declan Sanchez was the best when it came to computers. He didn't talk about it much, but over drinks in a shithole bar on the other side of the world, Dec had admitted he'd been something of a hacker in his teens.

"Illegal when I was a civilian," he'd said with a grin, "but my ticket to success in the service of Uncle Sam."

Sanchez would get into Bianca's phone and see if someone had planted a bug in it. Even better, he'd find whatever info Chay needed about Bianca's patients, her doctoral study subjects, even her family and friends and co-workers.

Nobody could be safe from scrutiny.

The law said you were innocent until proven guilty, but men in Chay's profession knew reality was exactly the reverse. People were guilty until proven innocent if your goal was to keep your balls from being blown off.

Chay headed for the shower.

• • •

Twenty minutes later, he sat down on the bed next to Bianca.

She was lying on her side with the duvet covering her from the tips of her toes to her chin. All he could see of her was her forehead, her nose, and the curve of her mouth.

The lovely curve of her mouth.

The desire to peel back that duvet and get into the bed with her was almost overpowering, but he'd let her sleep as long as he could and he knew it.

He laid his hand lightly on her shoulder. "Rise and shine, sweetheart."

Bianca murmured something, rolled onto her belly and tugged the duvet over her head.

"Honey," he said. "It's time to start the day."

"Mmmf."

He smiled. "Sorry, baby. *Mmmf* isn't gonna do it." Chay pulled the duvet down, just enough to expose her creamy shoulder, bent over and pressed his lips to it. "It's wake-up time."

"Not," she muttered, trying to wrest the duvet from him.

"Yes," he said gently, rolling her onto her back.

What a wonderful sight to start the day.

Tousled blonde curls. Pink mouth. Thick, dark lashes lifting to reveal spectacular blue eyes... Thick, dark lashes slamming down like shutters against the intrusive glow of the lamp on the night table.

"Wha' time izzit?"

"Early."

"How early?"

"Early," he said again, and brushed his lips over hers.

Bianca opened her eyes. She looked past him, at the windows where the vertical blinds were half open.

"Chayton. It's still night."

"It's morning."

"But it's dark out."

He kissed her again. This time, her lips clung lightly to his.

"It's five," he said softly.

"In the morning?"

The disbelief in her voice made him laugh. "Yup. That's what it is. Five in the a.m."

"Please don't tell me this is your idea of when to start the day."

"Certainly not." He paused. "I usually don't get moving until five-fifteen."

She groaned. He laughed, nuzzled a soft spray of curls away from her shoulder and pressed his lips to the side of her neck.

"I hated to wake you, sweetheart." He sat back. "But we have lots to do."

He saw the change steal over her face as she remembered what was happening and it damn near killed him.

"I know," he said gently. "Not the best way to start a Sunday. But we don't have much choice, honey. You know that."

She looked into his eyes. Then she sighed, held the duvet to her breasts and sat up.

"You're right. You want me to phone the psychiatrist treating John Cartwr—Treating my former patient."

He wanted more than that. For starters, he wanted the name she'd almost let slip, but this wasn't the time to get into that.

"Yes," he said, "I do."

"And I will, but, *mannaggia*, not at five a.m. Nobody's going to talk to anybody at this hour."

"True." His gaze dropped to her hand, clutching the duvet to her, then rose to her face. "But we have to go over what you're going to ask him. And we need to do a couple of other things."

"What things?"

His gaze fell to her hand again. Slowly, he reached out and tugged the edge of the duvet from her grasp. It fell to her waist. She made a grab for it.

He stopped her, and his eyes met hers.

"You have to provide me with lists of names," he said, and, Jesus, how could he sound so calm when all he could really think about was the sweet taste of her nipples?

"Chayton." She swallowed hard; he could see the action of the muscles in her throat. "I told you—"

"Your patients," he said. "The subjects in your study."

He ran the tip of his index finger lightly over one pale pink nipple and then the other. She made a little sound, a soft hum of desire, that sent a quick flash of heat straight to his dick.

"Chayton. I can't think when you—when you—"

He dipped his head, licked the pearled nipples.

She gasped and made another of those sweet sounds.

"Chay. If you do that…"

He looked up. Her eyes were wide and luminous. Her cheeks were pink. Her lips were parted.

And he—dammit, despite their conversation, he was swelling inside his jeans.

"I have to know about the people you deal with," he said, still calmly, still evenly, though he could feel his heart starting to race. "I can't protect you unless I know who they are and what they're like."

"But it is my duty to protect *them*, Chayton. Surely you are a man who understands duty…"

He framed her face in his hands.

"What I understand," he said, his voice gone rough and hot, "is that if I'm not inside you soon I'm going to go crazy."

She smiled.

It was a smile that spoke of everything he had ever

dreamed, everything he had ever wanted.

"Good," she whispered.

Chay brushed his mouth over hers. "Good that I'm going to go crazy?"

Her hands danced up his chest. Except for the jeans, he was naked and she loved the feel of his muscled body, his warm skin.

"Good that you need to be inside me," she said. "Because I'm going to die unless you—"

He pulled down the duvet.

She sank back against the pillows.

His hand moved down her body. Over her belly.

To her thighs.

"Open for me," he said gruffly.

Her legs parted. He grasped them and pulled them wider.

Then he stroked his fingers over her.

Ah, Jesus. She was wet. Soaked. She was ready for him. So ready, but he wanted her desperate. Pleading. He wanted her world narrowed down to this bed, to this moment, to him.

"Bianca," he said, and he ran his thumb over her clitoris.

She cried out.

"Look at me, Bianca."

She brought her gaze to his face. The hard, beautiful bones. The eyes as dark as emerald fire. The strong, straight nose with the little bump in it. The sculpted mouth.

"Tell me," he said.

"Chayton…"

His fingers moved against her. She moaned. Her body arched towards him. Towards that exciting, possessive touch.

"Tell me," he demanded.

"Chay." Her voice broke. "I want you."

"More than that."

"I want you inside me."

"More still."

"*I need* you inside me," she said, sobbing.

Quickly, he unzipped his fly and freed himself. Took his erection in his hand and rubbed it against her wet, welcoming heat.

He moaned at the feel of her. At the roll of her hips.

He rubbed the head of his penis against her again, and she cried out. She wept. She sighed his name.

He could feel everything inside him tightening, but he wanted more.

Wanted to give her more.

He pulled back.

"No," she said, reaching for him, but he clasped her shoulders and pulled her up.

"On your knees." His voice was a low growl, almost unrecognizable even to himself. Her eyes widened. "Do it," he said harshly, "and turn your back to me."

She obeyed his command.

Ah, dear God.

She was so beautiful.

The long, graceful line of her spine. The delicate shape

of her backside.

He leaned forward, pushed her hair aside and bit the nape of her neck in the most primitive declaration of ownership. She cried out, but there was no pain in the cry.

There was only acquiescence.

And desperate desire.

"Chayton," she said brokenly. "Please-please-please…"

The headboard was mahogany, a series of narrow sculpted posts.

"Lean forward," he whispered. "Wrap your hands around those posts."

She complied, and he put his hand between her thighs again, exulted in the feel of all that hot sweetness.

Then he clasped her hips and drove into her.

She cried out in ecstasy, and he drew back and thrust into her again.

She was sobbing.

He could feel her vaginal muscles starting to contract around his swollen penis.

She was on the brink of orgasm and he was there with her, but he didn't want to drop over it, not yet, not yet, not yet.

He grunted. Gritted his teeth. Rocked into her once. Twice. Three times…

She cried out, her muscles convulsed around him, and he threw back his head, gasped out her name, and lost himself on an endless wave of pleasure.

She fell forward and he fell with her.

It took a long time until he could think again. Until the

world stopped spinning. When finally it did, he gathered her in his arms, collapsed against the pillows and held her tight in the curve of his body.

"Okay?" he whispered.

She gave a little laugh. The sound went straight through him.

"Yes," she said, and she snuggled into him, her head on his hard shoulder, her arm over his chest.

He turned his face to hers and kissed her.

They had to get up.

He knew that.

But first he needed this. Bianca, in his arms. The feel of her not just against him, but inside him.

Inside his heart.

He was in a place he had never been before, a place he had not believed existed.

And of everything he'd ever faced, it was the most frightening.

• • •

"What do you mean, we're going to Santa Barbara?"

Chay looked at Bianca's reflection next to his in the bathroom mirror. He had showered again, with her, and they'd had another fruitless discussion about the ethics of sharing information about her patients with him.

"It's against the moral code of my profession," she'd said.

And he'd said that a patient trying to scare the shit out of his shrink was against the moral code of anybody's profession, and she'd said she understood what he was saying, but that it was against—

"—the moral code of your profession," he'd growled, and she'd put her hand on his arm, turned her face up to his and looked so unhappy that he'd sighed, kissed her, and told her he'd work something out.

The *something* was Sanchez, but why tell her that?

She was having enough difficulty dealing with what he'd just said—that they had some errands to run and then they were flying to Santa Barbara.

"Chayton? Why would I go to California?"

He considered telling her she'd go so she could be with him, but he knew she was too smart for that. So he wiped off the last bit of shaving cream from his face, dumped the towel, and swung around.

"Because it's where I can keep you safe."

Her eyes searched his. "I don't understand."

"Somebody's after you. Somebody who means to harm you."

"To frighten me. We don't know that whoever it is actually wants to—"

"If you mean, we have no proof, well, you're right. We don't." He clasped her shoulders. "But when you add up the phone call, the condom, the very fact that this—this—" *This lunatic, crazed, insane sociopath* was what he wanted to day, but logic warned that his beautiful shrink might object. "What I'm saying is when you tally things up and add in the fact that this person has obviously been in your home… Put all that together, sweetheart, and it's probably a safe bet to act as if you are, in fact, in physical danger."

He could see her thinking it through.

Then she nodded.

"Okay. Perhaps."

Perhaps? Well, at least they were making progress.

"I've gone through all the possibilities," he said. "One, we could stay on in the hotel, but I don't think either of us would be comfortable stuck here for much longer, no matter how luxurious the accommodations. Right?"

Bianca nodded.

"Two, we could stay in your apartment. Get the locks changed, but…" She shook her head vehemently. "Yeah. My feelings, too."

"I don't ever want to go back there," she said, and shuddered.

"Then there's option three."

"What's option three?"

"You have family in Texas."

"In New York, too. Well, some of them have condos here."

"Right. You could stay with family while I work this thing through."

He waited. Option three, while viable, was the one he didn't want her to take. He'd tried telling himself it was because it would worry him not to be at her side to protect her and that was true enough.

But there was another truth, a deeper one, and it was a lot more basic.

Option three would take her away from him.

And he wasn't ready to be parted from her.

Not yet.

He was a realist. He knew it would happen eventually. He'd find the man who wanted to hurt her, she'd be safe, and this—this episode would end.

Life would return to normal.

She'd go back to her job.

He'd be deployed.

Except for sex, he thought bluntly, a woman who saved souls and a man who took them would not have a hell of a lot in common, and anyway, he wasn't looking to tie himself down…

"Option four," Bianca said.

Chay frowned and brought his thoughts back where they belonged.

"Option four?"

She nodded. "I go with you to Santa Barbara." Her voice was soft. "If that's what you truly want…"

He kissed her, and gave her all the answer she'd need.

• • •

He ordered in breakfast.

In case someone had followed them here, why go somewhere public?

He'd considered throwing away her cellphone—he was almost sure Bianca's stalker had planted a GPS program in it—but it was too late for that. If he was right and her stalker already knew her location, it was too late to eliminate that knowledge. Besides, tossing the phone out would simply alert the stalker to the fact that they were on to him.

Besides, Chay had a better plan for the phone.

So he ordered orange juice, coffee, toast, scrambled eggs and bacon. The waiter set things up on the table in front of the window, and they sat down to eat.

Bianca said she wasn't very hungry. He knew that all the talk of stalkers and stalking had probably taken away her appetite. It hadn't done much for his, but experience had taught him that you ate when you could, so he downed some eggs and bacon, and encouraged her to at least have some juice and toast.

Then he got a pad and pencil from the desk and they got down to business.

He asked her to go through the last few hours of the rainy afternoon at her office.

"Tell me everything that happened as you best recall."

She did, starting with the impending storm. When she got to the part about Lacey coming in to say she was leaving, he stopped her.

"Spell her name for me."

Bianca did. Chay wrote it down.

"Do you know her number?"

"I have it in my phone... Chay. Surely, you don't think..."

"I don't think anything, honey. I'm simply trying to get all the pieces of the puzzle in one place. Maybe the receptionist saw something. Or somebody. She may have a bit of data that we can use."

Bianca checked her contacts list and gave Chay the woman's cell number and address.

"You say the power had failed before?"

"Uh-huh."

"And the building management said they'd had the electrical system updated after that."

"Yes."

"Do you happen to know the name of the company that manages the building?"

"Actually, I do." To Chay's surprise, she laughed. "It's Avido Management. Avido means 'greedy' in Italian. Dr. Epstein once mentioned the monthly rental that East Side Associates pays, and the name was amazingly appropriate. It just stuck in my head."

"Great. That makes things a little easier." He scrawled a couple of words more on the notepad and then he looked at Bianca. "Have you given more thought to those names?"

"Patients and study subjects?" She sighed. "Give me a little more time, okay?"

He leaned forward, cupped her chin and kissed her.

"I'll give you until we reach Santa Barbara. How's that?"

"That's fair enough, I guess."

"How about the names of friends?" Family, too, he almost said, but he could only imagine how she'd react to that.

"And your co-workers."

She frowned. "Co-workers? Well, that isn't a problem. I mean, the people at East Side are all listed right on the building directory in the lobby."

Chay pushed the pad and pencil towards her.

"Write down their names, honey. Their addresses and phone numbers, if you know them, or at least a general idea of where I can find them. And I'll want the same info for the people you work with in the psych department at the university."

Her face clouded over.

"Chayton. I do not want to involve all these good people in a witch hunt."

But they weren't all *good*. That was the problem. He knew that, and he was certain that Bianca knew it too. It was just hard for her to accept.

That was another difference between their worlds.

She believed people were innately good.

He knew better. The good guys weren't always good.

"Chayton?" She put her hand over his. "Why do you look so sad?"

He turned his hand over and clasped hers tightly.

Because we have no future.

The realization rang inside his head, as loud and clear as a rifle shot.

They had no future, even if he'd wanted one.

Even if he'd wanted one...

"Chayton?"

He took a breath, stood and drew her up with him.

"I'm not sad, sweetheart. I'm just thinking of all we have to accomplish before we get on that jet for California."

"What jet?"

As if on signal, the phone in his pocket vibrated. Chay dug it out.

"Olivieri," he said briskly.

"Dude, you're flying out at thirteen-oh-thirty from Stewart Air National Guard Base in Newburgh, New York. That's about sixty miles from Manhattan. Got you two first-class seats on a transport. Sound good?"

"Sounds perfect," Chay said. "I owe you one, Dec."

"Damn right," Declan Sanchez said, laughing. "See you soon. You and your lady." Dec paused. "She must be really special to you."

Chay looked at Bianca. Then he turned away.

"Yeah," he said softly, "but it isn't what you think."

"That's what we all say," Sanchez replied, just as softly.

And the call ended.

CHAPTER FOURTEEN

HE BEGAN TOSSING things into his carry-on.

Bianca was doing the same with her bottomless tote bag.

Suddenly, she stopped.

"Chayton?"

Hell. He could hear that tone in her voice. The one that said she was about to take a stand.

Telling a woman as determined as his Bianca that you were about to disrupt her life wasn't going to be a piece of cake. Yes, she'd seemed to accept it, but he should have known things were going too smoothly.

"Chay. I cannot do this."

"Can't do what?" he said, as if he had no idea what she was talking about, when, of course, he did.

He started towards the closet. She stepped in front of him, effectively barring his way. "I cannot simply leave New

York."

"Bianca." A muscle flickered in his jaw. "We've been all through this. You're not safe here."

She caught her bottom lip between her teeth. A couple of seconds went by. Then, to his relief, she nodded.

"No, maybe not. But I can't simply leave for the West Coast."

He moved around her, took a couple of shirts from the closet, walked back to the carry-on and placed them in it.

"Because?"

"Because…" She threw out her arms. "I have responsibilities."

"Such as?"

" I have appointments with patients."

"Reschedule them."

"I have to collate the data from my study."

"You have your laptop. You can work wherever you are."

"Well, yes. But—but—but—"

"But what?" he said. Stay calm, he told himself, but how could he? "Goddammit, we're talking about a maniac, and you're worried about appointments and notes?"

"You think I do not understand this? That someone wishes to turn my existence inside out? That someone hates me enough to—to want to hurt me?"

Shit.

Chay leaned over his carry-on, caught hold of her chin and kissed her.

"I'm sorry, baby. Of course you understand. But you also have to understand what I'm telling you, that there is no other way to end this thing except to keep you safe while I figure out who this crazy son of a bitch is."

She nodded. "I know." Her eyes met his. "The thing is, I cannot think of anyone who would do this to me."

"No one?"

"No one."

He'd been waiting to ask her that question, but she'd already been through so much that he'd intended to wait until they were on the plane, heading away from here.

"Think back, honey," he said gently. "Do you have enemies?"

She shook her head. "No."

"Somebody you inadvertently hurt."

Another shake of her head. "No."

"Someone who wanted something you had. A grade. A class. Anything, anything at all, because crazies don't operate the way the rest of us do."

She put her hand on his arm. "I know about mentally ill people, Chay."

"Yeah." He laughed, folded his hands, placed them on top of his head. "I forgot that."

"I know they see things differently, but I honestly can't think of anyone I've had a personal relationship with who would wish me harm. Harm like this, I mean. And it would have to be a personal relationship to trigger such behavior."

"Couldn't it be a relationship the stalker sees as

personal even though it really wasn't? What I mean is—"

"I know what you mean. And you are correct. Still, there would have been signs. Indications of interest beyond the norm."

"And you can't think of any situations you've been in that were like that?"

Bianca shook her head. "No."

"All the more reason I have to get you out of here." He bent to her and kissed her again. "I can't predict what this guy is going to do next. And I need you in a safe place while I work it out, a place this—this individual would never think of."

"California," she said slowly.

"Yes."

She paced away, then swung towards him.

"The man you thought you saw last night... Do you really think—"

"What I think," he said, "is that it's possible someone is keeping tabs on us. And if you think something is possible, the only way to operate is to assume that what you think possible is actually happening."

"But California..."

"I need a base, sweetheart, where I can coordinate and plan, where I don't have to keep looking over my shoulder, where we're not going to stand out. My cottage in Santa Barbara is perfect. I can come and go without anybody so much as noticing."

"Yes, but what about me? Surely people will notice that I'm with you..."

She paused and did that little biting-her-lip thing again. Any other time, he'd have caught her face in his hands and soothed the tiny bite with his tongue.

"…Or," she said quietly, "are you counting on the fact that they'll see me as just another woman spending a couple of days with—"

He kissed her. Deep. Hard. With enough passion to make her moan.

"They'll see me," he said, when he lifted his head, "as a man who's so crazy about a woman, he wants her all to himself for a while." Gently, he brushed his thumb over her lips. "And just for the record, I've never had a woman staying with me before."

"No?" she said, and told herself it was ridiculous that the admission should make her heart lift, because, after all, this was simply a matter of expediency, because what he'd said about what people would see and believe wasn't, couldn't be true…

"No," he said, and kissed her again. Then he smiled. "Is it really so difficult to think of trading hot, crowded city streets for a long stretch of blue water and white sand?"

She put her hands on his chest. "Sort of like that beach near the hotel," she said softly.

"Better."

"How could anything be better than that?"

Her smile almost brought him to his knees. He clasped her hands and lifted them to his lips.

"My beach is much more private."

"Oh. That's nice."

He kissed her. How could he not kiss her? Then he framed her face with his hands and looked into her eyes. "And I'll be able to keep you safe. Okay?"

She nodded. "Okay," she said, except he was wrong about keeping her safe.

Her heart would not be safe.

How could it be, when it was time to admit the truth to herself?

She had fallen for Chay. She had more than fallen.

She was head over heels in love with her lieutenant.

• • •

Leave no trace of yourself behind.

That wasn't often important when you were on a mission, but there were times it could be. In the field, it meant leaving behind no equipment, no footprints, no sign you'd been where you weren't supposed to have been.

Here, it meant something different.

What they couldn't leave behind was any sign that they'd left the hotel or the city, or any way to follow them.

That made the first thing he had to do the most difficult.

He put in another call to Sanchez.

"Dec. Remember, I asked you about GPS programs? A tracer that might have been programmed into a smartphone?"

"Yeah, dude, I got that."

"Is there a way for you to find out if something like that's on a phone without actually having the phone right in your hands?"

Sanchez snorted.

Chay rolled his eyes. "Is that a yes?"

"I assume you have the phone," Sanchez said.

Bianca's phone was on the table, next to his. Chay reached for it.

"Got it."

"Give me her number."

Chay read it off.

"Okay. Her phone's gonna ring. Take the call, but don't say anything. Then give me five minutes."

It took three. Then Bianca's phone disconnected.

"Son of a bitch," Sanchez said. "Yes, there's a tracer program in there. Dude. What are you into?"

Chay looked at the phone as if it had turned into a venomous snake.

"I'll tell you more when I see you."

"You want me to kill that program?"

"No," Chay said quickly. "Leave it just the way it is. But what happens if you were to download the contacts from the phone? I mean, will the bug be part of the download?"

"No."

"You sure?"

"Olivieri," Sanchez said patiently, "trust me. You want the contacts? You can have them. Bug free."

"Can you transfer them to my phone?"

Declan laughed. "This is gonna be quite a story when you finally get around to clueing me in. Yeah. Sure. Give me five minutes."

Sanchez worked his magic again. By the time Chay ended the call, he had Bianca's contact list.

He tossed her phone aside and took a deep breath.

On to the rest of the plan. Compared with all this, it would be easy.

According to his hotel reservation, he'd be leaving on Monday. There was no reason to tell the desk anything different. This way, if someone checked up, reception would say that yes, Chay Olivieri was still in residence.

He and Bianca would leave a few things in the room so the cleaning staff wouldn't raise any questions. Toothbrushes. A change of clothes. Stuff people would normally have lying around.

As far as the hotel would know, he'd still be here.

Excellent—except, he wouldn't be, which took him to the next part of the plan.

Leaving the hotel without a watcher knowing they were leaving.

Walking out the door and getting into a taxi? No way. That was far too visible.

But the hotel had a car rental company right on the property.

Chay made a quick call and requested a mid-sized, mid-priced, mid-everything vehicle. The clerk came up with the name of something so dull it made Chay's Harley-loving self shudder, but he knew that a car like that would be all but invisible on the teeming Manhattan streets and he arranged to pick it up in the hotel's parking garage.

Finally, it was time to get moving.

"Honey? You ready?

"Yes," Bianca said as she came out of the bathroom. "I'm ready."

He looked at her. She'd put on jeans, an oversized T-shirt, and flat-heeled sandals. No makeup, as usual, and she'd pulled her hair back into a ponytail.

She was, no question, the most beautiful woman in the world.

He didn't realize he was staring until she gave a nervous little laugh.

"What? Is something not right with how I am dressed? I thought it would be best to look, you know, unobstructed."

He smiled. "Unobtrusive," he said softly, and he took her in his arms and kissed her. She melted into him and he felt his heart, his soul, his head fill with her. He wanted to stand here forever, holding her, holding onto this moment that he knew could not, would not last…

"Chayton?"

"Yes?"

There was so much she longed to say, to tell him…

"Thank you," she whispered.

He tilted her chin up. "Hang on to that thought," he said, smiling, "after you discover that my house isn't much bigger than this room."

• • •

He told her about her phone just before they left their room.

Her face went white.

"What? Are you telling me that—that this person inserted something into my phone? That he has been following me by—by listening to my calls?"

Chay assured her that the program didn't work that way.

"The bug isn't designed to hear calls, only to bounce signals off a satellite that tracks where the phone goes."

"Where *I* go, you mean."

He'd deliberately tried to make the bug's function sound impersonal, but there was noting impersonal about Bianca's reaction. She was upset. Very. And though he hated seeing her like that, he knew her reaction at least meant that her final mental resistance to leaving the city was gone.

They took the elevator to the car rental office on the garage level, where Chay made a quick detour to a trash can. He dropped Bianca's phone into it. The phone was fully charged and it would continue broadcasting their location from the hotel. Tomorrow, when trash was picked up, her cellphone would broadcast their supposed travels through Manhattan.

By then, they'd be long gone.

The car he'd rented was waiting. Chay signed a few documents and they were on their way.

Bianca phoned Lacey on Chay's phone as they drove off. When Lacey answered, Bianca put her on speakerphone.

"Lacey," she said briskly, "it's Bianca. Would it be okay

to stop by your place for a minute?"

Lacey sounded puzzled. Why wouldn't she? She and Bianca had gone to lunch a couple of times, but nothing more.

"It's important," Bianca said quickly. "And—and I'll have a friend with me. Okay?"

"A friend?"

Chay put his hand on Bianca's thigh. "A building inspector," he mouthed.

Bianca nodded. "Actually, he's a friend who is a building inspector."

"Huh?"

"I don't mean to sound mysterious… We'll only take a few minutes of your time, I promise."

"You've got my curiosity up," Lacey said, laughing. "Sure. Come on over."

She lived on the Upper West Side. Sunday traffic was relatively light, but it took a few minutes to find a parking space. Then Chay and Bianca hurried back the couple of blocks to Lacey's building and walked up three flights to her apartment.

Chay put his hand over Bianca's as she reached for the doorbell.

"Remember," he said, "let me do most of the talking, okay?"

She nodded and he stepped back so Lacey would see Bianca, not him, when she looked out the peephole. The receptionist knew Bianca was bringing a friend—*is that what I am? A friend?*—but smart New Yorkers never opened the door without looking out the peephole, and Chay knew there were some people who might find a guy his height and build intimidating.

Why take chances?

"Go for it," he said, and Bianca took a breath and rang the bell.

A few seconds went by.

"Coming," a voice called.

More silence. Chay assumed Lacey was peering out the peephole. Then a lock thunked as it turned, a chain clinked as it was undone, and the door swung open.

"Hi, Lacey," Bianca said. "Thank you for seeing—"

Lacey's eyes had fastened on Chay. No intimidation there. Nothing but sheer female appreciation.

Chay smiled. "Lacey," he said, extending his hand, "it's nice to meet you. I'm Chay."

"Chay. It's a pleasure." She stepped back and Bianca and Chay entered a small, somewhat messy living room. "My roommates," she said, and gave an apologetic shrug. "Sorry I didn't have time to clean up. Can I get you guys anything? Coffee? Tea? Water?" She flashed Chay a huge smile. "A beer, perhaps?"

Bianca didn't give Chay the chance to respond. "Nothing, thank you," she said coolly.

"Water would be great," Chay said, his voice cutting across hers.

Lacey all but batted her lashes. "Water coming right up."

Bianca glared at him as Lacey left the room. Well, well,

well. Was his sexy shrink staking her claim? Jesus, he hoped so—but he didn't need her ruffling Lacey's feathers.

He reached for Bianca's hand and squeezed it. "Easy," he said in a low voice.

"Easy?" she hissed. "What does that mean, easy? I am easy. I am very—"

Lacey returned, with three bottles of water. She distributed them, her gaze touching on Bianca's and Chay's clasped hands, and then she sighed and looked at Bianca.

"You never mentioned your—friend," she said.

"No," Chay said quickly, "she probably didn't. See, we haven't seen each other in a while and I just happened to phone her yesterday and she mentioned the blackout Friday and since things like that fall into my job description—"

"What blackout?"

"The blackout in our building," Bianca said.

Lacey frowned. "There was a blackout in our office? East Side Associates?"

"In the entire build—"

Chay applied a little pressure to Bianca's hand.

"Bianca says you left before she did," he said.

"Uh-huh."

"The power was okay when you left?"

"Yes. It was fine. Well, it would be, considering that the entire electrical system had just been overhauled."

"Well, apparently not," Bianca said, "because right after you left, the electricity began shutting down."

Lacey looked puzzled. "See, that's impossible."

"It is not impossible. I am telling you what—"

Chay's hand tightened again on Bianca's. "What do you mean, it's impossible?"

"After the electrical upgrade was completed, Dr. Epstein and building management set up a new system. If the power were to go out again, she and I would both get automatic notifications. Hers would be just for administrative purposes. Mine would be so I could contact all the doctors. So they could, you know, get in touch with any patients who might have appointments."

Chay's eyes narrowed. "And you had no such notification?"

"No."

He nodded. "And when you left on Friday… Did you see anybody on your way out?"

Lacey shook her head. "Not a soul."

"You sure? No one in the hall? The elevator? The lobby?"

"Nobody… Well, yes. I did see a janitor."

"Where?"

"In the lobby. Heading for the service door to the basement."

"Did you know him?" Chay asked, trying to keep his voice calm. "Recognize him?"

"No. I mean, how could I? His back was to me. Plus he was wearing a uniform."

"Describe the uniform."

"It was the same kind all the service people in the

building wear," Lacey said, looking from Chay to Bianca and then to Chay again. "Charcoal gray. One piece. Long sleeves. With the name of the building management company stenciled on the back. *Avido*."

Chay nodded. "That's it? Nothing else?"

"No," she said, as she turned towards Bianca. "Doc? Something's wrong, isn't it?"

Bianca looked at Chay. He slipped his arm around her shoulders.

"Just some kind of mix-up," he said. "Nothing for you to worry about. Just one last favor…"

"Yes?"

"When you go in on Monday, I'd appreciate it if you didn't mention any of this to anyone." He flashed a quick smile. "You know what bureaucracy is like. Your boss calls management, management calls my boss, my boss calls me, and a problem that could have been dealt with in maybe an hour ends up taking a month."

Lacey sighed. "Tell me about it. Last week? I couldn't get any hot water in the bathroom. I should have just phoned the super, but no, I phoned the landlord and it took days until I had hot water again."

"Right," Chay said cheerfully. His arm tightened around Bianca as they all walked towards the door. "Oh, and one other thing…" He looked down at Bianca. "Honey? You want to let Lacey in on our little secret?"

"What little—"

"About us going away for a few days. To Miami."

Bianca's eyes widened. Then she nodded. "Oh. That."

"Miami? You guys are going to Miami?" Lacey stared at Bianca. "What about your patients? Your dissertation?"

"She'll call her patients," Chay said lazily. "Reschedule her appointments. See, we used to be, you know, very close. And now that we're in touch again…"

Lacey grinned. "Why, Doc," she said teasingly, "I'd never have imagined you doing something so cool."

"No," Bianca said. "Neither would I."

"You just go and have fun. I'll get in a little early and phone your patients for you tomorrow. Actually, if I remember right, I think you have a pretty light day Monday, don't you?"

"I—I—Yes. I think I do."

Lacey grinned. "You just go to Miami and have fun. And Doc?" She leaned in close. "What we both said about work before, you know, before other things?" She flicked Chay a fast look. "Not when *other things* look like that," she said, and giggled.

• • •

They took the George Washington Bridge to the Palisades Parkway, where Chay pulled over at what was labeled a scenic rest stop, not for the scenery or the rest, but that so he could phone the Avido Management Company.

"It's Sunday," Bianca whispered. "Who—"

Chay held up his index finger.

"Yes," he said briskly. "This is John W. Smith. I'm a

supervisor with the Department of Public Works. I need to speak with someone who has the authority to give me some information about the electrical system at..." He snapped his fingers, and Bianca rattled off the address of the building that housed East Side Associates. Chay repeated the information. "I know it's a Sunday, but I'm a born and bred workaholic." He barked out a laugh that made Bianca raise her eyebrows. "I'm trying to close out a file and I have a couple of simple questions. I'm sure we can do this over the phone. Of course, I'll understand if you prefer to wait until business hours tomorrow, when we can schedule an appointment for me to send in some of my people to go over things with you. Done that way, we shouldn't need more than, say, three or four hours of your time. Thank you, and please get back to me ASAP at 1-555-231-4752."

He disconnected.

Bianca looked at him. "Voice mail?"

Chay nodded.

"Really, Chayton. You cannot possibly think that anyone is going to respond to a message left on a Sunday by a man named John Smith..."

"John W. Smith. No joke, honey. The initial makes all the difference. Just give it a minute and—"

His phone rang. He tried not to look smug as he answered it.

"John W. Smith here." Bianca's mouth dropped open. Chay grinned and touched the tip of his finger to her bottom lip. "Yes, Mr. Garson. Thank you for returning my call so promptly..."

Ten minutes later, he'd confirmed what he'd already suspected.

There had been no power failure on Friday. If there had been, the system would have automatically relayed that information to Avido Management. The new system was programmed to deliver that sort of feedback.

Chay thanked Garson. Then he ended the call.

Bianca had been listening to every word. Now, she turned and faced him.

"So—so someone was in the building," she said. "Someone who wanted to—to—"

Her face was pale. She sat rigidly upright, her fingers tightly laced together in her lap. She was doing her best to remain self-composed, but he could see the fear in her eyes.

Chay cursed, reached for her and gathered her tightly in his arms.

"You are mine," he said fiercely. "And there's not a way in the world I would ever let anything or anyone harm you."

Had they been anywhere but inside the cramped confines of the car, he'd have made love to her; he'd have stamped her as his; he'd have given himself to her in the only way he understood.

Instead, he did the next best thing.

He kissed her again and again, until she was whispering his name against his lips…

Until the words he'd never dreamed he'd want to say were right there, unspoken—in his heart.

CHAPTER FIFTEEN

THEIR FLIGHT WAS waiting for them in Newburgh.

The pilot introduced himself as an old pal of Liam Sanchez.

"Heard you guys need a lift to Santa Barbara," he said cheerfully.

Chay nodded as they shook hands. "I can't thank you enough for this."

The pilot grinned. "No need, dude. Happy to do a favor for Liam—especially since now he'll owe *me* one."

Chay laughed. "What goes around comes around, right?"

"Abso-fucking-lutely."

The accommodations were sparse but comfortable. The flight was long. Bianca slept through much of it, but even though Chay hadn't had much sleep, he was too wired to do more than doze.

They landed at Vandenberg Air Force Base. The time difference made it late afternoon.

The Santa Monica Municipal Airport, where Chay had left his Silverado, was just a twenty-something-minute taxi ride away. The trip from there to Chay's place took another twenty minutes.

Soon, he was pulling the truck into the small garage that adjoined his house.

His cottage.

Hell. His shack.

He'd bought it because of its location on a mostly forgotten stretch of beach that was usually home to more sea lions and seals than people. Shorebirds danced at the ocean's edge, and sunsets were spectacular. As far as Chay was concerned, those things more than made up for what the place lacked in size and amenities, but as Bianca stepped down from the truck, it hit him that a woman accustomed to city living might not see things the same way.

At least she wouldn't find the place untidy. Years of military training had made him a stickler for neatness, but knowing things would all be in their proper places wasn't much comfort when he unlocked the door that led from the garage to the kitchen, stepped back and motioned her past him.

She stopped just on the other side of the threshold.

Not a good sign.

"Told you it was small," he said quickly.

Nothing.

He cleared his throat. "You know, I just realized...We

should have stopped to pick up some things. Toothbrushes. Well, no. I have this humongous pack I bought on my first and last visit to one of those giant discount stores. A comb and hairbrush, then. No problem. You can use mine. Although if you prefer..."

He clamped his lips together.

Jesus.

He was as nervous as a kid on his first date.

Maybe he'd been crazy to bring her here. Not to California. To his home. It wasn't too late. There were endless motels and hotels up and down the coast. Sure, they'd both said they'd had it with hotels, but—

Bianca swung towards him, her eyes, her lips, her entire face bright with pleasure.

"It's perfect!"

Perfect? He looked around him. Well, the room had all the right appliances, and two walls of glass-fronted cabinets. It had a Mexican-tile floor—the original owner must have had a thing for Mexican tile because the floors that weren't oak were tile. And, yeah, there was the kitchen table he'd made himself from one hell of a chunk of driftwood...

But perfect?

"Well," he said cautiously, "I don't know that I'd call it—"

Bianca put her arms around his neck.

"I grew up in a monstrosity my mother called an antique. The Wilde house is gorgeous, but you can get lost going from one room to another. My New York apartment... Well, you saw it. This—this is perfect."

Chay laughed, put his arms around her and linked his hands at the base of her spine.

"I think Goldilocks said something similar."

She shook her head. "It couldn't have been Goldilocks."

"I'm pretty sure it was, honey. You know: 'This one is too big, this one is too small, this one is just—'"

"I remember Goldilocks," she said softly. "And I remember Cinderella. And Sleeping Beauty. I remember all those fairy tale princesses who were surely happy wherever they were, because they had their princes with them."

Chay gathered her to him.

"Trust me, baby," he said in a husky whisper. "I am light-years away from being a prince—but you are a princess straight out of any one of those stories."

Bianca rose to him and kissed him.

"Aren't you going to show me the rest of your house, Chayton?" She smiled. "Especially, if it isn't too much trouble, the bedroom?"

Chay kissed her, swept her into his arms and carried her to his bed.

• • •

"I," Chay announced a while later, "am starving!"

As if in response, Bianca's stomach growled.

He laughed, tipped her face up to his, and kissed her.

"I take it that was a yes."

"It certainly was."

"Okay." He got up, stepped into his jeans, pulled on his T-shirt. "How about we get some food? Takeout okay? Pizza. Chinese. Thai. You name it, I'll find it."

"Do you have anything we could throw together?" Bianca zipped her jeans and smoothed down her shirt. "I'd rather stay right here, if that's all right with you."

He smiled. "It's great with me. Let's raid the kitchen and see what we can come up with."

What they came up with, according to Bianca, was a feast.

Steaks in the freezer. Idaho potatoes in the cupboard. A big Maui sweet onion. A couple of newly ripened tomatoes on the kitchen windowsill. And, in the fridge, romaine lettuce and a few bottles of ale.

"Sorry, honey. No *vino*. We'll pick up some tomorrow."

She smiled as he kissed her shoulder on his way past her to the charcoal grill on the deck.

Tomorrow, Bianca thought.

What a nice word.

She'd wake up in this house tomorrow. Wake up in her lover's arms. They'd make breakfast together. Go shopping together. Return here, to their private world, together.

It all sounded wonderful—as long as she didn't think about the—the artificialness of it.

Was there such a word? Or was the word *artificiality*? If not, there should be. Because it described things perfectly.

This wasn't a lovers' tryst. It was a necessary step in

the process of finding the person who wanted to hurt her. She knew, without question, that Chay *would* find him. That Chay would keep her safe until he did.

And that once all that was done, this—this lovely interlude would end.

"Hey."

She looked up from the onion she was slicing. Chay reached for her hand.

"Sweetheart? What's wrong?"

She shook her head. She didn't trust herself to speak.

"Honey." He drew her close. "You looked so happy a couple of minutes ago…"

She laughed. Laughing was often very close to crying. If she were careful, she'd be able to substitute the one for the other.

"It's the onion. I always have trouble slicing onions."

"They make you cry?"

She nodded.

"These sweet ones aren't supposed to do that. Tell you what. I'll do the onion. You cut up the tomatoes. Deal?"

"Deal," she said, and she gave him a quick kiss and turned away.

• • •

They ate on the deck, by candlelight, and talked about lots of things.

How delighted he'd been to make the SEALs, and how amazed and thrilled he'd been when he was selected for STUD.

How she'd loved growing up in the Sicilian hills, and what a shock it had been to discover she had half-brothers and half-sisters in America.

"A painful shock at first," she said, "but then, as I got to know them, I came to love them all. I know you—" She caught herself in mid-sentence. *I know you'll come to love them too,* she'd almost said, but wasn't that foolish? He'd spent time with them when Alessandra was kidnapped and again at Alessandra and Tanner's wedding, but there was no reason he'd ever see her family again. "I know you liked them when you met them."

He nodded. "But your father wasn't there."

"The general." Bianca stabbed a piece of tomato with her fork. "No," she said quietly. "He's pretty much been, you know, banished from our lives." She looked up. "I'd probably be accused of treason by the rest of my family if I ever admitted that sometimes I think maybe he's been punished enough. I mean, he did what he had to do."

"We all do what we have to do," Chay said. "The thing is, sometimes we're not sure exactly what that is."

She nodded. "Yes. Exactly." She smiled. "In fact, spoken like a true shrink."

They both laughed. She reached for his open bottle of ale. Surprisingly enough, it had a taste she thought she might just come to like.

"Tell me more about you," she said. "About what you were like growing up."

"What I was like," he said, with a quick smile, "was hell on wheels. I lived only for trouble. Riding horses. Hunting.

Fishing."

"Hunting?"

"Yeah. For meat. I get how some people feel about hunting—"

"No. I think it's different if it's for food."

"Well, that's what it was." Chay took the bottle of ale from her and tipped it to his lips. "In fact, Tanner and I had this thing we did whenever we came across trophy hunters."

"What?"

"We'd send them in the wrong direction. Or, if we knew there were animals they'd want in the area, we'd scare the animals away." He laughed. "One time, there was this big old male grizzly. We sent him running, except he apparently stopped and asked himself how come he was running when he outweighed us by a thousand pounds, so he stopped on a dime, turned around and took off after us."

"Oh my!" Bianca put her hand to her heart. "But you got away!"

"Did you ever see that old movie *Butch Cassidy and the Sundance Kid*? That scene where they leap off a cliff into a river?" Chay grinned. "That's exactly what we did."

"You could have been hurt. Or you could have died!"

His expression softened. "And what a waste that would have been," he said, "because then I'd never have found you."

• • •

His bed was oversized, but they slept tangled together.

And awakened to the buzz of Chay's cellphone.

"Mmmf," Chay growled.

Bianca gave a sleepy laugh. "That's supposed to be my line."

He dropped a kiss on the top of her head as he reached across her and fumbled for the phone, which turned out to be on the floor next to the bed.

"What?" he said.

"And a charming good morning to you too."

Chay sat up and ran his hand through his hair. "Sanchez?"

"Sorry if I woke you," Sanchez said, not sounding sorry at all.

"What time is it?"

"Seven."

"Not on the East Coast."

"Yeah, well, according to Liam, you're not on the East Coast. And if you were, it would be ten in the morning. Time to get your ass in gear, bro."

Chay sighed and swung his legs to the floor.

"You're right. And I would have called you in another couple of minutes."

"Bull," Sanchez said cheerfully.

"Yeah. Sorry, Declan. I just haven't had much sleep lately."

Sanchez chuckled.

"Things have been happening is what I mean."

"Right. So it would seem. Look, the reason I called is

because I'm free today. So if you're gonna need me, now's the time to say so."

"I need you," Chay said. "My place or yours?"

"Your choice."

"Here, then. Say in two hours?"

"Done. Just clear me a space and make sure your printer's up and running." Sanchez paused. "Okay if I bring someone along?"

"What someone?"

"A girl. She's a student. At UCSB. The University of California at Santa Barbara."

"Dude. Don't tell me you're into cradle-snatching."

"She's twenty-four."

"Hey. I was only joking."

Sanchez gave a long sigh. "Yeah, right. Anyway, she'll be happy to stay out of whatever it is we're going be doing with your lady's computer."

"She's not..." Chay cleared his throat. "Fine."

"Or she might be able to help. I don't know what the issue is, but Annie's working on her master's degree in psych—"

"She's a psych major?"

"Was a psych major. Now, she's going for her master's. Listen, if this is a problem—"

Chay shut his eyes. Another shrink in his life. Who would have believed it?

"Olivieri. Look, I'll just come alone."

"Chayton?"

Chay almost laughed. His very own personal shrink

was sitting just behind him, her naked body warm against his back, her breath soft in his ear.

"Bring her," he said into the phone. "Of course, bring her. I have the feeling it's gonna be an interesting day."

• • •

Showers.

One shower, actually. And during it, a fast but wonderfully sweet and sexy morning hello.

Then coffee. Toast. A promise to go out later to buy wine and whatever else they needed or wanted.

And, last of all, most important of all, a short conversation.

Chay took Bianca's hands in his.

"So," he said, "here we are. My magic guy is on his way. Will you give me the names and information I need, or am I going to send you off to walk the beach with the woman who's apparently his girlfriend—an amazing thing in itself, and remind me to explain that later—collecting seashells while Sanchez downloads the stuff on the sly from your computer?"

She blinked. "Wow," she said softly.

"Yeah. Wow." He smiled. "I can't lie to you sweetheart. I mean, I could—but I don't want to. The thing is, we need answers. And those lists in your computer might just contain them."

Bianca sighed. "I know. And I've been thinking about it." Another sigh. "Let your friend download everything you want."

Chay kissed her just as the doorbell rang.

Bianca smoothed back her hair. She knew what came next was all business, but meeting a buddy of Chayton's was still an event, and it made her nervous.

"Do I look okay?" she whispered.

"You look gorgeous," he whispered back, kissed the tip of her nose, and opened the door.

Declan Sanchez was tall, like Chay. Leanly muscled, like Chay. He had a killer smile—well, not as much a killer smile as Chay's, but Bianca could see that it could surely break a few hearts.

Everything else about him was precisely what his name promised.

He had the almost black eyes of a sexy Spaniard and the dark blond hair of an equally sexy Irishman. It was a dazzling combination.

He also had an easy grin.

"Lieutenant Declan Sanchez at your service, m'lady," he said, with a dramatic, sweeping bow.

Bianca returned the grin. "Bianca Wilde," she said. "It's lovely to meet you."

"And this," Sanchez said, sliding his arm lightly around the waist of the hazel-eyed brunette standing beside him, "is Annie Stanton."

Annie smiled shyly. "Hi. I've heard a lot about you, Lieutenant Olivieri."

"It's Chay," Chay said. "And whatever Dec told you,

don't believe a word."

They all laughed and Bianca felt herself begin to relax.

Sanchez had brought two laptops, his smartphone and what looked like a dozen different kinds of cables.

Annie had brought the really important thing.

A box of freshly made doughnuts.

They gathered around the kitchen table, drank coffee, munched on doughnuts, and then Chay turned to Bianca.

"Okay," he said. "It's time. I think I have to tell Dec what this is all about before he gets to work. Do you want to stay here while I do—or would you prefer not to hear it all again?"

Bianca's lips were dry. She went to the sink, poured a glass of water and took a long drink.

"I'll stay."

Annie pushed back her chair. "And I'll wait out—"

"No," Bianca said. "It's nothing you can't hear. Besides, you're a psych student, right?"

Annie nodded and shoved a strand of dark hair behind her ear. "I studied psych. Right."

"Well, you might just be able to offer some suggestions. Please. Stay."

Everyone waited while Chay went into the bedroom and retrieved Bianca's laptop. He put it on the table and opened it. It was an ordinary computer, but for a couple of seconds nobody did anything except stare at it.

Then Sanchez looked at Bianca.

"You have a password?"

She nodded.

"Okay. Type it in, but don't do anything else. I need to check for bugs."

Bianca swallowed hard. Entered her password. The screen lit and Sanchez leaned in. Typed a string of letters. The screen went black. The laptop gave a soft hum and the screen brightened.

Sanchez smiled.

"Clean as a baby's…bottom."

And they were in.

· · ·

Downloading was fast. Printing came next.

"Dec?" Chay said. "Are we going to be doing anything for, say, the next twenty, thirty minutes?"

Sanchez shook his head. "Not unless you think watching paper spew out of a printer is something special."

Chay nodded.

The small plastic bag that held the condom he'd taken from Bianca's apartment was in his pocket. He knew its value was limited. It probably could not be considered actual evidence, because it hadn't been logged in and entered in a police report, but once they had a solid suspect, the condom's contents would confirm his identity.

The law might not see that as evidence, Chay thought grimly, but there were different ways to mete out justice.

"I'll be back in half an hour," he said.

Bianca looked at him. "Don't…"

Don't leave me.

He could almost hear her unspoken words.

He'd phoned a friend, the CEO of a highly reputable lab. They'd been in the SEALs together until the guy was wounded, wounded badly enough that he'd had to take early retirement. His friend already had a degree in science; he'd added another in biomed, and that had led him to starting a lab often used by the military and the police.

"Sure," he'd said, after Chay clued him in. "Bring me the sample. I'll run a DNA check ASAP and then I'll put the rest in storage."

Chay hadn't intended to mention any of that to Bianca. She didn't need to be reminded of what they'd found in that dresser drawer.

But one look at her now and he knew he couldn't leave her. Besides, this was about her. She deserved to know what was happening.

He held out his hand.

"We'll be back in half an hour," he said, and the look on her face made his heart swell.

• • •

They were back in exactly that.

The baggie was safely stored—Bianca had been fine with that. They'd made another quick stop, and they were each carrying a big paper bag.

"Sustenance for tonight," Chay joked as they entered

the kitchen.

"And excellent timing," Sanchez said.

Dec had both his laptops going. As Bianca emptied the bags and put things away, he motioned for Chay to sit in front of the computer he wasn't using.

"I have a laptop," Chay said. "You didn't have to bring one for me."

Sanchez grinned. "You have something that probably says *Hey, look at me!* wherever it goes." His fingers flew across his keyboard. Sites flashed by on his screen and on Chay's. "Also, this pair is synched. What I see, you see. Plus they're superfast and totally discreet. No kiss-and-tell here, my man. Nobody will ever know we've been wherever we end up being. Got it?"

Chay laughed. Yeah. He got it.

"Okay," Sanchez said. "We're each gonna take a list. I'm gonna call up search engines. You check the names on your list. I'll check the names on mine. You come up with anything, anything at all, tell me."

They got to work.

At first, the sites were recognizable. Google. Bing. Nexis. Spokeo. Names on Bianca's lists turned up on almost all of them, but none of the information was anything unusual. Addresses. Phone numbers. DOBs. Places of work.

Dull. And useless.

Then the search engine names, the names of sites, grew less familiar.

Government names. Cryptic names. Some names that

were obvious acronyms. People on the lists began turning up.

Chay and Declan kept hitting the Print buttons.

There was lots of information. Medical data. Divorce data. Financial stuff. Things most reasonable people would consider private.

It got worse.

Sites appeared that were recognizable enough, secretive enough, that Bianca's whispered "*Mannaggia!*" pretty much summed things up.

Sanchez had taken them deep, deep into darkness.

Police records. Military records. Court records. Local and state records. Federal records.

They were in places supposedly walled off from prying eyes, but Sanchez found the keys to them all.

The printer kept pushing out sheet after sheet of paper. Bianca read each page. Sometimes she showed the data to Annie and the two would confer in whispers.

Chay phoned out for pizza. While they waited for it to arrive, Declan and Annie took a walk on the beach, and Bianca made a call to the psychiatrist treating her former patient.

The conversation eliminated the man from a growing short list of suspects.

"The mental condition of my patient—my former patient—deteriorated," Bianca said. "He's been hospitalized."

Chay started to say something, and Bianca shook her head.

"I know what you're thinking, but he was committed well before these latest incidents, and Dr. Abbott did me the favor of checking while we were on the phone. My ex-patient is still behind the doors of a locked ward." She gave a quick, sad smile. "I'm glad. Not that he's sick enough to have been institutionalized, but that he's finally receiving appropriate treatment."

Hell.

Despite the phone calls, the ugly and terrifying things the guy had said to her during those calls he'd made to her when she was in Texas, she was still worried about him, thinking of him and not herself.

"You're an amazing woman," Chay said softly, and hugged her.

SEAL and STUD operatives understood the importance of duty. So did his Bianca.

She would always put the needs of her patients above her own, even if it put her in harm's way.

• • •

The pizza arrived.

They ate out on the deck and spent a few minutes talking about nothing more important than the weather. Not much of a topic, considering Santa Barbara weather was almost always glorious, but they all wanted to put aside, at least for a little while, the increasingly gritty stuff turning up on the computers, stuff about people who were in Bianca's life.

Then they went back to what they'd been doing, Chay on one computer, Declan on the other, the printer tossing out pages that went straight into Bianca's hands.

Finally, when it was almost sunset, Sanchez groaned, pushed back his chair, raised his arms over his head and stretched.

"Man, I could use a break. And some food. How about getting to whatever you guys brought back this morning? Or we could send out for pizza again."

Chay got to his feet, flashed a smug grin and opened the refrigerator. "Do you think you could give up pizza for burgers, corn roasted on the grill, and a couple of bottles of Napa Valley cab?"

"Dude," Sanchez said with delight.

Chay grinned. "Man does not live by MREs alone."

"MREs?" Annie said.

"Meals Ready to Eat," Sanchez said, and shuddered.

"We picked up some cheese, too," Bianca said. "And a loaf of sourdough bread."

Chay handed her a wooden board. She put the bread and cheese on it. He grabbed silverware, plates and a corkscrew; Annie snatched up a stack of napkins. Sanchez took four glasses from the cupboard, and they all trooped out to the deck, ready to toast the spectacular Santa Barbara sunset. First, though, there was time for Sanchez and Annie to stroll the beach in the last glow of the dying sun.

"Whoops," Bianca said. "We forgot the burgers and the corn."

She started into the cottage. Chay grabbed her and pulled her into his lap. She sighed and settled against him.

"Tough day," he said softly.

She sighed. "Yes. I hate dipping into people's lives that way."

"No choice."

Another sigh. "I know."

He drew her even closer. For the moment, the reason she was here, the reason they were all here, faded into oblivion. There was only the beach, the sunset, and the woman in his arms.

And he thought, *A man could get used to this.*

Not just a man.

Him.

• • •

By midnight, Bianca was asleep on the living room sofa. Annie was sprawled in a big leather chair, snoring lightly.

"Breathing hard, she'd call it," Dec said with a little smile.

Chay looked up from his laptop. "So, what's the deal?" he said quietly. "This a serious thing, or what?"

Dec sat back. "You know me, Olivieri. Hell, you know yourself. No room in our lives for anything serious, particularly when it comes to women... Although I seem to see some kind of change goin' on with you."

Just days ago, Chay would have laughed.

Not tonight.

He sat back too and looked at Sanchez.

"Sometimes life catches you by the short hairs," he said, even more quietly. "Not that I know where this is taking me, you understand, but—but yeah, things, you know, things change."

Dec nodded. "Damn right. Like—like I'm the one who won't talk about anything beyond dinner tomorrow night or maybe, if I'm really into it, a weekend away." He sighed. "But…"

"But?"

"But," he said, jerking his chin towards Annie, "*she's* the one who won't talk about anything beyond tomorrow. Or, if I'm lucky, next week. And, man, you know how they say women are mysterious…"

Bianca sighed, rolled onto her back, opened her eyes and said, "What time izzit?"

Chay laughed. He rose from his chair, went over to her and drew her into his arms.

"My lady's favorite question," he said.

She flashed a sleepy smile. A minute later, Annie woke up. She and Bianca started making coffee, and Sanchez and Chay got back to work.

• • •

By two a.m. they had cleared all but five names on Bianca's lists.

Five names.

Five histories. Five serious histories.

One of the instructors in her department, a guy she

described as mild-mannered, even meek, had twice been arrested for assault. He'd beaten his ex-wife. Beaten her badly enough that she'd been hospitalized, but no charges had been filed, because she'd refused to press any.

A professor she'd studied with had a history of bizarre psychotic episodes. Under control as long as he took his meds, but who knew if he was?

A subject in her dissertation study had been arrested for—*Holy Christ,* Chay thought, reading the arrest report— murder. He'd beaten the charge on a technicality, but the only person—probably the only one on the entire fucking planet— who didn't think he was guilty was the guy's mother.

Another subject—a female—was a sex offender. She was forty-five. Her specialty was boys under the age of twelve.

And one of Bianca's patients was also a sex offender. He was a rapist, out on parole, facts he'd never bothered divulging.

Chay blew out a breath, sat back and folded his arms over his chest.

"We can eliminate the woman who digs little boys," he said, his voice hoarse with exhaustion. "She deserves to have her picture on a dartboard, but for our purposes only the others are candidates for Shithead of the Year."

"Couldn't have put it better myself," Declan agreed.

Chay rubbed his hands over his face. "It could be any of them."

"Or not." Bianca said. "The truth is, he might be nobody I know. Nobody I *think* I know. He could be a delivery man who dropped off a package at my apartment. A guy who lives in the building. A clerk I bought potatoes from at the greenmarket."

Her voice trembled.

Chay got up, fast, went to her, dropped to knees beside her chair and took her hands in his.

"We're all exhausted," he said. "We need to get some sleep."

Annie yawned in agreement. Dec began unplugging his equipment.

"I'm sorry," Bianca whispered. "You've all worked so hard. And I know we've made progress. It's just that—that I don't see how we're ever going to make sense of this mess."

"We'll start by interviewing some of these people."

"But they're all back east."

"I can do a lot by phone," Chay said. "And after a couple of days, when I think you're up to me leaving you here, I'll fly back to New York."

"You are not doing that without me!"

"Bianca," Annie said quickly, "you can stay with me. I have an apartment just off campus."

"Or she can stay right here," Sanchez said. "I can bunk on the couch until Chay's back."

Bianca looked from one of them to the other.

"You don't understand. Wherever Chay is, is where I want to be."

The room filled with silence.

Bianca wanted to crawl into a corner and hide.

Oh God! Had she really said that?

Everything she felt for Chay was in that admission. Everything. Declan knew it. So did Annie. She could see it in their shocked expressions.

Most of all…most of all, Chay knew it too. She'd stripped herself bare, told him something he certainly didn't want to hear.

"Honey," he said softly.

She had to remedy it. Say something. Twist the meaning.

A deep breath. A fixed smile. Then she tugged her hands free of his and stood up.

"I am the reason Chayton is knee-deep in this situation," she said. "And I am not going to remove myself from dealing with the problem. Whatever must be done next, I will be there when it is done. You know what they say. If you are not part of the program, you are part of the difficulty."

It wasn't what "they" said. Everyone knew it, but only Chay knew that Bianca was in distress. The question was, why? Because she thought she'd stepped on his plans—or because she'd admitted that she needed him. Wanted him.

That she—that she cared for him.

"Well," Sanchez said briskly, "I don't know about the rest of you guys, but I need to grab some shut-eye. Olivieri? You need anything else, just yell."

"I don't know what to say, Dec…"

"Hey, one for all and all for one. Who said that? A couple of Navy guys? Or a pair of French dudes a long time ago?"

Laughter. Back slaps. Hugs. Doors opening and closing.

At last, Chay and Bianca were alone.

She looked at him, then away. Amazing. This man knew her intimately. More intimately than any man ever had. And yet, because of a handful of foolish words, she felt embarrassed and awkward—and there was nowhere to hide.

"Well," she said, "let me just clean up…"

She got as far as reaching for an empty coffee mug when Chay's arms closed around her. He drew her back against him, kissed her hair, her earlobe, her throat.

"Bianca," he said.

She shook her head. Why pretend she hadn't made a fool of herself?

"I should not have said what I said," she whispered. "That—that I want to be wherever you are. I misspoke. You know how I sometimes do that. I get the words wrong…"

He turned her in his arms. "That's how it is for me too, baby." He brushed his lips gently over hers. "I want to be wherever you are."

Her eyes glittered with tears. "Do you, Chayton?"

He nodded. "That's the only place I want to be. Wherever you are."

She laughed. He kissed her. Then he led her into the bedroom and this time, when they made love, it was so sweet and tender that she wept.

• • •

Bianca came awake abruptly.

The room was chilly. It held the faint light of very early morning, and the bed beside her was empty.

She rose, wrapped herself in the blanket and padded to the bathroom.

Chay wasn't there. He wasn't in the living room or the kitchen. She opened the sliding doors and stepped out on the deck.

There he was! Wearing gray gym shorts, doing push-ups on the hard-packed sand near the water's edge.

And so beautiful he made her heartbeat quicken.

The morning light dappled his body with gold, and what a body it was. Hard. Powerful. A long, lean mass of incredibly delineated muscle. Her mother used to weave tales of the warriors who had tried to conquer Sicily, whose blood was part of hers. Phoenicians. Carthaginians. Greeks. Romans. Her half-brothers and half-sisters had grown up on their father's tales of the Viking and Celtic and Apache conquerors whose DNA was within them.

Chayton could have belonged to any of those warrior tribes. To the best of them. He had their strength, their courage…

And he had her heart.

She thought of what he'd said last night. Early this morning, really, just before he'd taken her to bed. That he wanted to be wherever she was.

But what did that mean? Did he love her? Or was she only important to him now? She wasn't a fool. Love—not that he'd ever mentioned love—did not always mean forever.

It would, for her. She would always love him. Adore him…

Dio. What was she doing? She was a scientist. She knew better than to theorize without at least some basis in fact. And she was a woman. She had watched her mother live for dreams.

It was far wiser to live for the moment.

Besides, she thought, as she went back into the cottage, she had work to do.

• • •

She sat up in bed, her computer in her lap, and checked her email. Some of it she dumped; some she put aside for later.

Only one message had to be dealt with now.

It was from Lacey.

Hope you and The Hunk are having fun! Canceled and rescheduled your appointments for the rest of the week. Hey, why would you only spend a weekend with Mr. Gorgeous? Told Epstein you were called away unexpectedly. A frown, but no complaints. Only one thing you might want to know about. Your patient Susan Abrams called. Sounded very upset. Gave me an earful. Know how you don't like to put personal details of patients in email, so give me a call and I'll fill you in. - Lacey

Bianca frowned. Give her a call. How?

She looked at the nightstand. Chay's phone lay on it. Of course! She'd use that. The bug had been in her phone, not his.

She grabbed the phone, pulled Lacey's home number out of her memory. It was nine back East; Lacey was probably up.

She was, and after some jokes about how Lacey was spending her weekend compared with Bianca's, Lacey told her about Susan Abrams and gave her Abrams's telephone number. She told her, too, about Dr. Epstein.

"She was surprised, like I said, but she didn't froth at the mouth or anything. But, you know, you might want to touch bases."

Bianca ended the call. She dialed her patient's number. Abrams's crisis, which hadn't been a crisis at all, was history. "See you next week," she said happily. "Ta-ta."

Two calls down. One to go, this one to Dr. Epstein.

No lies, but she wasn't going to tell her she'd left New York because someone was terrorizing her…or worse.

So she said that something very important had come up.

Epstein asked how she could reach her if that became necessary.

"Not that I think it will, but…"

"You can reach me at this number," Bianca said. "I'm staying with a family friend." True, more or less. Chay was Tanner's friend, and Tanner was her brother-in-law. "I can't use my phone. It, uh, it died."

"Ah. Too bad. And your friend is…?"

"Chay. Chay Olivieri."

"Great," Epstein said briskly. "Let me just write all this down. I probably won't have to call, but if I should... Oh. My son just walked in. Remember him?"

"Of course."

"David, I'm talking with Bianca Wilde. Do you want to say..."

Bianca rolled her eyes. "Marilyn. Look, I'm kind of busy..."

"It doesn't matter." Epstein lowered her voice. "David is in one of his moods. He doesn't want to talk to you. Nothing personal, you understand. He's just—"

Bianca stopped listening.

Chay had just entered the room.

Sweat glistened on his skin. His muscles stood out in sharp relief, and his gym shorts hung low on his hips. He was a walking advertisement for sex, and the look he gave Bianca left her breathless.

"I have to go, Marilyn," she said, even as she pressed the button that ended the call. Slowly, she opened the blanket that hid her from him.

Chay flashed a hot, wicked smile.

"Baby," he said huskily, and then they were in each other's arms.

CHAPTER SIXTEEN

FOR MOST OF the rest of that day, they did what they could to forget what had brought them together, what had brought them to this little piece of paradise.

They needed a break, Chay said, from everything.

Bianca knew the break was for her, not for him, but she didn't argue. Surely, nothing would change if they spent a handful of hours away from the nightmare that had taken over her life.

Hand in hand, they walked along the beach. Bianca oohed and aahed over the seashells given up by the sea to the sand, and after she'd filled the pockets of her shorts—Chay's shorts, really, and they were enormous on her—Chay said okay, he'd keep the overflow for her, but she'd have to tuck the shells into his pockets herself.

Dipping her hands in his pockets turned out to be a lovely price to pay, and ended with them racing for his cottage, laughing until they reached it—and then, once they were inside, the laughter turned to sighs.

The next day, they rode his Harley up the coast to a little café that almost overhung the sea. It turned out he had a couple of other leather jackets, but he offered to take the truck, if she preferred it.

Bianca batted her lashes. "I'm going to let you in on a secret, Lieutenant. The second best thing that happened to me the night we went to that Italian restaurant was riding your big, bad motorcycle."

"It's a good thing that came in second best," Chay said, laughing as he dipped her back over his arm for a kiss.

At the café, he ordered a huge platter of Santa Barbara Channel ridgeback shrimp.

She said they'd never finish so much food... But they did.

"Mmm," she said. "That was delicious."

"Wait until you taste spiny lobster."

She groaned. "Chayton. I couldn't eat another bite."

"Actually," he said, laughing, "you couldn't. Spiny lobster season doesn't start until October. You'll just have to dream about it until..."

He fell silent.

She looked at him.

Was he really talking about the future? She wanted to ask, but how did you do that? How did you say *I'd like another glass of sangria and by the way, are you asking me to—to—*

"Ice cream," he said, and he said it so briskly that

she knew he was trying to fill the uncomfortable silence, and maybe hoping she wouldn't misinterpret what he'd said. After all, telling her she'd have to wait to eat spiny lobster in the fall wasn't the same as saying they'd be together in the fall.

How could they be?

She lived in New York. He lived in California.

And, really, that was the least of it.

Her lieutenant wasn't a forever kind of man. You didn't need a degree in psychology to know that.

"Honey? You up for ice cream? Because there's a place in town that dishes up the most incredible orange-ginger stuff—"

"Orange-ginger," Bianca said brightly. "Don't be silly. Everybody knows the only flavor that matters is vanilla."

He laughed, as she'd hoped he would. He put some bills on the table, topped them with a water glass, got to his feet and held out his hand. She got up too, took his hand and as they walked to the Harley, she wondered what he was thinking...

Even as *he* wondered at that little slip he'd made, talking about the future, trying to figure out why he'd done it, why she hadn't picked up on it—and whether the very thought of a future with the woman he loved, because he did love her, Jesus, he loved her with all he was or ever would be...

Chay dragged air into his lungs.

Mostly, as he sent the Harley roaring onto the road, he was wondering if loving her, planning a life together, had a survival chance better than that of a snowball in hell.

• • •

They ate ice cream. Picked up something for dinner. They passed a small clothing shop and Bianca said she wanted to go in buy and bras and panties. She had deliberately not taken any from her apartment.

"I am," she said with determination, "tired of washing out my undies every night."

Chay tugged her close and said he had a solution for that.

"Just don't wear any," he whispered in her ear. "No bras. No panties. And I'll know you're naked under whatever you have on. Naked, just for me."

The suggestion made her blush. Not with embarrassment. With delight. It was a lovely idea and one she decided she'd work up the courage to try. For now, though, she went into the shop and bought undies, plus a couple of pairs of shorts, T-shirts, white canvas pants and an oversized linen cardigan.

All their conversation was light and easy. No talk of the future, and none of what had to happen next when Chay took the info they'd collected and put it to work. He'd said he could do a lot by phone, but Bianca had the feeling he'd probably have to do most of it on the ground, back east, and she just hoped he'd remember what she'd said, that she would go with him.

This was her problem, even though he'd taken it as his own.

Besides, what she'd left unspoken, yet come all too close

to saying, was true.

She wanted to be wherever her lieutenant was.

He was her joy, her comfort, her lover. He was her love, even though he didn't know it, and she was not about to lose a moment of precious time at his side.

· · ·

The next day, they finally got down to work.

They settled in at the round redwood table on the deck with the final list of names they'd printed out yesterday.

They went over those names. Over them again and again, taking short breaks for coffee, for lunch, for a walk on the beach.

For an hour in each other's arms.

A quick shower, and they returned to the list of names.

"None of these people leap out at you?" Chay said. "Something one of them said. Something one of them did. Something that seemed off."

Bianca shook her head in frustration. "No."

Chay huffed out a breath, opened the notepad in front of him and picked up a pencil.

"Okay. We'll check out every one of these people. Deeper background checks. Interviews with their co-workers, friends, families."

"How can you do that without making them suspicious?"

There were lots of ways. Some he'd talk about. Some he

wouldn't. But now wasn't the time for that discussion.

"Ve haf vays," he said with a leer, doing what he could to keep things light. "But for now, let's try something else. Think about people you didn't have listed in your computer. Consider anyone you might know, just casually, who raises an alarm bell. Even the faintest alarm bell. Remember what you said? That it might be anybody? A delivery guy who maybe seemed overly interested in you. A clerk at the supermarket. Somebody a little strange."

Bianca plopped her elbows on the table and rubbed her hands over her face.

"Some people who are perfectly normal can come across as a little strange. I mean, we're talking about Manhattan. Lots of people seem disassociated. Or withdrawn. Or just plain mean-tempered. Survival skills at work in a big urban environment."

She was right. Chay knew it. But there had to be someone.

"Think, honey. Isn't there anyone who stands out? Anyone you might have had a quick run-in with? Somebody who looked at you as if he wanted to do you harm?"

"It's impossible," she said, folding her hands in her lap. "I mean, what about the guy who steps on your foot in the subway and glares at you as if it's your fault? The woman who insists you tried to cut ahead of her at the supermarket checkout? Things like that happen all the time. People behaving strangely, I mean. Even at the little party they threw for me when I joined East Side Associates..."

"What about it?"

"Nothing worth talking about."

"Do me a favor and talk about it anyway."

"But it's silly. Honestly, it was nothing. Chayton, Don't look at me that way...Oh, all right. The wife of one of the doctors sort of suggested she didn't trust me."

"How?"

"She warned me that her husband would come on to me and I should just ignore him."

"Nice. What else?"

"One idiot told me that he and his wife had an arrangement—open marriage, he meant—and I ought to give him a call."

"Bastard," Chay muttered. "Anything more?"

"Well, the doctor I replaced got drunk and told me I wasn't up to the job."

Chay's eyes narrowed. "Was his name one of the ones Sanchez would have downloaded?"

"Probably not, but—"

"I want his name. In fact, I want to know which doctor is married to the woman who warned you off, and which is married to the piece of shit who invited you to a threesome."

"Chayton. He did not invite me to—"

"Is there more?"

She thought back to the party.

"No. Everyone else was very nice. There was one sad moment..."

"What was it?"

"Nothing to do with this. It was Marilyn Epstein's son. A sweet, sad young man. A boy, really. Brilliant, but uncomfortable around people."

Chay rolled his eyes. "Meaning, he was the only one who didn't say anything unpleasant to you?"

Bianca laughed. "Talk about reducing things to their basics... Really, it was a lovely party."

"Except for the assholes." Chay put down the pencil, picked it up again and rolled it between his fingers. "How about the opposite? Somebody who struck you as extra-nice? You know. Somebody who seemed to take a special interest in you."

"Nobody I can think of."

'What about that barista?"

"What barista?"

"The smooth dude at *Cuppa Joe's*."

Bianca frowned. "He's just a nice guy."

"He's a nice guy who'd love to get into your pants."

Her eyebrows shot skyward. Chay laughed, dropped the pencil, took her hand and kissed the knuckles.

"Sorry to be so blunt, sweetheart, but it's true. The barista has a thing for you."

"I don't think he does—but even if you're right, that doesn't make him a suspect."

Chay's expression turned grim. "Everything the least bit different makes a suspect a suspect. You happen to know the guy's name?"

She shook her head. "I have no idea."

Chay reached for his phone, Googled the *Cuppa Joe's*

they'd been talking about, got its phone number and made the connection.

"Yeah," he said pleasantly, when the call was picked up, "I hope you can help me. I'm looking for somebody, a friend of a friend who works at your shop. No. See, that's the problem. I forgot his name, and I was supposed to give him a call, say hello… Yeah. A guy. Maybe six feet tall. Light brown hair. Dark brown eyes. He was working Friday evening and I tried to get over there, but I got hung up." He gave a guy-to-guy chuckle. "My friend says he does well with the ladies, which is why I'm tryin' to get in touch, seein' as I'm new in town… Doug? Yup. That's it. Doug…? Vitali. Of course. Doug Vitali. He's not on until tomorrow?" Chay flashed Bianca a thumbs-up. "Too bad. I'll just have to call back then. Yeah. Sure. And thanks, man. You've been a big help."

Bianca shook her head. "Six feet tall. Light brown hair. Dark brown eyes. And you saw him for, what, all of sixty seconds?"

"What can I tell you? I'm an observant guy." Chay laughed, leaned in and kissed her. "I really am observant. It's part of my training—but the truth is, I knew our friend, the barista, was hoping to make a move on you. That's why I took such a good look at him. Just in case I had to track him down and explain, again, that you weren't available."

"Explain again?"

Another quick, sweet kiss.

"That night. I thanked him for being ready to come to your aid… And I warned him, very politely, that you were already spoken for."

A warm blush suffused her face. "Did you?" she said softly.

"I most certainly did."

"Such arrogance, Lieutenant."

"Not arrogance, Tigress. Determination."

"Tigress." She smiled. "You called me that before. Why am I a tigress?"

"Because you're sleek. Beautiful. Smart. A wild creature that needs taming." He reached out, threaded the fingers of one hand into her hair. "Taming by me," he said quietly.

A tiny shiver of excitement swept through her.

"And have you tamed me?"

"No. But, hell, why would I want to? Why would any man want a kitten when he could have a tiger?"

• • •

They had dinner on the deck.

After, Bianca nestled in Chay's lap while the scarlet sun slipped into the dark blue ocean.

"This has been nice," he said softly.

She nodded. "Yes."

"But tomorrow…"

"I know."

"I made some calls while you slept this afternoon."

"I didn't sleep." She smiled. "Maybe just for a little while."

He kissed her hair. "The thing is, I did what I could at a distance. Called in some favors. Got some more info." He paused. "But I don't have anything yet. So, tomorrow…"

"We're going back. To New York."

"I'm going back. You're staying here. Dec will sack out on the sofa. Fortunately, our unit hasn't been deployed yet and—"

"I'm going with you."

"No. See, things might get, you know, dicey. And there's no way I'd let you—"

Bianca turned in his lap and faced him. "I beg your pardon?"

"I said, there's no way I'd let you—"

"Lieutenant. I make my own decisions."

"Yeah." His voice hardened. "Except when I make them for you."

"Chayton. I am not a child. I am a grown woman."

"You are *my* grown woman," he growled. "And I intend to keep you safe."

A short while ago, days ago, his possessive words would have made her furious. Now they made her heart sing—but they weren't about to change her mind.

"You are not going without me, Chayton. I appreciate your concern, but—"

"I don't want your appreciation, goddammit! I want you here, where I don't have to worry about you."

"Ha."

"Ha?"

"Yes, ha! Is that what this is all about? Finding a way to keep you from worrying?"

"It's about you. You and what I—what I feel..." Chay took a deep breath. Leaned his forehead against hers. "Bianca. I cannot let anything happen to you."

She cupped his face with her hands. "Nothing will happen. When I'm with you, I'm safe."

"When you are here, you are safe."

"I won't do anything other than what you tell me to do, Chayton. I promise. I'll behave. I'll follow orders. I'll be good."

"Hell," he said, on a broken laugh, "I don't want you to be too good, baby."

She laughed too. Then he kissed her, led her back into the cottage, and they made love.

• • •

Chay called Declan.

He gave him the names of the barista and of the doctor Bianca had replaced, and asked him to take a look at the spouses of the two people Bianca had told him about.

"And check out this kid..." Chay looked at Bianca. "What's his first name?"

Bianca raised her eyebrows. "What's whose first name?"

"The kid you mentioned. Dr. Epstein's son. What's his first name?"

"Really, Chayton..."

"Really, Bianca. What's the boy's name?"

Bianca sighed. "David. His name is David Epstein."

"Dec?" Chay said. "Add one more name. David Epstein. The son of —Mary? Meryl?"

"Marilyn," Bianca said, "and this is silly."

"The son of Marilyn Epstein," Chay told Declan. "He's just a boy, but see what comes up."

"Will do. Just give me a couple of hours."

Chay ended the call. Bianca was glaring at him.

"It's called due diligence, honey."

"It's called being ridiculous."

"Will you look at that?" Chay said with delight. "My girl is pissed off."

"I am not pissed off, and I am not your—" Her expression softened. "Is that what I am?"

"Damn right," he said softly, and he took her in his arms.

• • •

At nine o'clock, they took the Harley to Dec's place. He looked rumpled and weary, and Annie wasn't with him.

"Problems?" Chay said softly.

Dec shrugged and said maybe.

"Hey, man, if there's anything I can do…"

Dec laughed. "Yeah. You can figure out why the female of the species is so impossible. With all apologies to the lady present, of course."

"No apologies needed," Bianca said, smiling.

Dec reached for a couple of sheets of paper, and handed them to Chay. "Here's what I found. It pretty much comes down to nothing. All the names came up clean, except for this guy. Douglas A-for-Anthony Vitali. Works at a coffee shop. Has a degree in electrical engineering. And he's not really dirty. Just some interesting stuff about him."

Chay took a fast look. The barista had a couple of old misdemeanor arrests for drugs. A breaking-and-entering charge during that same time frame, but the charge had been dismissed. He was in a drug treatment program and he'd kept out of trouble for the last two years, but you never knew.

Chay nodded at Sanchez.

"Thanks, dude."

"And the Epstein kid… Take a look at him too."

"Because?"

Sanchez shrugged. "There are lots of blank spaces."

"Yeah, well, he's young."

"Nineteen. Nothing too remarkable in blank spaces, but you check what I gave you and if you want, I'll go deeper on him and on the Vitali dude tomorrow." Sanchez cleared his throat and shot Bianca a quick look. "Speaking of tomorrow… Are we on?"

"Yes," Chay said.

"No," Bianca said. "Because if this is about baby-sitting…"

"It's about you being safe. We've been all through this."

"We most certainly have, Chayton. And I am going east with you."

The men exchanged looks. Chay sighed and told Dec he'd call him later.

They said goodnight. Chay tucked the printouts into one of the Harley's saddlebags and he and Bianca rode back to his cottage.

The weather had changed.

Clouds obliterated the moon and stars. A chilly wind was blowing in off the ocean. Bianca gave a little shiver as she got off the bike.

"It's so dark," she said. "And cold."

Chay dismounted and reached for the saddlebag. "There's a storm coming in."

She moved closer and kissed his jaw. "We seem to be destined for storms."

"Maybe this one won't be so bad…"

Roar!

As if this were a stage set and a backstage technician had just been waiting for his cue, thunder roared over the ocean. Half a dozen zigzags of hot white lightning arced from the sky.

"I told you," Bianca said, laughing, but her laughter turned into a shriek as rain came pouring down.

Chay handed her the keys. "Run for the house," he shouted, "while I get this saddlebag off. We don't want to lose the stuff Dec gave us."

She gave him a quick kiss and raced for the front door.

It took Chay a few seconds to release the saddlebag. It was already wet and slippery, and he sure as hell didn't want to drop it.

Then he took off for the cottage.

Bianca had already gone inside.

He clambered up the three steps to the small porch, grabbed the doorknob and flung the door open.

The living room was pitch black, even darker than it was outside, and he stood still, his eyes adjusting to the lack of light.

Without warning, the hair rose on the back of his neck.

He had a bad feeling. A sense of something evil.

"Bianca?"

Nothing.

Chay could feel his muscles tightening, his conscious thought narrowing and focusing on the room ahead and the yawning darkness.

Quietly, carefully, he eased the saddlebag to the porch floor.

"Honey," he said, trying to sound casual. "Turn on the lights."

Silence. A silence broken only by the patter of the rain, and then he heard a small voice.

"Chayton?"

Chay stepped forward.

"Bianca…"

"Don't come in," she screamed. "Chayton! Don't—"

She gave a muffled cry just as the lights blazed on.

For a second, Chay was blinded.

Then everything inside him turned to ice.

Bianca, his beloved Bianca, stood ten feet away.

A man stood right behind her. He had one arm wrapped around her throat.

A knife was in his hand, a long, curved, vicious-looking knife.

The blade rested right across her jugular, and a single drop of blood gleamed like a ruby against her skin.

CHAPTER SEVENTEEN

JESUS CHRIST!

Chay had been trained in hand-to-hand combat. Well-trained. Trained to be deadly, but not like this, not with all the odds against him.

Not with the woman he loved as a maniac's captive.

Bianca's attacker had everything he needed.

The element of surprise. The light blazing into Chay's eyes. A weapon that could do fatal damage in one single swipe.

Bianca's eyes were wide with fear.

And she was gasping.

Her attacker had dragged her onto her toes. Her hands were clutching his arm in a desperate effort to gain breathing room, but her assailant wasn't about to lessen his hold on her.

Just the opposite.

The more she struggled, the higher he lifted her.

Her gasps became pants.

She needed air.

If she passed out, if she sagged onto that blade, it would slice through her flesh.

Chay worked at sounding calm.

"Easy, baby," he said softly. He raised his gaze to her attacker's face. "I'm sure this—this gentleman doesn't really want to hurt you."

The guy laughed.

Chay knew he would remember the chilling sound of that laugh forever.

"You're a fool, Lieutenant Olivieri. Of course I want to hurt her—or do you think saying something so banal will soothe me?"

"Who are you?"

"I am the man Dr. Wilde spurned."

"No," Bianca gasped, "I never…"

A quick movement of the blade. A second drop of scarlet blood. Chay's vision blurred.   *Focus. Focus.* Giving in to rage might cost Bianca her life.

"She could have helped me," the man said. "She could have accepted me as her patient. But she refused."

"I'm Ms. Wilde had a good reason for turning down the chance to treat you." Carefully, barely moving, Chay shuffled forward an inch. "Why don't you let go of her and we can all sit down and discuss this?"

"She didn't have a good reason! She said it was because she wasn't a doctor yet. But I know the truth. She just didn't want to help me."

"I never…"

Bianca gasped as the arm around her neck tightened. It took all of Chay's self-control not to rush the guy and to respond, instead, in a steady, calm voice.

"Maybe it was a misunderstanding."

"Are you calling me a liar?"

"No," Chay said quickly, "no, of course not. I'm just suggesting that sometimes people get confused—"

The man's eyes flashed with rage. "You sound just like my mother! Have you been talking to her? To my mother? Ms. Wilde talks to her all the time. And that's why I know precisely what happened. Mother told me."

"Look, friend. I bet if you put down that knife and let go of Ms. Wilde…"

"Please," the man said coldly. "Don't try that nonsense with me. I'm smarter than you. I'm smarter than all of you."

"Maybe, but—"

Bianca made a strangled sound as the arm around her neck pressed even harder. Chay knew it had to be close to choking off her air supply.

"Did you hear what I said? I am smarter than everyone. That's the reason you're all against me. You're jealous of how smart I am." His face twisted. "Mother was always against me. I should have known she'd turn Bianca against me, too."

Fuck. "Your mother is Marilyn Epstein."

"*Doctor* Epstein," David Epstein said. "*Doctor* Epstein. You must not forget that title. *Doctor* Epstein is the success in our family. Not my father. Not me."

"David." Chay raised his hand and carefully moved another inch forward, slip. "Easy, son. I'm sure Ms. Wilde can help you if you'll just—"

"Didn't you hear what I said? I told Mother that I wanted Ms. Wilde to be my doctor. Mother said she would ask, and she did, and Ms. Wilde said no."

Chay's gaze flew to Bianca. She was standing so high on her toes that her feet were almost off the ground. She was panting. Still, she managed to give her head a tiny shake that said *No.*

Chay looked at David Epstein again.

"Well," he said evenly, "here's your chance talk to Ms. Wilde yourself. I bet if you put down that knife, let go of her..."

Epstein laughed.

"You're wasting your time, Lieutenant. See, I've got past that. The nonsense of wanting Ms. Wilde—of wanting Bianca to take me as a patient." His head tilted; his expression went from angry to sly. "I know a lot about psychology. And psychiatry. And I know that doctors shouldn't have intimate relationships with their patients. And when I had time to think about it, I realized that the true reason Bianca wouldn't treat me was because she wanted to have sex with me."

Ah Jesus! Chay felt the bile rise in his throat. They were finally getting down to basics.

"She told me so, over and over. She found a secret way into my head and I could hear her saying it, saying *David, I want to fuck you.* And for a while, I said no, we couldn't do that. Mother would have been so angry, so angry..."

"David," Chay said softly. "Let go of Ms—Let go of Bianca. You want to have sex with her. Fine. I understand that, but if you frighten—"

Shit! Another prick of the blade. Another drop of blood.

"You're right. I don't want to kill her. Not yet. Not before she gives me what I need."

"David. Listen to me—"

"She *was* going to be mine," David Epstein snarled. "She told me so, at night, in my bedroom. She said so each time I touched myself. She whispered it to me after I learned how to get into her apartment." The snarl became a beatific smile. "She said she wanted me to be with her all the time, despite Mother's interference, and that it was up to me to figure out how to do it. So I sent her an email, a silly kind of ad, and when she opened it, a wonderful little worm ate its way straight into the heart of her cellphone."

He giggled like a teenage boy with a crush on a girl, instead of like a lunatic with a knife at a woman's throat.

"After that," Epstein said, "I was with her all the time. *All* the time. I considered walking up to her some evening, or waiting for her in her apartment—I wanted to surprise you, Bianca," he said, for the first time directing his conversation at her, "but then I decided it would be more romantic if I left you a gift. " His voice hoarsened. "A gift to show you how much I wanted you."

The condom, Chay thought. God, that condom!.

"Oh, it was going to be so exciting! I stood across the

street, waiting for her to come home and find my present."
A look so cold, so ugly that it made Chay's gut twist flashed
across Epstein's face. "But she didn't come home alone, did she,
Lieutenant? She brought you with her, and anyone could tell
you were fucking her. The way you looked at her. They way she
looked at you."

Chay took another small step forward. Every instinct,
every sense he possessed warned him that Epstein was just
about all talked out.

"When the police came, I knew she'd found my gift and
that you'd made her call the police because you were jealous.
Because you wanted her to be *your* whore. *Your* vessel. And that
was when I realized she was not the pure virgin I thought she
was and I phoned her and you took the call, you made it clear
you were claiming her for your own." Spittle appeared in the
corners of Eptstein's mouth. "You—called me a sick bastard.
And—"

Chay was no longer listening.

He saw David Epstein begin to tremble, heard Bianca
gag as Epstein's arm tightened around her neck, saw the knife
blade began to move.

Years ago, one of Chay's martial arts instructors had
concluded an already dangerous training session in Krav Maga
with a move so lethal it could have resulted in death.

Pain, bruises—even an occasional torn ligament or
broken bone—were always possibilities in serious balls-to-the-
wall martial arts training.

A session that might have ended in death was not.

Even the STUD recruits, accustomed to Silat and Muay Thai and half a dozen other forms of the most dangerous martial arts, had been stunned.

"Here's the bottom line, gentlemen," the instructor had said. "Sometimes, the stakes are so fucking high that a man has to risk everything for a chance at winning."

And this, Chay knew, was that time.

He thought back to Krav Maga, thought back to high school football…

"Bianca," he shouted, lowering his head and charging David Epstein.

Epstein, taken completely by surprise, loosened his grip just enough so Bianca could sink her teeth in his arm.

He screamed.

The blade rose, but Chay was already there, smashing his shoulder into David Epstein.

Epstein staggered back, but not before the blade flashed. It nicked Bianca's throat, slashed Chay's arm.

"I'll kill you both," he shouted.

Chay kneed him in the balls. Then in the ribs. Cartilage cracked. Epstein screamed again. He doubled over but he came up still holding the knife. Chay smashed it aside with his elbow and took Epstein to the floor.

This time, Epstein's shriek was high and girlish.

Chay's fists moved with lightning speed.

Epstein's nose shattered. His blood spurted.

Chay saw nothing, heard nothing, knew nothing except that this man had tried to kill Bianca.

"Chayton!" Bianca grabbed his shoulders from behind. "Chayton, stop! Stop!"

She was screaming, but Chay was deaf to her screams. She was tugging at his shoulders, but he didn't feel her hands on him.

"You fuck," he gasped. "You sick, crazy fuck!"

"Chayton, you're killing him!"

Yes. He would. He fucking-A would…

A shudder went through him.

He pulled back.

Epstein was a bloody mess. So what? Bianca. That last flick of the knife…

He turned around, still on his knees.

Bianca's throat was bleeding.

"Oh God! Bianca…"

"I'm all right."

"You're bleeding, honey. Jesus, you're—"

"It's superficial. But you…"

Her gaze flew to his arm. His gaze followed hers. Shit. Blood was pouring from his upper arm. Epstein must have slashed his brachial artery.

"Honey. Get me a towel. Then call the police."

Bianca shot to her feet. Ran into the kitchen. Returned with an armful of of dish towels. She pressed one to the slash in Chay's arm. She held it there for a few seconds, then lifted it.

GodohGodohGod!

He was still bleeding. Too much. Much too much blood. Blood that was spurting from the wound.

"My artery," Chay gasped. "He must have—"

She leaned forward. Pressed a hard kiss to his lips.

Working quickly, she folded another towel. Pressed it against Chay's arm. She tried ripping a towel in half, but she couldn't, so she yanked off her T-shirt, used her teeth to tear into one end of it, then tore it lengthwise.

Good. Excellent. It made a perfect tourniquet.

Epstein began to groan. He tried to sit up.

Bianca swung towards him. She kicked the knife away and sent it spinning across the floor.

"You move one inch," she hissed, "and I'll finish the job the lieutenant started. Understand?"

When Epstein tried to sit up a second time, she muttered something short and ugly in Sicilian. Then she said, "You're sick, and I'm a shrink, and I understand that you're sick…but I swear I'll kill you if you move again."

The third time, she didn't say anything. She simply balled her hand into a fist, slammed it into Epstein's middle and and nodded with satisfaction when he fell back onto the floor.

Chay was laughing.

The sound was weak, but it was laughter.

"You'd better not give me a hard time, either, Lieutenant," she said, and she kissed him again, her face wet with tears.

Then she dug into Chay's pocket, found his phone and dialed 911.

Dio, his face was pale! And blood was seeping through the improvised dressing.

Bianca sank down beside Chay, wrapped her arms around him and pressed one hand, hard, against the tourniquet.

"Do not die on me, Chayton Olivieri," she said. "Do you hear me? You are not, repeat *not* to die!"

"Wouldn't...dare," he whispered.

She laughed. And cried. He lost consciousness, and she held him until the cops and the medics arrived, and even then, they had a hard time getting her to let go of him.

CHAPTER EIGHTEEN

CHAY NEEDED A blood transfusion and what he laughingly referred to as a lot of fancy stitching, but the doctors all agreed that in a couple of days, he would be fine.

Bianca needed little more than a couple of Band-Aids.

Epstein needed lots more than that.

A wired jaw. Three new teeth. Ten stitches over his eyebrow and, as Declan Sanchez joked, Epstein's prospects at fatherhood were up for grabs.

It turned out that David Epstein was sick.

Very sick.

And he had been sick for a long, long time.

His mother knew it. Her unwillingness to admit he was sick had been the underlying cause of Marilyn Epstein's divorce. The "blank spaces" Dec had found in David's background were the times his mother had taken him out of elementary school, out of middle school, out of high school to have him institutionalized.

Somehow, she saw her son's mental illness as a negative reflection on her as a psychologist. She was ashamed to acknowledge his sickness and she'd managed to use her influence to suppress his medical records.

All of that came out over the next couple of days, while Chay was in the hospital. He hadn't wanted to stay there, despite the pleading of Bianca and the doctor, but his CO dropped by and gave him a flat command.

"You don't leave this place until the doctor says you can leave," James Blake said.

Bianca, who hadn't been sure whether or not she liked Chay's captain, decided she liked him a lot.

David was charged with everything the law could come up with. Assault. Attempted murder. Breaking and entering. Stalking. Sexual harassment. Attempted rape. Some of the charges might not hold. All might be set aside if David pleaded to mental incompetence.

Whatever happened, he'd be locked away for a long, long time.

"And," Bianca told Annie, who'd sat with her in the hospital that first night, "hopefully, he'll get the treatment he needs."

She told Chay the same thing the day she drove him home, and Chay shook his head and kissed her and said that it took one hell of an amazing Tigress to show concern for a man who'd tried to kill her.

Lacey phoned in the middle of the week.

The office was buzzing over what had happened. And Dr. Epstein had stepped down as head of East Side Associates. One of the other doctors was taking over. The entire staff was going to have a reorganization meeting Monday morning.

Could Bianca be there?

Bianca knew that the word *could* was incorrect. There was no *could* about it. She had a job. An important job. She had responsibilities. She had to return to New York and resume her life.

She anguished over how to tell Chay.

What would he say? How would he react?

They still made love. A little more carefully than before, considering Chay's arm, but it was still wonderful.

They still held hands as they strolled along the beach.

They still talked about all kinds of things, but something had changed between them. It was a subtle change, but it was a real one.

Bianca knew what it was.

The situation that had brought them together was gone.

There was no more reason for her to be in California, or for Chay to talk about going to New York.

The mission, as she knew Chay would have put it, was over.

• • •

Thursday evening, Bianca poured two glasses of wine. "How about we go out on the deck and watch the sunset?" she said.

He nodded. "I was about to suggest the same thing."

He opened the sliding doors. They stepped outside and for the first time Bianca could remember, Chay didn't gather her into his arms.

Well, his arm was probably hurting. The wound was healing well, but there were times it twinged.

This had to be one of those times.

So they stood side by side, watching the sun as it dipped lower and lower in the sky, while Bianca told herself to stop being a coward.

She had to tell him about the meeting in New York. About her responsibilities in New York.

What would he say?

Would he ask her not to go?

She'd tried not to think about that, tried not to plan ahead…but if he asked, she knew what she would say.

She would say yes.

Really, it had been an easy decision to make.

Yes, she would stay in California. Or, to be accurate, she would move to California. Give up her apartment. Well, she'd do that anyway. She never wanted to set foot in those rooms again.

As for her job… East Side Associates would probably not be sorry to lose her. Marilyn Epstein was gone, but the memories—and the gossip—would linger. Bianca had been part of the mess. An unwitting part, but still…

So, it was time to go. To start over.

And California was a perfect place for that.

She had excellent academic credentials and she could find the same kind of work here, finish her dissertation here.

She could be happy here, with her lieutenant.

She'd never even imagined herself doing anything like it. Meeting a man. Falling in love with him, falling so deeply in love that she'd willingly make life changes to accommodate his career, because she knew that to ask Chay to leave the military would be like asking him not to breathe.

The real question was, would he ask her to stay? To be with him?

Or maybe the real question was, would he tell her he loved her? Because if he didn't love her, there was no point in any of it.

• • •

By that evening, Chay had decided he couldn't stand it anymore.

The suspense.

The not knowing.

The endless wondering.

It was time to ask Bianca, straight out, if she loved him. Because, Jesus, he sure as hell loved her.

The problem was that asking the question was only step one.

If she said yes—if she said yes, step two would be figuring out what to do next

She had a life back east.

He had one right here.

There'd been a time he'd never imagined leaving the service. Leaving STUD. Then Tanner had almost died and, well, Chay had done a lot of thinking. And what he'd thought was that he loved what he was doing, but maybe he'd only do it for another couple of years.

Thirty-four, thirty-five looked like good ages to retire.

He'd still be young enough to start a new, different kind of life. He didn't want to be one of those ex-military guys you sometimes ran into in bars, guys who talked endlessly abut the good old days because they really didn't have many good new days.

You could see that they'd never planned ahead.

Never planned something to do with the rest of their lives.

Bottom line? He'd be cleared for duty soon and that was what he wanted. He wasn't ready to leave STUD. He would be, in a couple of years, but a couple of years was a long time.

How could he and Bianca make that work?

She could stay in the east, he could stay in the west, and they'd spend all their free time together.

Yeah. Right. Like weekends, if he wasn't deployed. And when he was deployed? He'd leave from the West Coast. Return to the West Coast.

No good.

Okay. He'd explain things to her, say that he wanted to put in another two, three years in STUD, and he'd ask her to move here.

Jesus.

Ask her to give up her career, her position at one hell of a practice, and start all over again in California?

Chay glanced at her as she stood beside him on the deck.

He thought of how she'd dealt with David Epstein. How she'd, man, how she'd punched him right in the belly, put him flat on his back, and told him she'd kill him if he made any more trouble.

He thought of how she'd stopped the blood pouring from his arm.

He thought of what she'd said, that, despite everything, she was glad the man who'd tried to kill her was going to get help for his illness

There was nobody like his Bianca. His Tigress.

There never would be.

But how much could he ask of her?

And another question. How much would she do out of the goodness of her heart? Even if she cared for him. Hell, even if she loved him. Would she give up everything because he asked it of her?

Fuck.

That was the last thing he'd ever want her to do.

Goddammit, Olivieri, take a deep breath. Be a man.

"Bianca—"

"Chay—"

Each of them smiled.

"You first," she said.

"No, that's okay. You first."

She nodded. Looked away from him. Looked at the ocean. At the floor. At the sun as it slid into the water.

"I—I had a call from Lacey. You know. From my office."

"Oh?"

She nodded again. "Marilyn Epstein resigned."

Chay made a rude noise. Bianca laughed.

"I know. Amazing news, right?" She paused and searched for the right words. "So there's going to be a new person in charge."

Chay swung towards her. "You?" He was so happy for her. Still, he felt his heart drop. "Honey, they couldn't make a better choice."

"No. No, of course not me. I'm much too new. I don't even have my doctorate."

"Oh." Shit. He hated feeling relieved. "Who, then? Not the woman whose husband wants to be in an open marriage?" he said, trying for a smile.

"No. Not her. It's Carl Anderson. He's been part of the team from the beginning. Smart guy. Easy to get along with. It's a good choice."

"Ah. Okay. Glad to hear it."

"Right. Right." Bianca's hands were shaking. She dug them into the pockets of her shorts. "They voted."

"Without you?"

"Well, I voted, too. By phone. The thing is, they're going to meet Monday morning. To, you know, to reorganize."

"Monday morning," Chay said. Could she hear the hollowness in his voice?

"Yes. And—"

"And you have to be there."

"I—Yes. I should be there."

"Get back into the swing of things."

"Right. I mean—"

"Get back to work. Because your patients need you."

He sounded so calm. So matter-of-fact. Didn't the prospect of her leaving mean anything to him?

"They do need me." *Even though I won't be staying. I wouldn't feel comfortable there anymore. Now was the time to tell him that—or was it? Why did he have to sound so composed?*

"And your dissertation. I know you have to get back into that."

She did, but she'd just lost her advisor. No way would they work together anymore. Did she need a new advisor when she was this close to completing her dissertation? She had no idea, but she'd find out.

As for the dissertation itself… Not a problem.

She was almost at the finish line. Time to defend her dissertation. When she was ready, she'd fly back to New York and do it.

She'd explain that to Chay.

"Well, sure," she said. "I mean, yes, I have some last things to organize. But what I'm hoping is, since I'm fairly close to finishing my dissertation, to defending it…"

He laughed. The laugh sounded forced.

"How in hell do you defend a dissertation? I know how to defend a town. A hill. But a stack of papers? A bunch of statistics from something called *Interpersonal Relationships Among Millennials in the Digital Age*?" Another of those tight laughs. "I can't even imagine it."

Bianca stiffened.

"It's *Interpersonal Bonding Among Millennials in the Age of the Internet*. And it's a lot more than a bunch of statistics."

"Whatever."

"Not *whatever*. It's an important piece of work, Chay, and I've put a lot of time and effort into it."

Yeah, he thought. Right. It was an important piece of work, *her* piece of work, and what she was trying to tell him was that the fun was over and it was time she went home.

Well, it probably was.

He'd been a fool to think she would put him ahead of her work. Why would she? Hell, he wouldn't put her ahead of his work, either.

Of course he wouldn't.

The love thing...

The sex had been great.

Spending time with her had been great.

He'd never spent time with a woman before.

Well, he had. In bed. But out of it it? Not really.

Maybe he'd learned something. That man could not live by mission alone. Hadn't one of the guys in his unit said that one time and made them all roar with laughter?

Still, he—he cared for her. She was—she was an

interesting woman. An amazing woman. And she had a big heart. That evening in the coffee shop, when she'd told the idiot who'd been giving her a hard time that he needed help, and the other night, when she'd warned David Epstein she'd kill him two seconds after she'd assured him that she understood that he was sick. Plus that last bit of business, her saying she was glad Epstein was going to get some help...

Yes. She had a big heart.

And he wasn't going to make her feel bad about this.

He was going to make it easy.

"Bianca." He took a deep breath. "I know what you're trying to tell me."

She turned towards him. Was she smiling?

"You do?"

Chay nodded. "This has been—it's been an interesting week."

Where had that smile gone?

"Interesting," she repeated.

"Yeah. But, you know, but like all good things, it's come to an end."

"To an end," she said, and he realized he'd only imagined that smile.

He nodded again. He felt like one of those fucking dolls people put on their dashboards, head bobbing up and down in sheer idiocy.

"You have a job to go back to. And I'm going to be deployed next week."

"You are?"

Maybe. Assuming he could convince the STUD docs he was already up to it.

"Yes," he said with utmost assurance. "I'll be gone at least a month. So we're both moving on."

Were those tears in her eyes? No. It had to be a reflection from the candles on the table.

"Yes," she said. "Moving on."

He took hold of her shoulders. His heart was lodged someplace in his throat. For a second, he was afraid to speak, but that was dumb.

Men didn't cry.

Men never cried.

He'd learned that early, when his old man had beaten him almost senseless because he'd cried over the death of a puppy.

"So," he said, "so here's what I suggest. Let's go out to dinner. Go dancing." He swallowed hard. "Or—or, you know, we could just stay here and—and be together."

What he meant was make love. Have sex. Go to bed one final time.

She could almost feel her heart break at the thought, and she pulled free of his hands.

"I can't." Her voice shook. "I just can't. I—I called the airport. There's a flight out tonight. I really want to get home fast. I have so much to do before Monday..."

"Bianca." His voice was raw. "Honey..."

She swung away and fled into the house. Into the bathroom. She had a cellphone in her pocket—she'd picked up a disposable one while Chay was in the hospital—and with trembling fingers, she turned it on, found Annie's number and punched it.

Annie answered on the first ring. "Bianca?"

"Annie," she whispered. "Can you come and get me? Or are you with Declan? If you are—"

"I'm not with Declan. I'm not with anybody. Bianca, what's the matter?"

"Just come and get me. Please."

"Fifteen minutes," Annie said, and she was as good as her word. By the time she pulled her car into Chay's driveway, Bianca was packed and waiting outside.

CHAPTER NINETEEN

BIANCA LUCKED OUT.

There was a red-eye to La Guardia and she got the last available seat.

It wasn't a good seat. She sat jammed between a guy who unwrapped a salami sandwich when the plane reached cruising altitude, and a woman who must have bathed in a tub of cheap perfume.

It was hard to decide which smell was worse, but at least she was on her way home.

There was lots to think about, lots to plan, and Bianca wanted to hit the ground running.

She changed planes in Denver, crossed her fingers in hopes of getting a better seat, and ended up trapped between a man on her right who should have bought two tickets and one on her left who fell asleep as soon as the plane took off, and spent most of the flight snoring in her ear.

The plane touched down in a light drizzle.

Bianca hurried out of the terminal. Was rain going to accompany her through life?

She thought about taking the subway, but the idea of having to sit next to anybody else made her shudder, so she splurged on a taxi. It got stuck in traffic when she was half a dozen blocks from her apartment.

She'd tried to come up with a way of not going back to that apartment, but she needed her things.

Ten minutes and endless clicks of the meter later, she paid the driver, got out of the cab and walked the rest of the distance.

Her hands started to shake when she took out the key to her apartment.

"Stop being a wimp," she said, and she jabbed the key into the lock.

The apartment was just as she'd left it, except there was dust everywhere.

A glass stood on the kitchen sink, still filled with the wine Chay had poured into it.

And, in the bedroom, the drawer, her underwear drawer, still stood open.

Bianca shuddered.

No. No, she could not stay here.

Quickly, she pulled her suitcase from the back of the closet, opened drawers, tore down hangers, plucked her shoes from the rack on the closet floor and dumped everything into the suitcase.

Not the underwear.

She would never touch any of it again.

The furniture? She'd hire a moving company to get it out of here. Her books? Dishes? Glasses? Pots and pans, towels, pictures, books…You could pay movers to pack your things, and that was what she would do. It would be expensive, but she'd earned a good living at East Side Associates and she wasn't frivolous.

Alessandra always teased her about being frugal, but frugality was about to pay off.

She could afford to get out of here and let someone else worry about the packing.

She paused just long enough to pull the underwear drawer from the dresser, carry it into the kitchen and upend the contents into the trash. No way did she want some industrious moving guy to pack up the underwear and deliver it to her.

The suitcase was heavy, but she half-dragged, half-carried it to the street and hailed yet another cab.

"Where to?" the driver asked.

Bianca though about it. Where, indeed? Two of her half-sisters and their husbands, and both of her brothers and their wives had *pieds-à-terre* in the city, but there wasn't a way in hell she was going to show up on their doorsteps and try to explain what had happened to her.

"Lady? Where you wanna go?"

To a hotel, but not to the one she'd stayed at with Chay. Still, it was the only name she could come up with.

So she told the cabby to take her there, and when she

got to the front desk, she asked for a room. Not the kind she'd shared with Chay. She couldn't afford that, and she didn't want to be assailed by memories.

The clerk smiled. Nodded. Checked her in.

"Have a pleasant stay, Ms. Wilde," he said, and smiled again. "I remember you from a couple of weeks ago, and it's my pleasure to have given you an upgrade."

• • •

Oh, God! It was the same room.

The exact same room. The room she'd shared with Chayton.

The bellman hoisted her suitcase onto the luggage stand. Played with the blinds, the lights, the thermostat, until finally Bianca tuned in, took out her wallet and handed him a five dollar bill.

Then, mercifully, he left.

And she was alone with her memories. With Chay.

And wasn't that foolish? Any number of guests had stayed here since then. The room had been dusted. Cleaned. Vacuumed. There was nothing of him in it.

She sank down on the edge of the bed. The bed where they'd first really made love.

He was still here. If she shut her eyes, she could see him. That beautifully masculine face. That hard, work-toned body. She could hear his voice, feel his hands on her...

A choked sound burst from her throat.

"Chayton," Bianca whispered, and that was when the tears finally came.

• • •

By the time she showed up at the office Monday morning, she'd made a lot of progress.

She'd left a message for the head of the psych department explaining, briefly and succinctly, that she would be happy to come in to meet with him to determine whether she needed to arrange for a new adviser or not.

She'd gone online to StreetEasy and to Craigslist and found at least five apartments that looked as if they might work.

She'd found a moving company, also online, with a price list for packing and moving. Even at the room rate the hotel clerk had given her, she wouldn't be able to stay here more than a couple of weeks. She needed an apartment, and a job.

Finding a job would be harder.

In fact, it might be really hard. Who knew what the people in her tight little academic world were saying about what had happened to her? None of it was her fault, but she knew that didn't always matter.

In that same way, she had no idea how she'd be greeted at East Side Associates.

With caution, was the answer.

Lacey hugged her and led her into the conference room. There were cupcakes and bagels on the side table, coffee and tea. Someone—probably Lacey—had put up a sign that said

Welcome Home! Her colleagues applauded and cheered and said things like *We're so happy to see you* and *What a terrible ordeal for you to have gone through.* They used words like *shocked* and *stunned* and they all said they were so, so sorry this had happened, that no one could have possibly anticipated it, that they were sure it must have been devastating…

Then the room fell silent.

People looked at each other. At the walls. The table. The ceiling. At the new guy in charge, who kept moving his mouth as if he were chewing on words he knew he had to spew, sooner or later.

Bianca decided to make things easy.

"Well," she said briskly, "I want to thank you for this lovely welcome. And to tell you that I hope you'll understand when I say I think it's important for us all that I move on."

Nobody even tried to say *Please don't*, although Carl, the new man in charge, said he'd be happy to give her the highest possible recommendations.

Life in the fast lane, she thought, and then she told herself to keep it polite and pleasant, to shake the eagerly outstretched hands of her colleagues—her former colleagues— and exit stage left before she said something she would end up regretting.

• • •

By the following Monday, she had a job.

It wasn't exactly what she'd have chosen if she had the

time to choose, but it was a good job. She'd be working in a school. A private school, where she figured most of the kids' problems would be the kind that involved unhappiness over having to drive an Audi rather than a Sting Ray, but you never knew.

School started in another few weeks. Until then, to tide her over financially, she'd taken a job as a waitress. She'd waited on tables as an undergrad and she still remembered the right moves. The restaurant was not a fancy one, but it was near Times Square, so there was lots of tourist turnover and the tips were good. Between the tips and small, cautious withdrawals from her savings account, she figured she'd be okay until her job actually began.

She still needed an apartment.

She'd seen the places from Craigslist and StreetEasy. Three had been disappointments unless you were into having mice as roommates, but two others seemed fine—if she could snare one.

One landlord was away on vacation, but as soon as he got back, he'd let her know if she could have the place, or so his office said. The other landlord had a problem going, a "little" tenant eviction issue he was working out.

So she was still living at the hotel.

Still sleeping in the bed she'd slept in with Chay.

Still showering in the stall they'd showered in together.

Still having her meals at the table near the window, except her meals were from a Chinese takeout down the block and the McD's around the corner. She came home after work, changed into jeans or sweats or shorts, then headed out, bought her meal and smuggled it in—this wasn't the kind of hotel where you felt comfortable doing fast-food or takeout—but she couldn't afford room service, and besides, there just was something depressing about ordering from a fancy menu and having a server wheel in a cart when you were eating all by yourself.

One evening, she got back to the hotel, kicked off her shoes, changed into her sweats and decided it was time she did the thing she'd been avoiding.

She had to phone her sister.

Alessandra was surely trying to reach her on a phone that no longer existed.

Okay. No moo goo gai pan tonight.

She called room service and kept her order simple. It was a logical way to avoid overspending and feeling down about eating alone, and all in one easy action.

Bianca ordered a tuna salad. Tomato juice. And a pot of coffee.

"Twenty minutes," room service said.

Bianca said that would be fine. Then she took a deep breath and called her sister.

Alessandra's reaction to hearing her voice was close to explosive.

"Bianca! Where in hell have you been?"

"Hello to you too," Bianca said, but the touch of sarcasm was lost on her sister.

"Did you fall off the face of the earth? When I could not

reach you on your phone, I telephoned your office."

Bianca sat down and rubbed her hand over her forehead. "And?"

"And what? The receptionist told me that you had taken a vacation. A vacation? But you took one only a couple of months ago, when you met us in Texas. Bianca. What is going on?"

"Nothing is going on," Bianca said. "I am fine. I merely took a vacation. Must I inform you each time that I..." She groaned. "*Mannaggia*, A! Listen to us. Both of us speaking in stilted English as if we got off the boat only yesterday."

Alessandra laughed. "You are correct. *Merda*! What I mean is, you're right. We're both upset. B. The truth. Did you really just go on vacation?"

Bianca thought about her answer. Tell Alessandra that she'd been the victim of a stalker? That a mentally ill man had terrorized her? That he'd tried to kill her?

That was not a conversation to have over the phone.

"B? Tell me the truth! I know something is wrong."

"Nothing's wrong," Bianca said. And then, because she knew Alessandra wouldn't give up until she had an answer, she took a breath and said, "I went away with Chayton Olivieri."

She could almost hear her sister's jaw hit the floor.

"You did what?"

"I went away with him."

"But—but—but—"

"You sound like a motorboat. Is this so difficult to understand? We were attracted to each other that night in

California. He came east. He contacted me. We went out. And, you know, we got together."

"Does Tanner know? He couldn't, or he'd have told me."

"*Dio*, what does your husband have to do with this? Honestly, Alessandra—"

There was a knock at the door.

"A. I have to go."

"Go where? I want to know more. This makes no sense, Bianca. You said you didn't like Chay…"

The knock sounded again.

"Alessandra, I'll call you tomorrow. Right now, I have to go."

Bianca ended the call. Grabbed her tote bag, fished in it for her wallet. Charging the meal to her room was one thing, but she knew tips were shared by the service staff and she always felt bad about that, so she liked to give whoever delivered the meal something for him or her alone.

Knock. Knock. Knock.

Mannaggia! "I'm coming," she called out. "Just one second!"

Except, when she flung open the door, it wasn't room service.

It was Chay.

• • •

Great.

Bianca was staring at him as if he were an apparition.

Or a bad dream.

He couldn't blame her. He'd caught the first flight he could and, dammit, that meant changing planes not once, not twice, but three times. Three fucking times. In three fucking time zones. The last plane, he'd ended up in a seat so cramped his knees had been up around his chin until one of the flight attendants took pity on him and quietly moved him into an empty seat in first class.

And he probably looked like shit.

No shower. No shave. Not today, or whatever constituted today after all those hours in the air. Not yesterday, either. Probably not yesterday.

By yesterday, he'd pretty much given up on anything to do with being civilized or, hell, anything to do with being human.

Now he was here, and crap, this might have been the worst idea he'd ever had. The way she was looking at him…

God.

He didn't want her to look at him that way. As if he were the last man on earth she'd ever want to see.

"Chay?"

Her voice was soft. Full of bewilderment. Why? How come she hadn't thrown herself into his arms? All the way here, he'd imagined her doing just that…

Hell.

No.

Not all the way here.

Only last night. Or, fuck, the night before. Or whenever

it was he'd finally said *Enough*, climbed on his Harley, done better than ninety getting to the airport.

She loved him.

She had to love him.

One week and three days or whatever it was of rethinking what had gone down when she left him had convinced him that she'd been wrong to leave him.

Or maybe, okay, maybe he'd been wrong to let her go.

Whatever. She loved him.

At least that was what he'd figured until he was jammed into that last little seat, until he'd moved out of that little seat, stretched out his legs, had time to think, and that was when the doubts had set in. Maybe he'd read everything wrong, the way she used to look at him, touch him, kiss him, even the way she used to say his name, *Chayton*...

The possibility was more than he could take. It was agony, and the only way to survive the pain was to turn it into something else.

Anger.

"Goddammit," he growled, "did you really just open this door without checking to see who was there?"

She swallowed. "I—I thought you were room service."

"Yeah, well, I'm not."

"No," she whispered, "no, you are not."

The elevator gave a soft ping. Chay looked down the corridor. Shit. Room service. The guy was wearing an abbreviated version of a monkey suit. He looked foolish, but compared with him, Chay figured he probably looked like day-old dog poop.

"Leave it," Chay snapped, when the guy reached the door.

"But, sir—"

Chay pulled out his wallet. Took out a bunch of bills. Handed them over.

"Leave it," he said again.

The guy looked at Bianca. What could she do but nod in agreement? "Yes," she said, "please just leave it."

The room service guy turned away. Chay ignored the cart. So did Bianca. He stepped forward. She stepped aside. He moved straight past her. She hesitated, and then she closed the door and looked at him.

"What are you doing here?"

"What do you think I'm doing here?"

Her hand went to her throat. "I do not—I do not know. I have no conception of what you are doing here."

"You mean, you have no concept of what I'm doing here."

"*Si.* That is what I said. I have no conception of what you are doing here. I cannot imaginate a reason."

"Jesus! It's *imagine*, not imaginate…" Wait. Her speech was stilted. Her words were wrong. And she was trembling. He didn't want to see her tremble, but for a man reduced to reading signs, that was another good one.

Maybe there was hope.

"Please," she said. "Answer my question. Why are you here?"

He took a long, unsteady breath. *The only way to deal with fear was to face it.*

"I'm here to see you."

"But why?" she said. "Why would you want to see me, Chayton?"

Chayton. She had called him Chayton.

"Bianca," he said softly.

"Why? You have to tell me why. Because we said goodbye, do you remember? We said—we said we were done, that whatever had happened was over, that there was no more…"

He covered the distance between them in a couple of strides.

"Bianca," he whispered and then, just as he'd dared to dream, she was in his arms.

He kissed her mouth. Her throat. Her mouth again. He clasped her face in his hands and said her name, over and over, and her taste, her sweet taste, filled him.

She was weeping.

But, Christ, so was he. Except—except, that was impossible. Men didn't cry. They never cried…

"Honey," he whispered, "sweetheart, I love you."

She laughed. She dug her hands into the hair at the nape of his neck, rose on her toes and pressed her open mouth to his.

"Say it again, Chayton. Tell me."

"I love you," he said. "I adore you. I can't lose you. I *won't* lose you! Tell me it's the same for you, baby. Say the words."

"Chayton. *Il mio amore. Ti amo. Ti adoro. Ti desidero.*" Her eyes met his. "I love you. I adore you. I want you."

Could you laugh and cry at the same time? "But you left me."

"I didn't think there was room in your life for me."

"Baby." Chay kissed her again. "I have no life without you."

"Your career…"

"We'll find a way to make it work. If you can handle me flying back and forth, you flying back and forth…"

"It would be simpler if we were both on one coast," she said softly.

A muscle knotted in his jaw. He'd given that a lot of thought. And, hell, if it came down to that…

"Bianca." He slid his hands into her hair, tilted her face to his. "I'll give it up if I have to. STUD. If that's what it takes—"

She put her fingers across his lips.

"Foolish man," she whispered. "That last night we were in your beautiful house, watching that beautiful sun fall into that beautiful sea…"

He laughed. Kissed her. She smiled, though her eyes were still filled with tears.

"That night," she said, " I was going to tell you that I had made a decision." She took a deep breath. Despite everything he'd just said, this—what *she* was about to say—might be more than he was prepared to hear. Then she thought of what he had told her, that the only way to deal with fear was to face it. And she knew that if ever there'd been a time to take that advice, it was now. "That night," she said, "I was going to tell you that I was ready to give up my job. Move to Santa Barbara. Make a life with you."

He didn't say anything. He just looked at her.

Had she said too much? She could hardly breathe. Because if he didn't love her as she loved him, if he didn't want her forever and ever and ever...

"Bianca," he said. His voice was gruff. Raw. But his eyes were full of tenderness, and the hands that cupped her face were gentle. "Bianca, my love, will you marry me?"

Bianca laughed.

And said, "Yes."

EPILOGUE

El Sueño, the Wilde ranch in Texas, a late August weekend

CHAY HAD NOT thought about weddings.

For starters, he was male. And he'd never even imagined himself married.

Bianca hadn't thought about weddings either. She knew that some girls grew up planning their weddings, but she'd never been one of them. Finding a man, getting married—those things hadn't been on her To Do list.

Not at all

So, when Alessandra said, *You just let us plan everything,* Bianca and Chay figured, *Why not?*

Tanner, overhearing the long-distance conversation, had snorted.

"Dude?" Chay had said, and after some incomprehensible whispers on the other end of the phone,

Tanner had cleared his throat and said it had certainly worked out well for him and Alessandra.

Which turned out to mean the wedding was, well, kind of a production.

But, as even Chay had to admit, a pretty damn nice production.

Chay had met the seemingly endless bunch of sisters and brothers, half-sisters and half-brothers, sisters-in-law, brothers-in-law, babies and toddlers at Tanner's wedding. They'd all seemed nice enough, but it was different meeting them now, the weekend of the wedding, as his new in-laws.

Turned out they weren't just nice. They were great.

They were pleasant. They were fun. They could be serious, too, as Chay discovered the night before the wedding when the brothers—two of them—and the half-brothers—they came in a set of three—took him into the study for a drink and told him, earnestly enough to make him damn sure they meant it, that they were happy for their sister and happy for him—but that if he ever did anything to hurt her, they'd stake him out and skin him alive.

Chay had given half a minute's thought to some kind of snappy rejoinder, maybe along the lines of saying that, hey, he was the Lakota here and didn't that make him the skinning expert? And then he'd realized that this was a serious moment and a joke might not go over well, so he'd have to explain that he meant he was talking about skinning a buffalo, except he'd never skinned a buffalo in his life. Besides, by then, after those thirty-something seconds of silence, the men's eyes had all narrowed to slits. Logic had superseded being a smartass, which was why he'd hoisted his bottle of ale, nodded his head and said, in solemn tones, "Sounds like a plan to me."

The wedding arrangements belonged to the sisters.

"You're going to be so busy moving all your things to California, looking for a job, that kind of stuff," Alessandra had said, "we'll just handle the details for you."

It had seemed the kindest, sweetest of suggestions.

And, it turned out, it was.

Alessandra flew to New York for a weekend. Well, they all did. And they all trooped downtown to the atelier of a famous designer Alessandra knew from the days she'd been in the fashion business. The designer greeted them warmly and her assistants brought out half a dozen spectacular gowns.

Bianca tried on all of them. The sisters and half-sisters and sisters-in-law oohed and sighed and told her their favorites.

But Bianca knew her own mind.

She wanted the lace gown but with the off-the-shoulder neckline, and would it be possible to change the design of the sleeves so they were wrist-length, and perhaps narrow the skirt just a bit, and maybe shorten the train?

The sisters and half-sisters and sisters-in-law had tried not to laugh, but they laughed anyway.

"What?" Bianca said indignantly, but then she giggled, the famous designer giggled, and then, right on time, the driver of the stretch limo that had brought them to the showroom appeared with champagne flutes and chilled bottles of Dom Pérignon and the Wilde women had cheered and toasted Bianca with jokes that made her blush as much as they made her laugh.

She thought of all that now as the first chords of Wagner's *Wedding March* drifted up the stairs to where she waited with Alessandra, who was her matron of honor, and with her bridesmaid sisters.

"I know people use other music for the processional," she'd told Chay, "but if you don't mind, I'd like to stay with something traditional."

Chay wouldn't have given a damn if his bride came down the aisle to the sound of Chinese gongs.

All he wanted was her. His Bianca. His beautiful, strong, brave, smart Bianca, and when she reached him at the roses-and-lilies-of-the-valley-bedecked altar, he knew he had found all a man could ever want in life.

The wedding dinner was perfect.

Lissa-the-chef had planned, shopped, and supervised the preparation of the entire meal.

She'd asked for Bianca's approval every step of the way.

Each time, she smiled and said whatever Lissa did would be fine, and it was, though she did ask if the *petit pois* could be enhanced with mint. Not a lot, she said. Just a touch. And could there possibly be a choice of sour cream as well as whipped cream with the strawberries for dessert?

In the end, she forgot about all those things.

What mattered was being in her Chayton's embrace on the dance floor with his strong arms around her and his beautiful, perfect, elegantly simple, plain platinum band on the third finger of her left hand. There was a diamond ring on that finger too, one that had come as a complete surprise. Chay had given it to her during dinner at the Boathouse in Central Park. He'd gone down on one knee right beside their table between the main course and dessert.

There were some things he, too, wanted done traditionally.

And, it turned out, the entire Wilde clan, the Sicilians and the Texans, had a new tradition to institute.

They decided to invite their father.

General John Hamilton Wilde. The now retired four-star general they'd banished from their lives. The man who had lied to them for so many years, the man they'd all said they despised and never wanted to see again...

Except, a lot of time had passed.

A lot.

They were all older. Maybe even a little wiser.

They'd learned that life wasn't always quite as clear-cut as it seemed, and when Bianca had carefully brought his name up, when she'd said how anger and bitterness only reaped anger and bitterness, and how, perhaps it was time to forgive, if not to forget...

They agreed.

His Sicilian sons phoned him. His Texas sons phoned him. His daughters called, too. The calls were brief, because Johnny Wilde choked up during each conversation and—though none would admit it—so did his children.

The result was that he was at the wedding, a little quiet, a lot subdued, but he was there. Bianca didn't ask him to give her away—she wasn't ready for that much closeness. Not yet. Her brothers, all of them, gave her away.

But she danced a waltz with him, and she was happy for it.

• • •

The day went quickly, hours falling away into minutes. At last, it was time to leave.

Bianca's sisters hurried her upstairs so she could change into her going-away outfit.

Jeans. Motorcycle boots. The leather jacket Chay had given her and she'd never given back. They were leaving for California in Chay's Silverado, with the Harley safely secured in the truck bed.

The passel of brothers surrounded Chay as he headed upstairs too, along with Tanner—his best man—and the other guys from his unit, including Declan Sanchez.

"Will Annie be there?" Dec had asked, after he'd said, yes, damn right he'd come to the wedding.

Chay had checked with Bianca. Then he said yeah, she would be.

"Oh," Dec had said in a low growl, and Chay had almost asked what that *oh* meant, what that hard look on Dec's face meant—but he wasn't foolish enough to do either.

All the guests and the family gathered outside the mansion. They stood crowded together on the porch and in the driveway, laughing, joking, cheering as Chay scooped his bride into his arms and carried her to his truck. One last kiss and the truck pulled away in a scattering of Texas dust and rose petals thrown by the assembled crowd.

Everyone went back inside.

Everyone but Declan and Annie.

"Declan," she said softly.

Her eyes were dark. Full of pain. Well, dammit, he was in pain too.

"Goddammit, Annie," he said.

"Whoops. Sorry. I left my glass on the railing…"

Shit, Dec thought. Just what they didn't need. A fucking four-star retired general opening the door and stepping onto the porch.

But Dec was a military man.

"Sir," he said, politely if coldly.

Annie went a little pale and started to turn away.

"Your Highness?"

Dec turned a puzzled face towards the general.

The general was staring at Annie.

"Princess Anoushka? I thought that was you."

Dec saw Annie's shoulders rise and fall. Then, very slowly, she swung towards the two men.

"General," she said quietly.

John Hamilton Wilde smiled. "I thought I spotted you before, but then I thought, no, I must be wrong. What would the royal princess of Qaram be doing in a little town in Texas?"

Dec heard a roaring in his ears. "What?" he said. "What did you just call her?"

"I called her what she is, young man. The royal prin…" The general looked from Declan Sanchez to the woman who called herself Annie. He cleared his throat, snatched up his glass and went into the house.

The door swung shut.

Sanchez stared at Annie.

"A princess?" he said, on a choked laugh. "A princess from, Jesus H. Christ, from the kingdom of Qaram?"

She didn't answer.

He could see the pulse racing in her throat as he took a step forward. "Goddammit," he said, "*goddammit*, why didn't you tell me?"

Annie, or the princess of Qaram, whatever in hell the woman who haunted his dreams called herself, looked at him through tear-glazed eyes.

"I never told you," she whispered, "because you never asked."

THE END

DEAR READER:

THANK YOU FOR spending time with me. Thank you, too, for all your emails and messages. I absolutely love hearing from you!

Many of you know me from my career as a top author for Harlequin. I had a great time writing books for Harlequin, but the ones I'm writing now are longer, hotter and more complex, and I think they're even more sexy, romantic and exciting.

I hope you enjoyed **PRIVILEGE** and that you fell in love with sexy Chayton Olivieri. I know I did when I was writing him. Creating hot heroes and falling for them is one of the benefits of being a romance author!

STUD operative Tanner Akecheta and his bride, Alessandra, are in **PRIVILEGE**, too. If you haven't yet read their exciting story, please do! The title is **POWER**, Book 1 of my hot STUD series.

Some of you are already asking about Book 3. I'll tell you this much. The title of Book 3 is **RENEGADE** and it's is the story of STUD op Declan Sanchez—yes, you just met him in **PRIVILEGE**— and the woman he knows as Annie Stanton. When Annie breaks Dec's heart, he vows he never wants to set eyes on her again. But Annie has a dark and dangerous secret. She's actually the Royal Princess of the Kingdom of Qatar, and when Dec learns who she really is and what secret she carries, he knows that he'll give up everything he's ever believed in to save her—and to make her his forever.

My books are available through Amazon, iBooks, B&N, Kobo, Smashword and Google Play. You can find the complete list at

http://www.sandramarton.com

where you can also sign up for my newsletter. No spam, no ads, just news about my books and contests. Visit me @ SandraMarton at Twitter. And for all you Facebook fans, look for me at

https://www.facebook.com/SandraMartonAuthor.

Last thing. If you enjoyed **PRIVILEGE** or any other book of mine, why not leave a review at the online site wherever you bought the book? Your review doesn't have to be more than a couple of lines long, but reviews from readers like you mean the world to authors like me.

Until next time…

Sandra